KILL BOX

BOOK TWO IN THE ZULU VIRUS CHRONICLES

A Novel by
Steven Konkoly

Copyright Information

Stribling Media
Books. Games. Graphics.

Work by Steven Konkoly

The Black Flagged Series
Black Ops/Political /Conspiracy/Action thrillers

"Daniel Petrovich, the most lethal operative created by the Department of Defense's Black Flag Program, protects a secret buried in the deepest vaults of the Pentagon. A secret that is about to unravel his life."

ALPHA: A Black Ops Thriller (Book 1)
REDUX: A Black Ops Thriller (Book 2)
APEX: A Black Ops Thriller (Book 3)
VEKTOR: A Black Ops Thriller (Book 4)
OMEGA: A Black Ops Thriller (Book 5)
COVENANT: A Black Ops Thriller (Book 4.5) — Novella

The Alex Fletcher Books
Suspense/Action/Adventure/Conspiracy thrillers

*"Alex Fletcher, Iraq War veteran, has read the signs for years. With his family and home prepared to endure an extended disaster, Alex thinks he's ready for anything. **He's not even close.**"*

The Jakarta Pandemic (Book 1)
The Perseid Collapse (Book 2)
Event Horizon (Book 3)
Point of Crisis (Book 4)
Dispatches (Book 5)

The Zulu Virus Chronicles
Bioweapons/Conspiracy/Action thrillers

"Something sinister has arrived in America's heartland. Within 24 hours, complete strangers, from different walks of life will be forced to join together to survive the living nightmare that has been unleashed."

Hot Zone (Book 1)
Kill Box (Book 2)
Fire Storm (Book 3)

Fractured State Series
Near-future Black ops/Conspiracy/Action thrillers

"2035. A sinister conspiracy unravels. A state on the verge of secession. A man on the run with his family."

Fractured State (Book 1)
Rogue State (Book 2)

To my family, the heart and soul of my writing.
I couldn't do this without their tireless support and love.

About the Zulu Virus Chronicles

Two books into The Zulu Virus Chronicles, and I couldn't be happier with the trajectory of the series. You'll notice a familiar pattern in KILL BOX. The first few chapters revisit previously introduced characters that will merge with the core group of survivors from HOT ZONE, each playing key or supporting roles in the unfolding plot. Several new characters will appear, some very familiar to my Black Flagged readers—and they will prove pivotal as the series evolves! Everyone is important in The Zulu Virus Chronicles at some point, their decisions and actions shaping the saga—even if they don't survive.

The end of KILL BOX leaves The Zulu Virus Chronicles world wide open, and I already have already started FIRE STORM (Book 3). I designed the series so I could pursue several storylines after KILL BOX, focusing on specific aspects of the plot. My intention is to write slightly more compact stories, and release them more frequently; building on the foundation established by HOT ZONE and KILL BOX.

There's a greater conspiracy at work in The Zulu Virus Chronicles, which loosely ties in with one of my previous series—Black Flagged. I can't wait to tighten this knot. I guarantee you won't be disappointed.

Chapter One

A thin tendril of sunlight penetrated the dark room, causing Dr. Laura Hale to stir. Her eyes gradually registered the change, eventually reopening to the new reality she had desperately hoped had been a bad dream. No such luck. The living nightmare she'd experienced for the past forty-eight hours was real, with no end in sight. She started to drift back to sleep, thinking there was no real hurry to leave—and she needed the sleep. Hale could count the hours she'd slept over the past two days on one hand.

A sudden, distant burst of automatic gunfire triggered enough adrenaline to elevate her heart rate and put a temporary hold on her hopes of drifting off. The sound of gunfire no longer overtly startled Hale, but on a subconscious level, it still triggered her fight-or-flight response. A second burst cut through the morning, and she opened her eyes. Time to get up and figure out her next move. Not that she had a lot of options.

Last night's drive from the hospital to Dr. Chang's apartment had revealed a frightening shift in the city's dynamic. Her previous trip to the apartment, less than twenty-four hours earlier, had been mostly uneventful. Aside from a few police or ambulance sirens, the streets had been empty. Last night, the streets teemed with people, most of them engaged in looting or "glitchy" behavior.

Hale had witnessed a number of attacks by small mobs, unable to tell if the victim was one of the infected or the other way around, but she didn't stick around long enough to figure it out. Vehicles drew unwanted attention, evidenced by several new dents in the side of the SUV she borrowed from Dr. Owens. A sizable swarm of crazies nearly trapped her at the intersection of Delaware and Michigan when she slowed to observe the sea of flames engulfing the nearby Old National Theatre. If someone had smashed her window, they could have dragged her onto the street. Panicked by the realization of her vulnerability, she quickly drove straight to Chang's place without slowing.

A quick glance around the apartment indicated that the power was still on in the city. The microwave's green digital display read 6:50 a.m. Her wristwatch concurred. Hale truly had no idea what she'd do with the rest of the day. Probably sleep, eat and wait for sunset. She couldn't help but presume that she'd have a better chance of safely slipping out when it was dark.

There was no way to hide during broad daylight. Then again, the crazies had been up all night, from what she could tell. Maybe it got quiet in the morning, while they slept off a long night of looting and murdering, or whatever they were up to. There would be no way to tell until she hit the streets—on foot.

The SUV was no longer a viable option. Even if she avoided running into another mob, she couldn't dodge the government. The quarantine boundary sounded serious. The military would either turn her around or put her in a quarantine camp. Neither option sounded promising.

Another round of gunfire erupted, this cluster of shots sounding a lot closer than the last. The sharp crackle and pop of semiautomatic fire intensified while she lay on the couch, quickly reaching a frenetic cadence that lasted several minutes. It sounded like a protracted street battle had taken place a few blocks away. So much for the city going quiet.

Hale swung her legs onto the hardwood floor and rubbed her face. First order of business would be coffee and food. Her brief inspection of the apartment last night had revealed that Chang kept the place reasonably stocked, especially for a bachelor. She found a lot of dried foods like rice, beans and other grains on the shelves of the walk-in pantry, along with rows of various canned goods. Several cases of bottled water sat on the pantry floor, which would come in handy when she left.

A little later, she'd inspect the other rooms for camping gear or anything that might make her trek more bearable. Hale had no delusions about what lay ahead for her. Walking out of here was going to be a challenge on every level. The crazies roaming the streets were only part of the problem. Living off the land, or whatever she could find here, until she could sneak out of the quarantine zone would challenge her limited outdoor skills.

She stepped cautiously across the dimly lit floor to the patio slider, opening the curtains halfway to let in the orange rays of sunlight peeking between the buildings on the other side of the street. A quick glance down at her favorite breakfast spot told her she was stuck with whatever she could create from the pantry.

The restaurant's front window lay shattered on the parking lot asphalt. The tables and chairs on its fenced patio were overturned and strewn in disarray. It was hard to tell from this angle, but she thought she could see a body under one of the broken tables. Did that happen after she arrived last night? She hadn't noticed when she parked on the street. Of course, the only thing on her mind had been getting through the building's front door as fast as possible.

Hale leaned forward, peering up and down the street.

"Holy crap," she muttered.

Several bloodied bodies lay contorted on the sidewalks and street in both directions. She briefly considered her duty to render aid, but just as quickly dismissed the thought. The corpses looked slashed and torn, like they'd been mangled with a weapon. How had she slept through that? It must have sounded like a riot had passed by.

Hale closed the shades and took a few steps back. Maybe she was better off staying in place. The apartment had enough food and water to last several weeks. She could lie low and hope everything blew over. Even if the electricity failed, she should be fine. Might get a little stuffy inside without air-conditioning, but she could think of worse things. Much worse. If she could avoid detection, this place might work. It was something to think about.

Chapter Two

Paul Ochoa, Vampire team leader, relaxed on a leather couch set about fifteen feet back from the street, facing floor-to-ceiling windows of the apartment they had commandeered. The couch was far enough back to prevent most street-fired bullets from hitting him, but close enough to give him a wide view of Fletcher Terrace's ground floor. Dan Ripley, the team's sniper, sat on the other end of the couch, his scoped rifle, resting on its bipod, pointed across the street.

Ochoa caught movement behind the shades obscuring Chang's patio sliders, immediately raising his binoculars. He didn't need to tell Ripley what to do. The sniper had already nestled into his scope.

"Still weapons free?" said Ripley.

"If you positively ID Chang, take the shot," said Ochoa. "Don't wait for me."

"Got it."

A moment later, the shades parted, revealing a young, dark-haired woman.

"Negative shot," said Ripley.

"Keep watching," said Ochoa. "Might be the girlfriend or a friend."

The woman looked across the street for several seconds, seemingly in the direction of Jay Stansfield, who was situated inside the neighboring restaurant. His earpiece activated.

"Is she staring at me?" said Stansfield.

"Are you visible from her apartment?"

"Shouldn't be."

"Let's hope not," said Ochoa.

The woman leaned closer to the glass, panning her head back and forth. A look of shock overtook her tired face. Seeing dead bodies had a tendency to do that. The shades slid back into place seconds later.

"Did you catch anything behind her?" said Ochoa.

"Negative," said Ripley. "But it was pretty dark inside. You thinking about hitting the apartment?"

"I don't know. If he's not already here, what are the chances he'll still show?" said Ochoa. "The city is out of control."

"Where else would he go?"

"That's the big question, and command doesn't give us any answers. That's the infuriating part of this. Everything is done in a fucking silo. For all I know, Larsen and his band of idiots are sitting in the building right next to us."

"That would be awkward," said Ripley.

"It really depends on how important this guy is," said Ochoa.

"He's important enough to kill," said Ripley. "Important enough to change our orders at the last minute. I'd say he's pretty damn important."

"Which is why we might not be the only team working this. Four teams jumped over Indy," said Ochoa.

"We don't know if the other teams jumped over Indianapolis," said Ripley.

"Well, we assume they did," said Ochoa. "And we can

assume that one of them doesn't plan on executing their orders. You think Larsen would comply with a capture/kill?"

"Probably not," said Ripley. "But Peck would."

"Peck won't have a say in it. The rest of Larsen's team wouldn't follow that order either."

"So we wait?"

"We'll give it until noon or so before we move on the apartment," said Ochoa.

"And if Larsen shows up before noon?"

"We take his team out," said Ochoa. "Including Peck. No witnesses."

Chapter Three

Major Nick Smith dropped his exhausted carcass onto one of the emergency room chairs and removed his helmet, placing it on the seat next to him. He took a long sip of tepid water from the CamelBak hose secured to his shoulder and closed his eyes for a few moments.

"Major?"

A few moments seemed to be all this mission would spare.

"In here, Sergeant Major!" said Smith, pushing himself out of the seat and mumbling. "Just taking a two-second nap."

Sergeant Major Riddle strode through the ER's swinging doors and stopped just inside the waiting room, hands on his hips. The man didn't look the least bit tired or fazed by the night, which had been the longest in Smith's life.

"The convoy is clear," said Riddle. "Just reached the interstate. Should be smooth sailing."

"Didn't sound smooth on the way out," said Smith.

"They hit a mob of crazies approaching Eleventh Street. Chased the convoy all the way up the on-ramp," said Riddle. "Took some small-arms fire, too. Mostly pistols and hunting rifles. No casualties on our side."

Smith nodded. "How big was the mob?"

"Bigger than last time," said Riddle. "Captain Gresham

estimated a few hundred."

"And now they're using firearms against us," said Smith. "This is gonna get really ugly, really fast. Make sure we report the increased mob size and organized use of weapons to battalion."

"I have the radio section drafting a contact report with the relevant details," said Riddle.

"Very well," said Smith, refastening his combat helmet.

Riddle watched him for a few moments, a pained look on his face. He started to open his mouth to say something, but stopped.

"What's on your mind, Sergeant Major?"

"It's probably not my place to—" he started.

"Guard doesn't pay you to be diplomatic, Jeff. What's up?"

The grizzled-looking sergeant major chuckled before going deadpan. "I'm just thinking about the latest orders modification. It doesn't make sense."

"Nothing we've seen makes much sense," said Smith. "First they tell us this is some kind of pandemic virus, but send us in here without protective gear. Then they say it might be a bioweapons attack, but what kind of bioweapon turns people against each other like this?"

"None I've ever heard of."

"And now the infected population shows signs of cooperation," said Smith. "Frankly, I don't know *what* to believe. I just want to complete the mission and get the fuck out of here—before the city implodes on us."

"That's what I don't like about the new orders," said Riddle. "We can't leave the staff and their families behind to fend for themselves. They've earned a ride out of here."

"I agree. I just don't see how we can get all of them out of here. It's going to take us most of the day to execute the last two runs for the people we've been ordered to evacuate," said Smith. "And the vehicles will be jam-packed on both runs. We're talking close to two hundred extra people."

"I'd gladly swap them for the deadweight they want us to transport out of here," said Riddle.

Smith frowned, torn by the sergeant major's statement. Deep down he agreed, but they couldn't turn their backs on the infected patients, even those strapped down by their wrists and ankles. Still, he had no intention of abandoning the men and women who had tended to these patients, keeping the hospital intact in the face of an unprecedented catastrophe and the constant risk to their safety. He just didn't know how the hell he was going to get another two hundred people out of here without tipping his hand. If regimental headquarters caught wind of this, they'd shut him down hard.

"That's not an option, Sergeant Major," said Smith. "We'll have to come up with something else. Something that doesn't tip off the battalion and regimental commanders."

"Let me think it over, sir," said Riddle. "I'm sure I can cook something up."

"Don't think about it for too long. I'm guessing we'll need to start fudging numbers sooner than later. We can't suddenly *find* two hundred patients."

"Well, it has been a rather long and confusing night," said Riddle. "And it's not like we're trained for this sort of thing. Mistakes will be made."

Smith grinned. "Mistakes have already been made. That was apparent the moment we drove into the city. A few more shouldn't attract any attention. Keep me posted."

Sergeant Major Riddle saluted crisply. "The less you know, the better, sir."

"You're probably right," said Smith, returning the salute. "Let me know if you run into any snags."

After Riddle disappeared through the same doors he'd entered, Smith headed for the sliding doors leading to the parking lot. He was met by muggy air on the other side and slivers of new sunlight poking between the taller downtown buildings. The soldier standing sentry duty next to the door straightened as he emerged.

"At ease, Painter. And no more saluting. We're in a tactical environment," said Smith.

"Sorry, sir," said Painter, relaxing a bit.

"What do we have out here?"

"Nothing, sir," said Painter. "Sounded like the convoy got in a scrap."

"They ran into a mob of armed civilians," said Smith. "Infected."

"Crap. I hope that shit stays clear of the hospital."

"Me too."

Private First Class Chris Painter was one of the newer members of the battalion's headquarters and support company, temporarily assigned to Bravo Company specifically for this mission. Due to his relative inexperience, Smith had assigned him to Bravo Company's command group, where he would be somewhat insulated from the mess outside the hospital.

Smith had stacked the convoy with the most experienced soldiers, retaining enough of the "been there, done that" crowd to bolster the hospital's perimeter defenses. Not that the forty-three soldiers guarding the facility constituted an effective defense given recent developments. If a three-hundred-strong mob of gun-toting crazies hit the perimeter right now, they were seriously screwed. His people were spread thin covering the vulnerable entrances.

Without an early warning, he'd have trouble massing the defenders in one spot quickly enough to stop a mob that size. The thought triggered an idea he'd been too busy to consider until now.

"Painter, have you seen Staff Sergeant Vaughn?"

"Yes, sir," said Painter. "She's sitting in back of the leftmost HUMVEE."

"Thanks," said Smith. "Carry on."

Vaughn climbed out of the heavily armored vehicle right before he arrived. She reached into the vehicle and retrieved her rifle before addressing him.

"All is quiet on the block, sir," she said. "For now."

"For now is right," said Smith. "I think it's time to put up one of our drones. The convoy reported a sizable mob not too far from here."

"How big?"

"A couple hundred," said Smith. "Some armed with pistols and rifles. I'd like to get eyes on that mob, or any other mobs out there."

"I'll grab Sergeant Chase," said Vaughn. "We'll have a Raven up within fifteen minutes, as long as the satellite links are good."

"Last time I checked, we had full Satcom support," said Smith.

"We'll get to the roof immediately," said Vaughn.

"Patch into my command net," said Smith. "I want to know what you see out there."

"I can do you one better and transfer the feed to one

of our ruggedized laptops," said Vaughn. "You can see what we see."

Smith nodded, not sure he wanted to see what was out there.

Chapter Four

Laura Ragan, Specter team leader, crouched behind the brick fireplace, pointing her rifle at the sliding patio doors. It was still dark enough outside to tell that no lights had been left on inside the house. She peered beyond the rough-hewn stone table standing between her and the house for several seconds. All quiet inside and outside. The motion-activated lights mounted under the overhangs should have bathed her in light at this distance—unless the power grid was out on this side of town. A distinct possibility given the odd circumstances Specter team had encountered since hitting the ground.

The mission had started fine; her team had landed without incident outside a gated research park several miles to the east of Indianapolis. The target building, an unmarked chemical laboratory facility believed to be part of NevoTech, where Chang worked, had been completely deserted, a fact they confirmed firsthand. After reporting the results of their reconnaissance, they were instructed to take up surveillance positions outside the building and watch for Eugene Chang, their "high-value individual" (HVI).

Intelligence provided by Control indicated that Dr. Chang lived in Indianapolis and worked at the NevoTech facility in the city. However, he also had a second home east of the city and spent time at the second research facility near that house.

Distant emergency sirens drifted across the research park while they waited, her first indication that something widespread might be amiss. The order to proceed immediately to Chang's second home, by any available means (A2M), had been her second warning. An A2M authorized her to steal a vehicle at gunpoint, which thankfully hadn't been necessary. They'd hotwired an SUV sitting in a neighborhood driveway less than a mile from the research park and followed the highly specific driving directions on her CTAB.

The night's surprises continued en route. Ragan was informed that Zombie team had landed at Chang's house an hour ago—and had ceased responding to all queries. CTAB tracking data indicated that Larsen was still on site, and Ragan's job was to determine his team's status, exercising extreme caution. The only status choices provided by Control painted a grim picture of the possibilities.

☐ROGUE
☐NEUTRALIZED
☐CAPTURED
☐UNKNOWN

The only additional detail provided was that Larsen had reportedly entered and searched the house, failing to locate Chang. *Reportedly*. A small, but important indicator that Control wasn't confident about Larsen's report, which she found strange. Larsen was a little too laid-back and smart-alecky for her taste, but he was probably the most competent CHASE team leader at the Grissom Air Base Center, and everyone knew it, including Control.

There was a reason her team had been sent to an abandoned research park at two in the morning, instead of Chang's primary residence. The thought made her nervous. If someone could get the jump on Larsen's team, then what chance did her team have? And if his team had gone rogue? Same scenario.

So far, her team hadn't detected anything unusual. Zombie team's parachutes sat in the field behind her, crudely stuffed into their harness rigs, a few loose ends fluttering lazily in the weak breeze that flowed through the clearing. A detailed visual sweep of the home's entire exterior showed no signs of forced entry. If Larsen's team had accessed the house, they'd done it without breaking or disturbing anything, which she found unlikely.

Hell, if Ragan didn't know better, it almost looked like Zombie team had just walked off the job after landing. Then again, maybe they did. Her team was already having doubts. She could read it on their faces and barely blamed them. Halfway through their trek through the forest, after they had parked the confiscated SUV on the road at the edge of Chang's property, a massive explosion had lit up the northwestern sky, followed by a vicious firefight.

Not long after that, the unmistakable buzz of miniguns echoed through the forest. One hell of a battle had erupted nearby, convincing her that the mission was real—and the world around them had fallen apart. Maybe Larsen had heard something similar soon after landing and came to the same conclusion.

From what she remembered, he had a young family waiting for him in Colorado. Ragan didn't have kids, but she had been an adoring aunt to her sister's three munchkins for seven years. Long enough to know that family came first. Especially kids. Her money was on this scenario, but she still had to search the house to know for sure. Zombie could be inside, lying dead in pools of their own blood, or tied to chairs and gagged.

Ragan scanned the darkened interior again before shaking her head. There was no easy way to do this. She wanted to gain swift access to the house without bunching her team up in a constricted area like a hallway, so the glass sliders looked like her best option. They could quickly shatter both sliders with McDermott's shotgun and simultaneously fan out inside the spacious, two-story great room. She started to ease behind the fireplace, when something caught her attention.

A smooth rock the size of a fist lay on the patio below the rightmost sliding door. She slowly walked her gaze up the glass, noticing a scratch at about chest level. Looked like the rock had just bounced off the glass. Shit. It occurred to her that the shotgun trick might not work. Only one way to find out.

"Specter, this is One. Firing a single shot at the back patio slider," said Ragan. "Hold your positions."

After all team members responded, she pressed the trigger, firing a suppressed .223-caliber bullet at nearly three thousand feet per second toward the center of the slider. The bullet snapped off the glass before her finger reset—having almost no impact. What the living hell?

"This is One. Firing again."

She repeated the process, getting the same result. Barely a nick in the glass. Damn. If the windows were bullet resistant, she imagined the rest of the house was built the same way. They weren't getting inside the easy way. Maybe Larsen had come to the same conclusion, and that had sealed his decision to abandon the mission. She had to admit there was something very strange about a bulletproof house in the middle of nowhere.

"Specter, fall in on my position behind the patio. Watch your surroundings. The sliding glass doors are bullet resistant."

"That's not a good sign," said McDermott.

"No. It's not," she said, hearing a low-pitched alert tone in her earpiece.

She pulled her CTAB from a pouch attached to her vest, checking for the update signaled by the insistent tone.

—SPECTERXC32 MISSION STATUS UPDATE—
-PROCEED TO LOCATION SPECTER-D73M ASAP
-AVOID ALL CONTACT WITH
LOCAL/STATE/FED AGENCIES
-DO NOT ATTEMPT TO DRIVE THRU
INTERSTATE 465 QUARANTINE
-BOUNDARY CHECKPOINTS
-SEE MAP FOR RECOMMENDED BOUNDARY
APPROACH LOCATIONS
—IMMEDIATELY ACKNOWLEDGE RECEIPT—

Seriously? A third location? She acknowledged receipt of the change to her team's orders and checked the MAP tab. SPECTER-D73M was located in the heart of Indianapolis. Twenty-two point four miles away by the recommended route. Fifteen of that on foot, since they would have to abandon their vehicle before reaching Interstate 465—a federal quarantine boundary line. Quarantine for what? They'd soon find out.

"This is One. Change to orders. Proceed to southeast exfil point," she said. "I just received a new location."

Chapter Five

Stan Greenberg skeptically eyed the group loading gear into the pickup truck. Four wouldn't be enough. Not if his suspicions were correct. A platoon of Navy SEALs wouldn't be enough. The group looked hardcore enough, but it would take more than combat skills to survive in an infected urban environment. The little he knew about the destruction of Monchegorsk, a city that had been destroyed by a similar virus, painted a grim picture of what this motley crew faced, and that had only been a city of seventy thousand. The population of Indianapolis was ten times that number.

"You look worried," said a voice next to him.

He flinched, nearly jumping in place.

"Jesus. You people move like ghosts," said Greenberg.

The leader of this operation stood next to him, one hand on a hip, the other sipping coffee from a stainless steel insulated mug. He looked oddly familiar, but Greenberg couldn't place him. Definitely someone that had spent some time in the spotlight around D.C. Undoubtedly ex-military, the buzz cut and athletic physique a dead giveaway. Upper echelon, if he had to guess. The guy had the presence of a general, and his people treated him like one.

"Occupational hazard," said the man, surveying the

work like a proud father before turning to him. "They'll be fine."

"I don't know," said Greenberg. "They might be the best in the business, but this is unlike anything anyone has faced before, except for the Russians, and they've swept that information completely under the rug."

The guy grinned, pausing for several moments before responding.

"How much do you know about Monchegorsk?" said the man.

Greenberg tried not to appear surprised, figuring it would tip his hand. He still knew next to nothing about these people. Only that they had presumably saved his life, and that they had a keen interest in learning as much as possible about the virus that had been released in dozens of U.S. cities. Keen enough to send people into one of the quarantine zones to retrieve Dr. Chang's lab analysis—and hopefully Dr. Chang himself.

"We didn't pick you at random, Dr. Greenberg," he said. "You've worked at Edgewood for twenty years, specializing in emergent and potential weaponized biological threats. I can't imagine Monchegorsk slipped past your radar."

"No. It didn't," said Greenberg, unsure how much he should reveal about what he knew.

After a short pause, the man spoke. "I understand your hesitation," he said. "The circumstances surrounding the Russian city were uniquely terrifying, to say the least. The virus and its creator? Incomparably evil. I've spent the past several years chasing this down in one form or another. You and I share that in common."

"Who are you people?"

"We don't really have a name, but two of the four

operatives headed into the Indianapolis quarantine zone completed a similar mission in Monchegorsk. They understand the risks and know how to navigate them."

Impossible. This couldn't be the same group. He'd heard the stories, but considered them legend. The "head in a cooler" story had persisted for a number of years, though nobody could, or would, corroborate it.

"Trust me, Dr. Greenberg. We're on your side," said the man.

"Call me Stan," said Greenberg.

The man extended a hand. "Terrence."

General Terrence Sanderson? The stuff of legends.

"General?"

"In a former life," said the man.

"Unbelievable. Never in a million years did I suspect our paths would cross," said Greenberg, now recognizing his face.

"I *sincerely* hoped they wouldn't cross," said Terrence.

Greenberg nodded, his attention pulled back to the team loading the truck. A tough-as-nails-looking woman heaved two serious parachute rigs into the pickup bed, catching his eye when she turned around. A quick nod and she was off, replaced by two men carting a black case labeled OXYGEN.

"You really think they can pull this off?" said Greenberg.

"I know they can pull it off," said Terrence. "That's the easy part. Figuring out what to do with the information is the hard part. I still haven't worked that out."

"Maybe I can help fill in the blanks," said Greenberg. "After I get a cup of that coffee."

Chapter Six

Dr. Eugene Chang led the group deeper into the NevoTech building, guiding them directly to the main campus building's security hub. He needed to acquire a replacement ID card to access his laboratory in the research center, where he'd stashed copies of the data analysis he'd conducted on the infected blood. Emma Harper's ID card limited them to common areas, which was fine for now, but at some point today, he wanted to get his hands on that data. Greenberg had suggested it might help unravel whatever insanity had descended on the country.

When he last talked to Greenberg, Chang had no intention of returning to NevoTech. His friend should be quite pleased to hear that he was in a position to retrieve the data. The only question remaining was *how to deliver it?* His private plane could handle another trip. No doubt about that. He just wasn't sure they could safely get back to the plane at this point. They certainly couldn't travel the same route they'd taken this morning from the plane to the facility. It hadn't taken more than a few minutes to attract a mob of infected. By nightfall, it would be worse. Way worse.

Chang pressed Emma's ID against another card reader, relieved when it turned green. It was impossible for him to tell which doors they could access. They'd already taken a few wrong paths.

"How much farther?" said Larsen, leaning against the wall opposite Chang.

Larsen's stoic mask had begun to wear thin, the pain in his leg obviously worsening the farther they walked. Incredibly, it only showed on his face—and barely. He didn't limp or favor the leg at all, a testament to the soldier's training. The superficial wound to Chang's back had nearly driven him to the point of tears several times during their seemingly endless journey through NevoTech's expansive, winding passageways.

"We're pretty close," said Chang, pulling the door open.

"Maybe we should split into two groups," said Larsen. "One with guns. One without. Give you a chance to explain our situation to security. The last thing we need is a jumpy security guard waving a gun around."

"The security force doesn't carry firearms," said Chang. "Not even in the research building. Firearms aren't allowed on campus."

"You might be surprised," said Larsen. "Personally—I don't like to be surprised. I'm sure the guards don't like it either. We should split the group in two now, before we get too close. Given what's going on in the city, they'll be watching the cameras guarding all approaches to the security hub."

"It's a smart idea," said David Olson, a Westfield police officer. "Chang and the Harpers can square things away with security. You're all NevoTech employees. We'll wait here for you to come get us."

"What if you're right, and they're armed?" said Chang. "Why would they suddenly be fine with our weapons, even after they've cleared our identities?"

"Because you're going to tell them I'm with the Department of Homeland Security," said Larsen, digging through a pocket on his vest. "And give them this ID card."

Chang took the card from Larsen's bloodied hand and examined it.

"Special agent with the Department of Homeland Security?" said Chang. "Is that true?"

"Technically. The title is more administrative than anything," said Larsen.

David gathered close to him, checking out the ID. "Looks real enough."

"It's real," said Larsen. "You should add your badge to the pile."

"Good idea," said David, handing over his wallet.

Chang opened it. A golden Westfield Police Department badge on one side, David's police department ID card on the other.

"Three NevoTech employees, a Homeland Security agent, a local cop and his son. Makes a respectable group."

"I don't know about this," said Jack Harper. "Why don't we stash the weapons in a bathroom or something and get them later?"

"Not happening," said Larsen before lifting his rifle. "This is the only thing standing between me and whatever is out there."

"Aside from an eight-foot iron fence," said Jack Harper. "Plus a reinforced building."

"Let me rephrase that. This is the only thing I *trust* that's standing between me and whatever's out there."

"*Us* and whatever's out there," said David.

"Right. *Us*," said Larsen, giving David an approving nod. "Plus we have no idea if the rest of the perimeter is fully intact."

"And we've all seen *The Walking Dead*. They always get in," said Joshua Olson.

The group simultaneously nodded, like they all knew what David's teenage son was talking about.

"I'm sorry," said Chang. "What does that mean, exactly?"

"You've never heard of *The Walking Dead*?" said Larsen, winking at the group. "Jesus. Even I've heard of *The Walking Dead*, and I don't even watch TV."

"It's a zombie show. A little too scary for me," she said, sharing a grimace. "At least it used to be."

"Interesting," said Chang. "Unfortunately, what we're facing here is far more insidious than the mythical zombie. In many cases, infection won't be obvious."

"Like when they run at you with a machete?" said David, weakly chuckling at his joke.

"Exactly. If my suspicions are correct, temporal lobe damage caused by this virus could run the gamut of behaviors, from simple confusion and disorientation all the way to the *run at you with a machete* level."

"Or the *shoot at you from a window* level," said Larsen.

"That's the intriguing part," said Chang.

"I'd call it terrifying," said Emma.

"Same thing at this point," said Chang. "New behaviors not previously observed in patients infected with similar viruses. Working together is another example. A mob rush is one thing. Timing an attack is another."

"Felt like a bum rush to me," said David.

"It was and it wasn't," said Larsen, nodding at Chang. "Right?"

"Most of the people had clearly lost any sense of inhibition and attacked on sight, but a small percentage appeared to have varying degrees of higher-level functioning."

"What does that mean for us?" said Jack.

"It means you shouldn't make any assumptions out there," said Chang. "I think it's fair to say that the vast majority of infected will show obvious and outward signs of a problem. Torn clothing. Dried bloodstains. Weapons. Disheveled appearance. The longer they're out there, the clearer it will become. But some won't be so easy to detect."

"What about in here?" said Emma.

"We keep our distance from anyone inside," said Larsen. "And our weapons close by."

"I guess that's all we can do," said Chang, stepping through the open door. "I know where we are. The security hub is just a few more doors away. There should be a break room or lounge right before that, where Larsen and the Olsons can wait. They have some nice vending machines in the lounges."

"I didn't bring any cash," said Larsen. "Or a wallet."

"They take credit cards," said Chang.

"I'll spot you," said David. "My guess is you're good for it. If we survive."

"I'm a lot more interested in taking care of this gunshot," said Larsen. "I'm bleeding, in case nobody noticed."

"We can head to medical after I square things away with security," said Chang. "Maybe the cafeteria after that if it's not too crowded."

"No cafeteria. Vending machines will have to do," said Larsen. "We need to avoid contact with other employees. On top of the obvious reasons, we can't afford to add anyone to this group and expect to fly out of here."

"The vending machines have sushi," said Emma. "At least they do in my building."

"Sounds like we'll survive," said Larsen, patting Chang on the shoulder. "As long as I don't bleed to death."

"Are you bleeding?" said David, grinning.

"Just a little," said Larsen.

"We'll be right back," said Chang. "Then we'll head straight to medical."

Chapter Seven

Emma Harper got an uneasy feeling as soon as she stepped through the door leading to the security area. Three security officers outfitted like riot police approached them immediately, holding rifles similar to Larsen's. They kept their weapons pointed down, but the nervous looks on their partially hidden faces gave her the sinking feeling that they would shoot first and ask questions later. Chang pushed in front of her.

"Gentlemen, I'm Dr.—"

"We'll get to that in a minute," said one of the security officers. "Close the door behind you and don't take another step."

Emma raised her hands slowly, her husband and Chang doing the same a moment later.

"We're not infected," said Chang.

"One thing at a time," said the officer. "Where did the other three members of your party go?"

"How did you—"

"We registered your access through Gate 15," said the guard. "And every door after that. Where are the armed members of your team?"

"The employee lounge a few doors back," said Chang. "We thought it would be better to keep the weapons out of sight until I could explain what happened."

"We almost got killed out there," said Emma. "We're all NevoTech employees."

"Emma Harper. Jack Harper. Dr. Eugene Chang," said the officer. "Facial recognition confirmed your identities. I'm far more concerned with the others."

"May I show you something?" said Chang. "Two of the three people back in the lounge are law enforcement officers. One is a federal agent with Homeland Security. The other is a local police officer. I have their badges. The police officer's son is the third."

"Are any of you carrying a weapon?" said the officer.

"I have a revolver tucked into my waistband," said Jack. "Right hip. My right."

Emma sensed motion in her peripheral vision and turned her head in time to see another body-armor-clad officer appear directly to their right, near the corner of the room. Unlike the other guards, he pointed his rifle directly at them.

"Dr. Chang, walk forward until I tell you to stop. Everyone else remains in place with their hands held high."

Chang complied, stopping when directed.

"Slowly retrieve and place their badges on the floor at your feet. Raise your hands when you're done," said the officer. "No fast movements."

One of the guards in the group raised his rifle, pointing it at Chang. NevoTech must have seen some problems already. The guards weren't taking any chances. When Chang finished placing the badges on the floor, the guard instructed him to step backwards. The third guard quickly grabbed the badges, handing them to the leader, who took a few moments to examine them.

"Stay right there," he said.

"Where is he going?" said Jack.

"Jack," said Emma, trying to quiet him.

"What?" said her husband.

"You can talk," said the guard before disappearing behind a secure-looking door. "Just don't move."

They spent the next few minutes in silence, nobody keen to talk with guns pointed at them. When the security officer returned, he signaled for the other guards to stand down.

"Everyone checks out. Sorry about the drama," he said, returning the law enforcement badges. "Why don't you grab your friends, and we'll check your temperatures before we head to the food court. We do a temperature check every four hours, just in case. Can't be too careful. We've had a few cases of the infection develop during the night."

"I'll grab them," said Chang. "What about the weapons?"

"I'm a little leery about mixing weapons with the employee population," he said. "But we are talking a federal agent and a police officer—so I don't see a problem."

"Thank you," said Chang. "Be right back."

"Oh, Dr. Chang? You'll need this," said the officer, offering him a security badge. "This gives you access to all rooms in this building except the security hub, plus any areas you were cleared to enter under your previous clearance. I have passes for everyone else, including the nonemployees."

"Perfect," said Chang, disappearing through the door.

He returned less than a minute later with the rest of their bedraggled crew. Larsen handed Chang the spare rifle, leaving Emma wishing she and her husband hadn't left their weapons on the ground outside the gate turnstile. They'd likely need those when they returned to the plane later tonight, if they even left. Things seemed to be under control on the NevoTech campus.

"Now that we're all here," said the security officer. "I'm Dan Howard, head of NevoTech tactical security. If you don't mind, I'd like to take your temperatures."

Emma nodded, along with the rest of them, and one of Howard's security officers started moving among them with a digital thermometer, pressing it against each of their foreheads.

Larsen scanned the security team and smiled. "Maybe this is the safest place for us."

"I didn't know we had anything like this," said Chang.

"Nobody knows," said Howard. "We're entirely invisible to the employee population."

"How big is your team?" said Larsen.

"When fully staffed, a four-person team rotates through the research cluster twenty-four hours a day, three hundred and sixty-five days a year. A second rotating team is situated here during working hours."

"They're all normal," said the security officer with the thermometer.

"That's great news," said Howard.

"I mean now?" said Larsen. "How many do you have on the tactical team now?"

"You're looking at it," said Howard.

"Shit," muttered Larsen. His smile evaporated.

"It's not as bad as you think. I have a dozen or so security officers positioned in the food court area, where we keep the entire evacuee population. Everyone is in one place, so we can focus our limited security resources on their protection. I also have three two-person teams roaming the campus perimeter, looking for external problems, and a three-guard detail at the research center. We've cleared this entire building. Easier to detect a breach that way. Anything moving outside of the food court or medical is considered a potential threat until proven otherwise. We've been watching your group since it arrived at the gate."

"We could have used a little help," said Larsen.

"It would have been over by the time we arrived, exposing us to gunfire," said Howard. "We've been down that road before—unsuccessfully. I cut my losses at two security officers. One killed. One lying in medical with a bullet lodged in his thigh."

"Sorry," said Larsen. "It's crazy out there."

"Have any of the buildings been breached?" said Chang.

"No. But we've had a few outer perimeter breaches. Given what we've seen outside, it's only a matter of time before one of those mobs gets inside the fence. Compartmentalizing in one place is the only way we can protect this many people."

"How many people are here?" said Jack.

"Two hundred and thirty-eight. Employees and family. Some friends. We averaged about ten to fifteen arrivals an hour during daylight hours and the early evening. That slowed to two or three an hour until…" he said, uncomfortably glancing at the guard next to him. "You're the first group to make it inside the gates since around two in the morning."

Emma caught his meaning immediately.

"How many have tried?" she said, not sure she wanted to know the answer.

"Fifty or so, from what we can tell," said Howard. "Most of them never made it close to one of the gates."

"Without these," said Larsen, lifting his rifle, "we would have joined them."

"We barely made it with the rifles," said David.

"Perimeter sentries have reported sustained automatic fire throughout the night and heavily armed helicopters passing over the city," said Howard. "My guess is the National Guard will clear the city by the end of the day."

"I wouldn't count on it," said David. "They've set up two federal quarantine boundaries. The National Guard is set up along Interstate 465 around the city. The other is set about ten to fifteen miles beyond the interstate—in every direction. The 10th Mountain Division has been called in for that one."

"Based on what I know about this kind of emergency-response scenario, the government will initially focus on quarantine," said Chang. "They won't clear the city until they are one hundred percent certain that the virus has been contained. In a case like this, we could be talking weeks."

"Shit," said Howard. "What the hell happened out there? First we heard it was a pandemic flu, but that doesn't come close to explaining what we've seen."

"Bioweapon. Terrorist attack. It's a long story," said Larsen. "Which I'm sure Dr. Chang would be happy to shed some light on—after I get some medical attention."

The tactical officers shared uncomfortable looks that Emma immediately deciphered. Until just now, they thought this was a short-term problem and that they'd be home with their families by tomorrow at the latest. Possibly even tonight.

"Let's keep this under wraps for now. All of our

families are safe," said Howard.

"Stuck inside the secondary quarantine boundary," said one of the officers.

"Things are relatively calm in the suburbs," said David. "Most of the violence is within families, which I know doesn't sound good, but as long as none of your family members are infected, they should be fine."

"And none of our families showed any signs of fever before we lost communications," said Howard before turning to Larsen. "Let's get you to medical. It's close to the food court. We can get the rest of you something to eat."

"I think we might be better off keeping our distance from the rest of the evacuees. We won't be staying very long," said Larsen. "In fact, a few of us will be heading back out into the city as soon as I clean this up and apply a compress."

"What? Wait. Back out there?" said Howard before shaking his head. "I don't think that's a good idea."

"Neither do I, but this is going to require a little more than a compress," said Larsen, pointing at his leg wound. "Dr. Chang is in contact with an emergency room doctor holed up a few blocks from here. My plan is to bring her here."

Howard considered Larsen's words for a moment.

"Man, I hate to sound excited about sending you back out there, but we could really use a doctor here. Especially an ER doctor," said Howard. "At least a quarter of the people here are injured—some quite severely. We have some nurses in the group that are doing one hell of a job keeping the wounded stable, but the most critical patients are running out of time. We looked into transporting a few of them to one of the hospitals, but the emergency rooms have stopped accepting patients. I'd be willing to come with you."

"And I'd be happy to take you up on that offer," said Larsen. "If all goes well, you should have a doctor on staff within an hour."

"I'll go, too," said the youngest-looking security officer.

"I appreciate the offer, Mitch, but the tactical team can't afford to lose more than one officer," said Howard.

"Count me in," said David, immediately turning to his son. "Don't even think about it. You're staying right here."

"Come on, Dad," said Joshua. "I can handle myself."

"Josh, you've handled yourself extremely well tonight, but three is the best number for this. Fewer moving parts and enough firepower to get us out of a sticky situation."

"You can barely run," said David's son.

"I can run if I need to," said Larsen. "And I make up for any loss of speed with my shooting. I'll get your dad back in one piece. Promise."

"Dad," started Joshua.

"The decision is final, buddy," said David. "I can't be worrying about you out there, too. I need to focus on getting back safely."

"I don't want to lose you," said Joshua.

"I won't let that happen," said David.

"Neither will I," said Larsen. "Your dad will be in good hands. No risky shit. Pardon my language."

"He's heard worse," said David.

Joshua didn't look convinced by his father's argument, but he let it go, which relieved Emma. She couldn't imagine how Larsen was going to pull this off during the daytime—or any time for that matter. As soon as one of those lunatics spotted them, all bets would be off. Three guns or a hundred wouldn't make a difference against one of those mobs.

Chapter Eight

Larsen pursed his lips while he wiped an antiseptic sponge across the surface of his wound. It stung like hell. The bullet had creased his leg, taking a two-inch-long, half-inch-deep slice out of his thigh muscle. When he finished with the iodine sponge, he unwrapped a square piece of hemostatic gauze and placed it over the wound, keeping it in place while he tightly rolled an Israeli bandage around his thigh, securing it in place. A minute later, he was back on his feet, his thigh holster back in place over his bloodied pants.

"Good as new," he said, wincing a little as he took a few steps.

The wound needed stitches. Deep stitches that he couldn't do anything about—but they didn't have time for that. He'd done more with worse injuries. He could do this.

"Looks like it still hurts," said David.

"Of course it still hurts. It's a bullet wound," said Larsen, reading between the lines. "I'll be fine. Dr. Hale can stitch me up better when we get back. Dan? I assume we can access all of the external cameras from the security hub?"

"Right. We have a diagram of the campus, with additional sensor input. Motion detectors. Pressure plates.

Perimeter tamper detectors. We should be able to form the best picture from there."

"Then let's get the show on the road," said Larsen.

The walk back to the security hub felt better with the compressed bandage in place, but it was far from ideal. The pain was manageable but persistent. He imagined it would worsen with another dead sprint like before. He'd done the wound no favors during the last few minutes outside the campus gate, and it had punished him with steady bleeding, despite the hemostatic powder he had packed into it. That said, the worst-case scenario out there was more pain. The bullet wound was mostly superficial, presenting no life-threatening complications other than slowing him down, which could be quite lethal under the circumstances.

When they reached the hub, Howard let them inside the surveillance core, where a single uniformed security officer sat at a semicircular desk that faced a one-hundred-and-eighty-degree array of curved flat-screen monitors. At least three dozen camera feeds appeared on the screens, panning and shifting almost constantly.

"This is Gary Hoenig. He's the only security operations officer that showed up yesterday, and pretty much the only person in this building that knows how to operate the high-tech surveillance system. How does it look at Gate 15?"

"Still a few stragglers," he said. "But most of them have lost interest. I counted about sixty or so in the group that chased you to the gate. Another minute out there and—well, you know what would have happened."

A massive section of screens in the center of the array blinked, almost instantly displaying a color camera feed labeled G15:0710.35. Larsen counted five figures stumbling aimlessly within view. A woman pressed against the fence, hands grasped around the iron bars, appearing to be looking inside the campus.

"Check this out," said Hoenig, splitting the screen into two feeds.

The new video image was labeled D38:0711.04 and showed the person's head pressed through the bars.

"She's stuck," said Dr. Chang.

"Ripped her ears right off jamming that melon through," said Hoenig.

"That's fucking crazy," said David. "The rest of them don't attack her?"

"Oddly, no," said Howard. "We've seen them turn on each other all night."

"What did you mean by 'you know what would have happened'?" said Jack Harper.

Hoenig swiveled his chair to face them. "I meant if you got caught in the open by the mob."

"What would have happened?" said Jack.

"What do you mean?" said Hoenig, a confused look on his face. "You've been out there all night, right?"

"We landed in the city ten minutes before we arrived at the gate," said David.

"Landed?" said Hoenig.

"On Interstate 70 by South East Street exit, in a small plane. We came straight here."

"Will someone tell me what happens with these mobs?" said Larsen.

"People get torn to pieces," said Howard. "Literally torn to pieces."

"Bullshit," said Jack. "Things are bad out there, but not that bad."

"You want to see for yourself?" said Hoenig. "I can

replay some of the video captured last night."

"Please don't," said Emma.

"Yes. Please don't. I think our short trip from the interstate clearly demonstrated that the mobs are lethal," said David.

"Agreed," said Larsen before moving closer to the enlarged center image. "Can you get us a Google Earth map of the area right around this campus? Satellite version?"

"Sure thing," said Hoenig. "I think we're still connected to the internet by satellite. Even if we weren't, I have a full package of maps that would do the trick."

The oversized video feed switched to a satellite map of downtown Indianapolis, which the security officer adjusted to center directly over the NevoTech campus.

"What's your address, Dr. Chang?" said Larsen.

Hoenig typed the Virginia Avenue address, shifting the image slightly northeast.

"That's not far at all," said Larsen. "Can't be more than a half mile. Maybe less. Is that a gate connecting to Merrill Street? Jesus. We could drive there in thirty seconds."

"What about your friends out there?" said David, raising an eyebrow.

He was right. They had to approach Chang's apartment as quietly and discreetly as possible. The team assigned to the apartment had likely received a warning that Larsen had gone rogue. It wouldn't take Control long to link the airport escape to Larsen's communications blackout.

"What friends?" said Howard, eyeing him skeptically.

"I was part of a Homeland team assigned to locate and escort Dr. Chang to safety. Like a VIP protective detail.

My team was presumably one of four that parachuted into the greater Indianapolis area. I can only assume one of the teams is watching the apartment, which complicates things."

Hoenig and Howard spoke at the same time, each sounding extremely concerned by the information he just shared.

"One at a time, please," said Larsen. "Howard?"

"You don't have communications with the other teams?" said Howard.

"Negative. The program is extremely compartmentalized. No communication is allowed between teams. Control directs everything."

"Can't you ask this headquarters or Control place to deconflict our arrival?" said Howard before muttering a few obscenities under his breath. "Wait. Where's the rest of your team?"

"That's what I was going to ask," said Hoenig. "Among other things."

Howard shared a very uncomfortable look with Hoenig, which spread to the other tactical officers positioned around the room. Shit. This could spiral out of control quickly if he didn't adequately ease their fears. Keeping his hands clear of his rifle, Larsen started to explain, but was immediately cut off by Chang.

"I saw what happened to his team," said Chang. "Eric Larsen disobeyed an order to kill me, sparking a mutiny among his teammates. In the span of a second, everyone was dead except him. There's absolutely no doubt in my mind that this man is one of the good guys. Unfortunately, the same can't be said about the rest of the teams out there."

"Everything he said is the truth. My orders went from

locate and protect to capture or kill within the span of fifteen minutes. I didn't sign up for an assassination squad," said Larsen, looking around the room. "That's why I can't contact Control—and why we need to be very careful approaching the apartment. I wouldn't be surprised if the other teams have been warned about me."

"Man, this whole thing is one giant shit show," said Howard, still looking entirely apprehensive about the situation.

"A shit show that could get us all killed," said one of Howard's officers.

"Seriously," said Howard. "And why would the Department of Homeland Security want Chang dead or captured?"

"Dr. Chang has a few theories," said Larsen.

"Without boring all of you—"

"Trust me. You have our attention," said Howard.

"This is high-level nondisclosure information…but I suppose we're past that point now," said Chang. "I'm currently developing a preventative vaccine against herpes simplex one and two, which would theoretically double as a preventative measure against a herpes simplex-based bioweapon, which is what I strongly believe this to be."

"I guarantee you that a herpes outbreak didn't cause what I've seen on my screens," said Hoenig.

"Technically, it did, but not in the traditional sense of how we view herpes simplex. I had a chance to examine a blood sample, which contained a modified strain of herpes simplex one. Weaponized might be a better word. This strain aggressively seeks out the central nervous system and triggers herpes simplex encephalitis, a particularly nasty and typically rare condition."

"And this causes people to kill each other in the streets

like psychopaths?" said Howard.

"That's the theory. Herpes simplex encephalitis impacts the temporal lobe, lowering or eliminating inhibitions—which has long been documented to cause aggression."

"This is more than aggression, Dr. Chang," added Howard. "They are literally ripping each other apart like animals out there."

"I wish I could give you a definitive scientific answer, but I would need weeks to unravel the DNA coding variations to determine precisely how this virus turns people into murderous lunatics," said Chang.

"So why do they want you dead or in custody?" said Howard.

"Because I'm one of a handful of scientists with enough experience in the herpes simplex virus research field to authoritatively determine that the virus in question has been extensively weaponized. The government had a vested interest in my vaccine project. Certain state sponsors of terrorism have been trying to weaponized herpes simplex encephalitis for years—unsuccessfully for the most part."

"For the most part?" said Howard.

"A similar virus may have been used against a Russian city several years ago. All rumor. I became interested in this field based on that rumor. It was too terrifying a prospect to ignore."

"Maybe I'm missing something," said Hoenig. "But it sounds like the government would want to do everything in their power to keep you safe—unless they suspected you were somehow behind this outbreak."

"Or the government was behind the attack," said Chang. "Twenty-four cities have been hit."

"Bullshit," said Hoenig. "I heard something about Fort Wayne and Columbus, but those are pretty close. An easy few hours' drive for a scientist carrying a beaker full of nightmares."

"Add Cleveland, Cincinnati, Louisville, Milwaukee, Des Moines, Minneapolis, St. Louis, Detroit, Pittsburg, Nashville and Memphis to that list. You have internet access. Try to get any live coverage from inside one of those cities. Then check out Chicago, San Francisco, San Diego, Los Angeles, Boston, Atlanta, Denver, Philadelphia, Hartford and Seattle. Actually, start with one of those. Those cities weren't under full lockdown last time I checked. You'll immediately see some similarities to what was happening in Indianapolis a few days ago," said Chang.

"I will," said Hoenig, typing furiously at his keyboard.

Several smaller screens changed around the fringes of the satellite map, all of them displaying *HTTP ERROR 500 (INTERNAL SERVER ERROR)*. The typing continued, but the screens remained the same.

"I just hope none of those represent the bigger cities," said Chang.

"I haven't gotten to them yet," said Hoenig. "I have to admit this is fucking odd. Not a single local affiliate link works. Radio or TV. I've even tried a few municipal sites."

"Most of them went down early in the afternoon," said Chang.

"Gentlemen, we need to get this show on the road. The longer we wait, the worse this will get out there," said Larsen. "Do you trust us or not?"

"Looks like this is bigger than Indianapolis and the Midwest," said Hoenig. "Check it out."

The satellite map changed to a live news report from Seattle, which highlighted the recent activation of Washington National Guard units to assist hospitals and emergency responders with the worsening flu outbreak. They watched in silence for nearly a minute.

"Are we good?" said Larsen.

"I'm good," said Howard. "Gary?"

Hoenig nodded. "We're good."

The rest of Howard's team agreed, dropping the tension level back to normal.

"I still think you're biting off more than you can chew trying to get to that doctor," said Hoenig. "How do you discreetly infiltrate an actively watched apartment building with a horde of lunatics chasing you down?"

"We get close enough without attracting their attention," said Larsen, "then deal with the apartment."

Hoenig shook his head, sending the map back to the screen. "Good luck with that," he said, moving the mouse cursor to trace the closest approach to Chang's address. "The chances of crossing this ground unobserved are slim to none. The street may look deserted, but it fills up fast whenever someone walks by."

"What about the dead-end street just above it?" said Larsen. "Looks like it leads to a parking garage next to Chang's apartment."

"The garage is connected on the second floor," said Chang. "The apartment comes with a space in the garage."

"Perfect," said Larsen.

"They'll be watching that entrance," said David.

"Doesn't matter," said Larsen. "If the garage is connected, I can figure out a way to get into the apartment building. Might take a little climbing or parkour, but I'll manage."

"You still have the same problem. Possibly worse," said Hoenig. "The map is a little deceptive. Warsaw Street is across from the main campus parking lot, which isn't fully enclosed by the campus fence. A lot of people have died there, but that's mostly because they drove in and parked...drawing a lot of attention."

"They parked?" said David.

"In neat rows. Some in their assigned spaces," said Hoenig.

"Why the fuck would they do that?" said David.

"Most employees don't realize the lot is essentially wide open. They drive up and there's a gate with a guard shack, all connected to a formidable-looking fence, but the fence only extends to the trees about a hundred feet on each side. After the first few killings, we drove out there and posted signs, but nobody paid attention. Then we disabled the gate, but that just made things worse. People left their cars and climbed the gate, only to be torn apart fifty feet into the parking lot. We keep it open now. If anyone shows up, all we can do is try to get to them before they get out of their cars."

"We'll have to create some kind of diversion," said Larsen.

"One that doesn't alert the other teams," said Howard.

"Right. That's the trick," said Larsen, studying the image for a few moments. "What exactly happens when a car pulls into the lot?"

"A dozen or so crazies spill out of the trees and bushes that ring the parking lot, running full speed toward the car and whoever gets out."

"From different directions?"

Howard nodded. "Yeah. That's why it's so dangerous.

We don't know where they'll emerge the next time."

"They go back into hiding after a kill?" said Chang. "To the same hiding spots?"

"Yes to both questions. They don't like to linger in the open," said Howard.

"Does this frenzy draw any infected from outside the lot?" said Larsen.

"If it goes on long enough, they start streaming in from the surrounding streets," said Howard.

"That could work to our advantage," said Larsen. "How long are we talking?"

"We had a few vehicles pull in and get mobbed before anyone got out. Those lasted the longest," said Howard. "The people inside put up a fight, but got yanked out eventually. I'd say anything lasting over five minutes will start to pull crazies from the streets. Longer than five minutes and we could empty the side streets, especially if it's loud. Gunfire draws them in like moths to a flame."

"Gunfire might alert anyone watching Chang's apartment," said Larsen.

"You're gonna have shooting no matter what. That's the new norm with the mobs," said Howard. "However, if we can get you to the other side of East Street unobserved, you could hide out and let things quiet down. Trust me. If the team sitting on Chang's apartment has been here for most of the night, they won't think twice about a flurry of gunshots."

"Then that's the plan," said Larsen. "We drive one of your vehicles to the opposite side of the parking lot and create a lot of noise."

"We?" said Jack Harper. "I thought the mob pulled people out of the cars and ripped them apart?"

"Shit. I just assumed you have at least one hardened

vehicle?" said Larsen.

"We do," said Howard. "A bullet-resistant Suburban. Run-flat tires. The works."

"And you want one of us to drive it?" said Jack.

"I'll do it," said Joshua Olson.

"No, you won't," said David.

"I want to do something," said his son.

"Negative," said Howard. "Mitch will drive the vehicle. It'll get extremely dicey out there. Imagine forty to fifty people swarmed around you."

"Thanks a lot," said Mitch jokingly.

"Hey, you're the one that volunteered to go on the rescue mission," said Howard. "Careful what you ask for."

The group laughed nervously.

"The rest of my team and a few of the perimeter guards will be split between the perimeter vehicle gate and the roof, ready to thin the herd around the car so we can get Mitch back in one piece."

"Do you have any smoke grenades?" said Larsen. "I was thinking we could plop a few down in the eastern end of the parking lot to cut down on our chances of being spotted by any swivel heads in the mob."

"I have an array of goodies that might pique your interest," said Howard.

"Then that's it," said Larsen.

"The last time you said that, things went sideways pretty quickly," said David.

"As I recall, the plan was a complete success," said Larsen. "Just a little more dramatic."

"If you consider nearly getting shot down by a helicopter a 'little more dramatic,' I suppose I might agree with you," said David, and the rest of them laughed.

"Technically, my plan ended when the plane took off," said Larsen, exposing a wicked grin.

"Touché," said David, smiling. "Let's just make sure the plan for our little foray this morning ends with getting us back inside the NevoTech campus—alive."

"Well met, sir," said Larsen, before turning to Howard. "Let's take a look at those goodies you mentioned."

Chapter Nine

David Olson ran his hand over the ballistic vest borrowed from the NevoTech tactical team armory, tugging on the magazine pouches to make sure they had been attached properly. He'd been reluctant to give up the tactical rig he'd spent hours "getting right" at home, but the addition of front and back level IV composite body armor plates convinced him to make the swap.

His own vest consisted of a single front-facing level III plate and fewer rifle magazine pouches, trading the weight and space for longer-term survival gear. It was designed to balance tactical and travel needs. The rig he took from Howard's armory had been assembled with one purpose in mind—gun fighting—a much better match for their impending mission.

He crouched next to Larsen, who kneeled next to a window near the emergency exit they'd take to reach the pedestrian gate at the northeast corner of the campus. Thick bushes and mature trees would conceal their short trip to the gate from the outside world, but once they got through the gate, they would be exposed to the parking lot and the streets adjacent to the campus. Their plan almost entirely relied on Howard's parking lot diversion.

"I can't seem to shake the feeling that this is a bad idea," said David.

Larsen turned his attention from the scene beyond the window. "That's because it's a terrible idea."

Howard cast David a concerned look.

"He's kidding. Sort of," said David. "Takes a little while to adjust to his sense of humor."

"Actually, I wasn't kidding," said Larsen. "It's a horrible idea—but it's the best plan we have."

"Is that more of his humor?" said Howard.

"I hope so," said David.

Larsen gave them a wry smile. "Everything will be fine."

"Until it's not," said David.

"You're just as bad as he is," said Howard.

"If things get too dicey on the way to Chang's apartment, we pull the plug on the mission," said Larsen. "I'm not getting myself killed to help this leg."

"I would hope not," said David. "That would almost be the literal definition of cutting off your nose to spite your face. A Pyrrhic victory kind of situation."

"A Pyrrhic victory would be losing two of us to bring back the doctor," said Larsen. "I'm pulling the plug if it starts to look like one of us might not make it back."

"I hate to bring this to your attention," said David. "But I think we're starting out at that point."

"True enough," said Larsen, waiting a few moments before smirking. "Seriously. If this goes sideways en route, I'm bringing us back."

"No arguments here," said Howard.

"Or here," said David. "I'll let you know if my definition of things going sideways conflicts with yours."

"I expect nothing short of brutal honesty out there—from both of you."

"You don't have to worry about that with me," said

Howard. "The only question I won't answer honestly is 'does this outfit make me look fat?'"

"Smart man," said Larsen.

"Maybe that's why I'm no longer married," said David, and they all quietly laughed.

David's earpiece crackled a few moments later.

"Dan, this is Mitch. I'm ready to drive through the delivery gates."

Howard pressed his transmitter. "Copy that, Mitch. Proceed with your mission."

"Opening the gate," said Mitch.

"Sean? How are we looking?"

"Ready to make it happen," replied Sean Fitzgerald, the security officer stationed on a roof overlooking the parking lot.

"You and Roscoe are our eyes and ears up there," said Howard. "We move when you give the word."

"We're on it," said Sean. "Roscoe is dialed in. Never fired that thing before, but it doesn't look complicated."

"It isn't," said Howard. "May take a few tries, but he'll get the hang of it."

"I hear the tactical vehicle," said Sean, pausing for a few moments. "And so do the crazies. I have movement on the western edge of the parking lot."

"Keep a close eye on Mitch's situation," said Howard. "They can't get at Mitch from the outside without concentrating gunfire in one spot. You start to see something like that, you thin the herd around his vehicle. If they try to flip it, same thing."

"Nobody's flipping this mother," said Mitch.

"Don't count on that," said Howard. "Alright. I'm turning this over to you, Sean. You're calling the shots until we get back. Be ready for any of the contingency plans we discussed."

"Understood."

Howard took a deep breath, releasing it before continuing. "All stations, this is Howard. I have transferred tactical command of NevoTech security to Sean Fitzgerald."

After all of the security officers acknowledged the change of command, Howard edged toward the emergency exit.

"Now we wait for them to take the bait," said Howard.

David formed a snarky comment in his head, but kept it to himself. There was no point. The plan sucked. Even Larsen knew it. Any of a hundred things could derail it and get them killed. A part of him questioned why he had volunteered for this borderline suicide mission. Most of him still knew the answer. To serve and protect. Some things never changed, and that was a good thing—as long as it didn't get him killed.

"Mitch is in position," said Sean. "And they're already coming out of the trees."

"Copy," said Howard, turning to David and Larsen. "Won't be too long."

A car alarm sounded outside the window next to David, drawing his attention to the thick bushes on the outside of the campus fence. A few previously undetected figures stirred in the greenery, rising to investigate the growing ruckus on the other side of the parking lot. They took off as soon as they were upright, moving at a disturbingly fast pace.

"I hate that they can move fast," muttered David.

"Yeah. It ain't a *Walking Dead* scenario," said Howard. "Not a lot of time to react once they get excited."

"Which means we need to be proactive out there," said Larsen, putting a hand on David's shoulder. "You shoot as soon as you have a target. Doesn't matter if it's sitting pretty at a picnic table."

"What do you want me to do?" said Howard. "Aside from nothing."

"We only have two suppressed rifles," said Larsen. "You only fire in extreme self-defense—or in the unlikely event that we get mobbed."

The spotting team on the roof radioed in.

"Looks like we've got their attention," said Sean. "I have a few dozen crossing East Street directly from the area you're headed. We have them streaming in from every other direction as well. I think we'll let this develop for another minute or two."

"They're rocking this Suburban pretty fierce," said Mitch. "Man, this fucking sucks."

"Keep him safe, Sean," said Howard.

"He's fine. The truck is barely moving," said Sean.

A gunshot erupted outside.

"And now they're shooting," said Mitch, followed by a rapid string of gunshots. "A lot!"

"Jesus. They're shooting each other to get to the Suburban," said Sean.

Howard moved to the emergency exit. "I think it's time. I don't want Mitch stuck out there any longer than necessary."

"Let's go," said Larsen, pushing the door open. "Safeties off. Howard in the middle."

David followed the security officer through the door, shifting his rifle to cover their right flank as they walked briskly toward the pedestrian gate at the northeast corner of the campus. He detected movement beyond the bushes along the eastern fence line. Two or three figures scrambled up East Street, their features concealed by the overlapping greenery. Larsen slowed, tracking the rapidly moving shapes with his rifle.

He found himself silently wishing that one of them would spot his group and put an end to this insane mission before it started. No such luck. They ran past the gate and turned left at the corner of the fence, headed straight for the commotion in the parking lot. By the time David's group reached the gate, four more gaggles of crazies had materialized on East Street, sprinting toward the mayhem unfolding around Mitch's SUV.

A sudden, extended volley of nearby gunshots dropped them to the stone path. David lifted his head a few seconds later, confident that the gunfire hadn't been directed at him. He hadn't heard any of the telltale snaps and hisses signaling a near miss. He was about to rise into a low crouch when another group of crazies spilled by the gate, causing him to freeze in place.

One of them, a bloodied woman in a pink and gray yoga outfit, momentarily paused on the other side of the gate to fiddle with a hunting rifle. David tilted his rifle into an upright position on the ground, easing his face toward the holographic sight. She vanished before he could center the reticle on her chest. He let out his breath, relieved she had moved on. They couldn't reliably fire at her through the gate, due to the tightly spaced steel turnstile bars. If the woman had looked up from the rifle for any reason, they'd more than likely be headed back into the building.

Larsen led them to the right of the stone path, where a passerby on the other side of the gate couldn't so easily spot them. They stacked up next to the gate, pointing their weapons toward the street. This close to the fence, an astute observer on East Street should be able to pick them out from the foliage—though he strongly suspected that the infected didn't have that kind of focus. From what he'd seen so far, they appeared to be driven by base instincts. Reacting to stimuli rather than proactively seeking it. Still, they weren't taking any chances. A crazy with a pistol could barrel headlong through the bushes and put one or more of them in the medical bay—without an ER doctor to dig the bullet out.

"We ready?" said Howard.

"I think this is as good as it will get," said Larsen.

"I don't know. They keep coming out of the woodwork," said David.

"We can handle small groups," said Larsen.

"I hope so," said David before nodding at Howard. "I guess we're ready."

Howard transmitted to the rooftop over-watch team. "Sean, we're in position at the gate. Ready to make the run."

"Copy. Give us about thirty seconds to get the screen up," said Sean.

"Let us know when we can cross," said Howard.

"Roger that. Smoke grenade out."

A familiar, hollow thump sounded in the distance, the first of several smoke grenades sailing in an arc toward the center of the parking lot. Howard stepped forward and pressed his ID badge against the card reader, simultaneously typing a short code into the digital pad next to it.

"No need to individually swipe badges," said Howard. "I enabled the group passage function used for evacuations."

"That's one way, right?" said Larsen.

"Correct. I used the outbound code," said Howard. "If we're not being chased on the way back, I can expedite our return with the inbound code. Just hang on to your temporary IDs in case something happens to me. We all have a spare for Dr. Hale."

"Let's do this," said Larsen.

The former Navy SEAL cycled through a few deep breaths and exhales before pushing the turnstile, which moved freely. He slid to the other side and crouched on the sidewalk next to East Street.

"Shit. Contact right," said Larsen, spinning to face the unseen threat.

David shoved Howard out of the way and spun through the metal barrier, nearly colliding with Larsen, who had already started firing. He immediately regained his balance, nestling into a tight crouch next to Larsen.

"Jesus," he muttered, centering the holographic reticle on a hammer-wielding man less than twenty feet away—and pressing the trigger.

He had no time to think, only react, as he worked methodically with Larsen to clear the small mob of blood-soaked, raging lunatics headed full speed in their direction. Several seconds later, at least ten people lay contorted on the street and the sidewalk in front of him, a few still twitching. One of them started to lift its head, and Larsen fired a single suppressed bullet through the bottom of a man's chin, snapping the head against the pavement with a thud.

"Check the parking lot," said Larsen, turning to Howard, who was still on the other side of the gate. "We could use your help."

"Sorry," said Howard. "I wasn't expecting that."

"None of us were," said Larsen. "It's going to be a lot of fun out here."

Larsen jogged to the corner of the fence, turning briefly to watch Howard slide through the turnstile. Just beyond Howard, David kneeled before carefully peering around a bush at the parking lot. A thick cloud of white smoke obscured the far end of the parking lot, where Mitch's SUV was under attack. A few stragglers remained visible on the eastern side of the parking lot, but they were headed away from the gate, focused on whatever was happening on the other side of the chemical cloud. David triggered his communications link.

"We're good. The rooftop team put down a nice smoke screen," said David.

"Let's get moving," said Larsen. "I don't want to get hit by another group like that."

"You're not the only one," said David, turning to join Larsen and Howard, who had already started across East Street.

Chapter Ten

Larsen pressed against the cinder-block wall and checked his surroundings. So far so good. The smoke screen held in place thanks to a breezeless, humid morning, allowing them to shift the bulk of their attention to a one-hundred-and-eighty-degree arc facing the city. He listened for a few seconds before moving through a wide gap in the wall leading to a rough gravel driveway.

"Clear," he said, pushing deeper.

A two-story red brick house stood in the middle of the well-manicured lot, the green grass, lush vegetable garden and bright flower beds a stark contrast to its drab urban surroundings. Larsen kept a close eye on the home's window as he made his way up the driveway and took a knee behind a parked SUV. Howard's voice filled his earpiece.

"Fitzgerald, this is Howard. Get Mitch out of there. We're off the street."

"Copy that. Good luck."

They were going to need a lot more than good luck. More like divine intervention. He glanced over his shoulder, relieved to find that David and Howard had taken positions inside the wall, on opposite sides of the driveway. Right where he wanted them. David peeked around the wall, looking in both directions on East Street.

"The street is clear," said David.

"Maintain position until we're sure we haven't attracted a following," said Larsen.

"Staying put," said David.

He felt safe with the police officer watching his back. David had more than proven himself over the past six hours, saving Larsen's life more than once. He couldn't say the same about Howard, but the fact that the security officer had volunteered for this mission, on behalf of the NevoTech refugees under his protection, spoke volumes about his commitment. Larsen could count on these two. He just hoped the mission didn't get one or both of them killed. He'd have a hard time living with that. Then again, if things got that bad out here, he was more than likely to end up dead with them.

Tires screeched in the distance, followed by a cascade of gunshots. They might need to sit still for a while. The ruckus was bound to alert the team watching Chang's apartment. He assumed it was one team at this point. Maybe that wasn't a good assumption. Probably not. If Larsen detected the presence of more than one team, they'd have to abort the mission. He could deal with four operatives spread out around the apartment, but not a concentrated and likely coordinated mass of gunfighters. That was the true definition of a suicide mission.

"Howard, it's Fitzgerald. Mitch made a clean escape," said Fitzgerald.

"Good to hear. Sounded like hell out there."

"The bad news is the SUV took a beating. They flattened at least one of the tires," said Fitzgerald. "The run-flat system didn't perform as advertised."

"Damn. I need you to assess the damage to the SUV and report back," said Howard. "Keep Roscoe on the roof with the grenade launcher and sniper system—in case we need some long-distance help."

"Copy that. Heading down right now. Out," said Fitzgerald.

Howard shook his head. "We can't count on the SUV right now."

"I wasn't counting on it, anyway," said Larsen, eyeballing the side door to the house. "I'm going to give the side door to the house a try. We can use it as a safe house if things get dicey. Wouldn't mind finding the keys to this 4Runner, either. A ride is a ride."

"Hold on. I'll move up and cover you," said Howard.

When the security officer reached the back of the SUV, Larsen moved between the vehicle and the house, arriving at the door. He let the rifle dangle on its sling and drew the suppressed pistol strapped to his thigh in case someone was waiting for him on the other side of the door. The pistol would be easier to maneuver and use in tight quarters. He reached out with his unoccupied hand and tried to open the screen door, finding it locked. His knife was out in a flash, opening a fist-sized slash in the screen near the handle. He released the latch inside the screen and swung the door out of the way, propping it open with his shoulder.

He wasn't hopeful about getting into the house without making a lot of noise. The windowless metal door inside the frame looked formidable, and the doorknob didn't budge. In fact, it didn't even rattle, almost like it had been welded in place. He glanced over his shoulder and shook his head before signaling for them to follow.

The backyard contained a spacious stone patio featuring a long wooden table and rough-hewn tree stumps for seating. Strings of lights crisscrossed the patio, supported by thick wooden poles sunk into the ground at each corner. A large vegetable garden occupied most of the remaining square footage, leaving just enough room for a potter's shed in the far corner of the yard. He didn't see a gate or any way into the lot behind the property, which was a little concerning. The thought of climbing over and exposing himself to easy observation didn't sit well. Never did.

"David, keep a close eye on the house. Could be someone holed up inside. The door looked reinforced," said Larsen.

Larsen led them through the extensive garden, which he guessed had been picked clean very recently. Lettuce and kale bunches, which he recognized from his garden back home, had been completely cut to the new growth. Most of the carrots were gone, too, along with all of the season's other produce. He stopped to check the end of a long row of carrot plants, pulling a pinkie-sized carrot from the dirt. The row must have been planted late. Everything else was in the growing phase. Pole beans. Bush beans. Tomatoes. Cucumbers. Peppers. Cabbage. Everything. He looked back at the house, certain someone was inside—watching them very carefully.

He gathered them against the cinder-block wall next to the locked shed, taking a momentary break to reevaluate their situation.

"Dan, give me a quick lift," said Larsen. "I want to see what's on the other side of this wall."

"Should be a gravel lot," said Howard. "Wide open to the parking garage. Probably not our best approach."

"Let's see," said Larsen.

Howard kneeled next to the wall and interlocked his

fingers, nodding at Larsen, who gently placed a foot in his gloved hands.

"Ready?" said Larsen, and Howard nodded.

Larsen pushed up on his foot, grasping the top edge of the wall with both hands. Howard moved into a standing position, giving Larsen just enough height to see over the barrier. He cocked his head and inched upward until he could see the top of the apartment building and the parking garage attached to it. Shit. Wide open on the other side of the wall. He took a few moments to analyze other possible approaches before telling Howard to lower him.

"What's your read?" said David, not taking his eyes or rifle off the house.

"Wide open like Dan said," said Larsen. "We need to push north across Warsaw Street and approach obliquely."

"We can't go back out the way we came," said David. "The smoke screen will be gone, and all of those crazies will be headed back home."

"Whatever we do, it needs to happen right now," said Howard. "We'll be exposed to the northern side of the parking lot when we cross Warsaw Street."

"Then let's get moving," said Larsen.

"How are we doing this?" said David.

"Over that wall," said Larsen, pointing to the other side of the shed. "Stay low going over. Howard goes last. You have to stay up there and give him a hand over."

Larsen stepped onto Howard's locked hands and counted down from three, pushing off the foot on zero and pulling his body up. He kept his chest pressed flat against the top of the wall as he swung his feet over to the other side. As soon as his legs cleared the wall, the rest of him followed, giving him less than a second to assess the situation on the other side. Nothing jumped out at him before he landed on his feet or after he scanned the house and yard for a few seconds. He did see one major problem.

The corner lot was a quarter of the size of the one he'd just left, and the house occupied nearly the entire northern edge of the property, extending to the front gate. They'd have to go through the house to get onto the street adjacent to it. It was the best of their shitty options.

"All clear," said Larsen.

Several moments later, David and Howard dropped to the dead grass next to him, fanning out to cover the approaches.

"This is a dead end," said David. "We can't go out the front here either. Same problem."

Larsen had already started for the back door of the house. "Watch the front. I might have to make a little noise."

Miraculously, he didn't. The door was unlocked, opening into a scene right out of a slasher flick. The smell hit him before he could start to process what might have happened inside this quaint white house. Howard started to gag a few feet behind him.

"What the hell?" said Howard, barely getting the words out.

"Decomposing bodies," said David. "A few days old."

"I think some of these have been here longer," said Larsen. "I'm walking straight through to the front door. Cover the left."

Larsen shifted the rifle to his left shoulder, pointing it toward a dark hallway leading deeper into the house. He couldn't imagine a threat emerging from the family room on his left. In fact, he couldn't imagine what had happened here at all. It looked like a family had been slaughtered in place on the family room furniture. The corpses had been hacked so badly, he could barely tell them apart, aside from the size differences and remnants of long hair. Mom. Dad. Boy. Girl. An innocent family murdered in their own house by a pack of raving lunatics. Or was it their house? And had they been uninfected? He didn't plan on sticking around long enough to find out.

"Oh, God," said Howard. "I don't think we should. I don't—"

A fire hose stream of tan vomit gushed past Larsen's right leg, splashing off one of the kitchen island stools. He kept his focus on the dark hallway, continuing to move toward the front door.

"Take shallow breaths through your mouth and keep your eyes on my back. Nowhere else," said Larsen. "We'll be out of here in a few seconds."

A second round of vomiting erupted, the remaining contents of Howard's stomach hitting the floor somewhere behind him with a forceful splatter. David had become noticeably quiet, causing Larsen to take a quick peek over his shoulder. The cop was transfixed by the ghastly scene, still standing near the back door.

"Keep it moving," hissed Larsen. "We need to get across the street five minutes ago."

"Sorry," said David. "This is fucking unbelievable. These people were butchered."

"Same thing will happen to us if we don't get the fuck out of here right now," said Larsen, putting his hand on the front door. "We ready?"

"Good to go," croaked Howard.

"Ready," said David.

Larsen opened the door inward and took a quick look through the screen door. The street was empty, but he could already see movement in the thinning cloud of smoke to the west. A lot of movement. A concrete alleyway directly across from them seemed to be their best option. They'd be momentarily exposed to observation from the parking garage, but there was no other choice. He pushed the screen door open and bolted into the nearby street.

Halfway across, one of the figures emerged from the parking lot haze and stopped, clearly looking in their direction. Larsen took a knee in the middle of the street.

"Keep going," he said, centering the rifle reticle on the man's upper torso.

Howard and David passed behind him as he fired twice, dropping the crazy to the parking lot before he reacted. Larsen swiftly crossed the street, closely watching the shapes visible inside the dissipating cloud. He reached the alleyway, where David crouched behind the corner of the nearest house, monitoring the same situation. Howard stood next to him, with his hands on his knees, breathing deeply.

"I think we're good," said David as he passed by.

"We need to get off the streets," said Larsen, pausing in front of Howard. "You good?"

"Yeah. Just catching my breath," said Howard, standing up. "I wasn't expecting that. I knew things were bad, but this is something completely different. I have to get back to my family."

Larsen put a hand on the trembling officer's shoulder. "Dan, I need you to stay focused—so we can all get home to our families. I have a wife and baby daughter in Colorado that I'm worried sick about. David left his son back at NevoTech, and his wife is out there somewhere."

"Ex-wife," said David, still peeking around the corner of the house.

"But still your son's mother," said Larsen. "I'm sure you'd like to find her, for Joshua's sake."

"I would."

"Then let's focus on the mission. A successful mission gets us closer to seeing our families again, and it gets a qualified emergency room doctor back to NevoTech," said Larsen. "We all good?"

Howard took a deep breath and nodded. "All right. I'm ready."

"Good," said David. "I count about twenty hostiles walking in this direction."

"Shit," said Howard. "That's too many."

"We're fine as long as we get off the streets," said Larsen.

"We haven't had much luck finding shelter," said David.

"There's another apartment building attached to the parking garage. On the other side," said Larsen. "I bet it connects with the garage. Could be an easy way into Chang's building."

"How do we get in quickly, without making too much noise?" said David.

"We'll figure it out," said Larsen.

"We don't have to," said Howard. "Damn. I don't know why I didn't think of this earlier."

"Walk and talk," said Larsen, starting down the alleyway.

"One of NevoTech's key executives owns the top floor of that place. Actually, he owns the entire building. He's paranoid about being kidnapped, so there's a special arrangement with my tactical unit. It's part of the reason we have an armored SUV."

"You have the codes to get in?" said Larsen.

Howard grinned. "Regular and police override codes."

"Well, there you go," said Larsen. "We're gonna be just fine."

Chapter Eleven

Paul Ochoa peered through the binoculars at the smoke rising behind the apartment building, noting that it had already begun to dissipate. The gunfire had died down a few minutes ago, too. He didn't know what to make of it. Intense shooting sprees were nothing new on the streets, but the smoke was different, especially since it seemed to be fading. If a car caught fire, he'd have expected it to burn a lot longer, and darker. That was the other thing. The smoke was uniformly grayish-white. Maybe a National Guard patrol got ambushed and put down a smoke screen. But why didn't they return fire with heavy machine guns? The 240s had been zapping people north of here all night. Probably nothing. Skip Rocham's voice cast some doubt on that assessment.

"Ochoa, did you guys just smoke someone street side?"

"Negative, Rock. Nothing going down over here. Haven't heard any gunfire in a few minutes," he said, getting up from the couch.

"I could have sworn I just heard two suppressed shots. Couldn't determine a direction because of the parking garage."

Rock guarded the parking garage entrance to their target's apartment building. Nobody had come or gone from the apartment since Rock had taken up a position inside the garage. No cars had entered or exited either. The only vehicle-access point was located on Virginia Avenue, observable from Ochoa's perch.

"Wasn't us. Anything behind the apartment building?" said Ochoa.

"I'm on my way to take a look," said Rock. "Motion sensors haven't picked up anything near the rear entrances."

The first thing Ochoa's team had done upon arrival at the target building was scout the access points. He immediately determined that they would need to deploy several sensors to cover all of them. A small parking lot behind the building presented the biggest challenge. Two doors spread out over three hundred feet. With Rock focused on the most likely exit, the sensors were essential to complete their coverage. If one of the sensors activated, Rock could sprint to the back of the garage and make a quick assessment—all within easy rifle range.

"Be careful," said Ochoa. "Could be another team out there."

"That wouldn't exactly be bad news," said Rock. "We're spread a little thin here."

"Just watch yourself."

Forty seconds passed according to Ochoa's watch, a fucking eternity for Rock to visually check the area.

"Rock is killing me," said Ochoa, offline.

Ripley shrugged, keeping his binoculars trained on the target's apartment.

"I don't see anything out of place back here," said Rock.

"What took you so long?"

"I was being thorough—and careful," said Rock. "I've got a bunch of creepers coming from the west. They don't seem to be in any hurry."

"Copy that. Get out of sight," said Ochoa. "The last thing we need is one of those mobs harassing us."

"Already on my way back," said Rock.

"Stay alert out there," said Ochoa. "If another team got orders to take down Chang, you might have company at that door."

"Then what?" said Rock.

"Depends on who shows up," said Ochoa. "Out."

Ripley put the binoculars on the table in front of him. "Why don't we hit the apartment right now and get out of here while we can?" said the sniper. "If the National Guard is pushing up this way, things could get complicated."

"Because the intel update said he wasn't in the apartment, but it might still be a fallback position," said Ochoa. "It also said he more than likely had access to remote security features. If we bust inside, he'll never show."

"The woman might have some intel," said Ripley.

"If he doesn't materialize by noon, we'll have a talk with her," said Ochoa.

Ripley shook his head and smirked. "Who the fuck is this guy?"

"Doesn't matter. Control wants him—dead or alive. The sooner we make that happen, the sooner we get out of here."

Chapter Twelve

David edged along the back of the tiny house, a pristine, nine-story brick and concrete apartment complex towering over them. Larsen quickly pulled his head back from the corner, scrambling to open one of the pockets on his vest. He removed a small black electronic device the size of his thumb and stuck the top of it past the edge of the house, pulling it back a few moments later.

"What the hell is that?" said David, nervously glancing between Larsen and the alley behind them.

"Hold on," said Larsen, lowering some kind of visor on his combat helmet.

"What is that?" said David.

"Interactive visor," said Larsen. "Mostly useful during a free-fall jump, but it does have a few other uses. The little device in my hand is a high-resolution camera. I saw someone on the second floor of the parking garage."

"Shit," said Howard.

"Give me a second…there," said Larsen. "I can't really show you without putting my helmet on your head, but there's a guy with a rifle and a throat mike on the second level of the parking garage. I'm trying to enhance the image enough to identify him."

"I'd say we should turn back, but I don't think that's an option right now," said David.

"It isn't," said Howard. "Not until they get the SUV patched up enough for another diversion."

"What if they can't?" said David.

"We can hide out in the apartment building until another opportunity arises," said Howard. "Or we come up with a different diversion plan."

"I bet half of that apartment building is infected," said David.

"Damn. I didn't think of that," said Howard.

Larsen raised the built-in visor and muttered a curse.

"What?" said David.

"We have to get the doctor out of there immediately," said Larsen. "I know the guy staking out the second-level entrance. Guy likes everyone to call him Rock."

"Like The Rock guy?" said David. "From the movies?"

"No. Just Rock. Real name is Skip Rocham," said Larsen. "He's part of the team I'm the most concerned about. Real knuckle-dragging assholes. I can guarantee you they won't have *any* problem executing orders to capture or kill Chang—and anyone that gets in their way."

"Wonderful," said Howard.

"We'll be fine," said Larsen.

"You keep saying that," said David.

"And we keep being fine," said Larsen before taking a quick peek around the corner of the house. "All clear. Let's go."

They sprinted diagonally across the alley to a darkly tinted glass and steel door, taking up defensive positions facing the way they came. Howard punched a long code into the sheltered screen next to the door and waited a few moments before pulling on the thick door handle.

The door remained in place.

"Probably missed a number," mumbled Howard, trying the code again.

Howard yanked on the door handle again, with the same result.

"What's the problem, Dan?" said Larsen.

"The door override isn't working," he said. "The code shows up as valid when I hit the enter key, but the door won't open."

"Is this a problem you can solve in the next thirty seconds?" said Larsen. "That's about all the time we can spare right here if this door isn't an option."

"Yes," he said before transmitting on the tactical net. "Gary, you there?"

"Unfortunately," said Hoenig.

"I need the kill code for Mr. Abbot's apartment building. Right now," said Howard, turning to David and whispering, "Someone has to write this down."

"Just a second," said Hoenig.

"Can't you just remember it?" said David.

"It's twenty-four fucking numbers," said Howard.

"It's not like I carry a notepad with me!"

"Why don't you just enter it at the same time?" said Larsen.

"Just trust me," said Howard.

"David, use your phone. Just enter the numbers like you're making a call!" said Larsen.

David wrenched the smartphone out of one of his cargo pockets, still fumbling to remove one of his gloves to use the screen when Hoenig started passing the numbers.

"Jesus. Hold on," said David, throwing a glove to the ground.

He activated the phone screen and nodded. "Okay. Now."

Twenty-four digits and about twenty precious seconds later, David held the code up for Howard, who pressed the "CALL ATTENDANT" icon on the door screen.

"What are you doing?" said Larsen.

Howard held out a finger as a warbled voice emitted from the small speaker set into the screen.

"Sorry, Mr. Howard, I can't let you in."

"I need to get inside right now," said Howard.

"I can't do that," said the voice. "Mr. Abbot entered a code that neutralized any overrides to the external doors. He left with his family early yesterday. You have no reason to enter the building."

"Who is this? Jeremy?" said Howard.

"Doesn't matter who I am. I have strict instructions from the remaining residents. Nobody gets in. Not even Mr. Abbot if he returns."

"Listen very carefully, Jeremy," said Howard. "I have a code that will instantly kill the building's security system, requiring a complete on-site reboot by OMEGA Security Solutions. If I enter that code, every door connected to the system will unlock and stay unlocked, indefinitely."

"That's every door in the building," said Jeremy.

"Internal and external," said Howard. "You have three seconds to open this door before I use the code. I promise we're not here to hurt you or anyone inside. There's a situation nearby that needs our attention."

"I really shouldn't—"

"Three," announced Larsen, quickly adding, "Two."

"One," said Howard, starting to type the kill code numbers.

"The door's open."

Larsen yanked the door free, motioning for them to get inside while he covered the alley behind them. Once inside, Larsen tested the door by putting a shoulder into it. A figure stumbled into view a few houses down, followed by another.

"Is this ballistic-grade glass?" said Larsen.

"Yes. You could take a fire ax to the doors and windows on the ground level," said Howard.

David detected movement at the end of the wide hallway and instantly leveled his rifle.

"It's just me. Jeremy!" said a man stepping into the hallway with his hands above his head. "I'm not armed. Tell them, Mr. Howard."

"He shouldn't be armed," said Howard.

"Shouldn't being the operative term," said David, keeping his rifle pointed at the building attendant. "Keep your hands high! Stay right there."

"I'm cool. Not moving an inch," said Jeremy, frozen in place. "I'm probably going to lose my job for this. And the bonus they promised me."

David approached the young man cautiously. Jeremy looked harmless enough, but that was no reason to let his guard down. Desperation changed everything, and this guy was one newsflash away from reality. A newsflash he was about to deliver.

"Jeremy, I don't think you have to worry about losing your job," started David.

The oblivious look on the attendant's face instantly shifted to something a little more recognizable and appropriate for the situation. Fear.

Chapter Thirteen

Larsen ignored the attendant's pleas and opened the stairwell door.

"Guys, come on," said Jeremy. "You can't just break into one of the suites. Why don't you use the roof? Nobody will get upset that way."

"We're not breaking in," said Howard. "I have a code that can override any door in the building. No breaking."

"You know what I mean," said Jeremy. "The residents have security cameras. Shit. There are cameras everywhere. The Holtzes are going to see that you broke in, and they're going to know I let you in the building."

He was about to set Jeremy straight, but David beat him to the punch.

"Dude, what don't you get about the situation here? The Holtzes aren't coming back. The Abbots aren't coming back. Nobody is coming back. Not for a long time. The city is under military lockdown. In fact, I strongly suggest you follow us up these stairs and make 403 your new home, because you're not leaving the building—unless you're suicidal."

"I'm not," said Jeremy.

"Not what?" said David.

"Suicidal."

"Jesus," muttered Larsen, barely able to comprehend how clueless he was.

"Good. Because you won't make it one block out there without a National Guard escort," said David before following Howard into the stairwell.

"I need to get my girlfriend over here," said Jeremy.

"Brother, if she hasn't shown up by now, I think it's fair to say she isn't showing up," said Larsen, holding the door open. "You coming up?"

"I probably shouldn't," said Jeremy.

"We'll leave the door propped open for you," said Larsen. "I didn't see any vending machine on the lobby level."

"I'll have to think about that," said Jeremy.

"Don't think about it for too long," said Larsen. "I guarantee that the few remaining residents here have already planned their break-ins."

"The people here would never do that," said Jeremy.

"Are you willing to bet your life on that?" said Larsen.

"How long will you be up there?" said Jeremy.

"Hopefully not very long," said Larsen, grinning. "Make sure you lock the window after we leave. Wouldn't want one of the neighbors crawling in."

Larsen caught up with Howard and David on the first-floor stairwell landing.

"Don't let your guard down," said Larsen. "Young Jeremy doesn't have a clue what's going on outside the lobby."

"How long do you think he's been here?" said Howard.

"Long enough to know who's here and who's not," said David, pulling on the locked door next to him.

"Don't be fooled," said Howard. "The doors open freely from inside the resident hallways. Fire regulations."

"Good to know," said David, pointing his rifle at the

door as they moved past.

They reached the fourth floor and opened the door with Howard's override code, moving in single-file formation through a well-appointed elevator lobby. Larsen didn't detect any hint of an unusual smell, which was a good thing. Dead-body smells tended to permeate a space, even behind closed doors—especially in an enclosed structure. He'd missed the dead-smell cues at the house on Warsaw Street, most likely because the air was contaminated with the chemical smoke from the parking lot. Little misses like that could get you killed under the wrong circumstances.

"Air smells normal," whispered Larsen, stopping at an emergency exit placard with a basic diagram of the floor. "Which apartments are occupied?"

"401, 408 and 410," said Howard. "We have to pass 401. The others are on the opposite side of the building."

"Treat every door like it's occupied," said Larsen.

"Copy that," said David.

The entrance to apartment 403 was at the end of the hallway, near a window conveniently overlooking the parking garage. Located on the right side of the hallway, the apartment faced the rear of the building, hopefully giving them cover from any likely observation points used by Ochoa's team. Given that Rock had appeared at the back of the garage to visually survey the area behind Chang's apartment building, he figured that the rest of the team was hidden on Virginia Avenue, directly in front of the building. They were probably using motion sensors to cover the rear entrances. Maybe a false reading had drawn Rock out to take a look.

Larsen would have deployed his team the same way to cover the building if his mission was to observe and report—but it wasn't—and neither was Ochoa's. Why hadn't Ochoa breached the apartment? He felt like he was missing something. It didn't really matter right now. They needed to get Hale out of the apartment and back into this building before Ochoa detected a problem. He still wasn't sure how they were going to pull that off.

Before they reached the apartment door, Larsen moved David and Howard to the left side of the hallway, away from the window, and told them to wait. He lowered his helmet visor and removed the thumb-sized camera from his vest before sliding into position against the wall next to the windowsill. The Bluetooth-enabled device streamed a high-definition image to the visor, which he could manipulate with the buttons inside his helmet.

He liked what he saw. Most of the three-story apartment building across Virginia Avenue was blocked by Chang's apartment building. All of it would be blocked from the window they would use in apartment 403. The backs of a few flat roofs were visible directly across and in front of the parking garage. He wasn't worried about those. The threat would come from the three-story building. Ochoa would be in the third-floor unit facing Chang's balcony—watching and waiting. Ripley, the team's sniper, would be co-located with Ochoa, leaving Stansfield unaccounted for. For all he knew, Stansfield was with Rock. He doubted it, but it was possible.

Larsen backed up several steps and slowly approached the door to 403, watching the view through the window. Deeper in the hallway, all he could see was Chang's building.

"I like what I'm seeing. No exposure," he said, making room for Howard at the door. "Remember, we clear the apartment first. Every nook and cranny."

Howard typed several digits into the pad next to the door marked 403, deactivating the lock. Larsen turned the handle and gently pushed the heavy door open, relieved that the air smelled neutral—with a hint of lavender. He checked behind the door and continued down the marble foyer, sweeping the visible areas with his rifle. Apartment was a bit of an understatement for these digs. Palace might be a better term.

He came up to a closed door on the left side of the entry hallway, signaling for David and Howard to check it out. While they moved quietly behind him, he kneeled and scanned the rest of the unit. From what he could see, the apartment opened to a spacious living area just past a hallway on the right. Wide sliding doors led to a balcony beyond a black dining room table. A leather couch and chairs sat in the left back corner, turned toward floor-to-ceiling glass windows with a view of the Indianapolis city skyline.

"Bathroom and storage room clear," whispered David through his earpiece. "No signs of recent activity. Full toilet paper roll. Sink is bone dry."

Larsen clicked his transmitter three times, the agreed-upon quiet signal that he copied the transmission and everything was fine on the receiver's end. Two radio clicks asked for a repeat of the transmission. Four clicks meant trouble. They'd developed this system for silently clearing spaces that required them to split up.

When Howard and David returned to the hallway, he continued the search. Next stop was the hallway before the great room area. He checked the hallway, finding it empty, before scooting to the opposite side. From there, he scanned the massive open-concept kitchen, dining and family area. Seeing nothing out of place, he stationed Howard at the corner of the hallway, where he could watch the kitchen area and the entrance to the apartment.

Three bedrooms, three bathrooms, an office—and a laundry room bigger than his dining room back in Colorado—the two of them returned to the entry hall.

"Check behind the kitchen island," said Larsen, looking around the space. "I'll take that door. Probably a pantry."

Larsen was right about the door, though he hadn't imagined it would lead to a room the size of another kitchen—with shelves packed like a grocery store.

"You clear out there?" said Larsen.

"Yeah," said David. "Unless someone's hiding in the fridge."

"That's not funny," said Howard.

"Take a look at this," said Larsen. "Jeremy might want to reconsider his sturdy position on breaking and entering. He could probably survive up here for months."

Howard stepped into the pantry and surveyed the shelves. "Wow. Gourmet stuff, too."

"What the fuck, are we stopping for brunch now?" quipped David, appearing in the doorway. "Wow. That's a lot of food. Grab some of those snack bars."

"Now it's okay," said Larsen, taking a box of granola bars off one of the shelves. "Grab what you can in, like, thirty seconds. Nothing that's going to hinder you. I think I know how we're going to pull this off."

"Think?" said David, pocketing a fistful of breakfast bars.

"Nothing's set in stone with me. You should know that by now," said Larsen.

"More like floating in mud," said David, stopping for a

second. "And I mean that in a friendly, ball-breaking kind of way. I trust you. Sort of."

Larsen laughed, shaking his head. "They must love you back at the station."

"You know it," said David.

He led them to one of the smaller windows that faced north, toward Chang's apartment. Like he'd predicted, the three-story building facing Chang's was completely obscured, along with the rooftops of the smaller structures in front of the parking garage.

"Unless they have someone posted in Chang's building, looking this way, we're good to go," said Larsen.

"Why would they do that?" said Howard.

"They wouldn't. And it's no more than a fifteen-foot drop to the top floor of the parking lot. We can use a bedsheet if your old legs can't handle that distance," said Larsen, nodding at David.

"Funny," said David, looking through the window. "On a serious note, the sheet isn't a bad idea, especially with your leg. No reason to make it worse."

"True," said Larsen. "I'll grab some sheets from the linen closet. We can tie some knots in it or something."

"I thought that was a prison movie thing," said Howard.

"It works," said Larsen. "Been in a few pickles before."

"We're obviously not climbing back up here, right?" said David.

"No. Chang's place is on the third floor. My plan was to send you and David in to grab Hale while I staked out the ground-floor entrances. If they suspect that Rock has been taken out, they'll either hit the building together or send a scout."

"What if they send that scout to the parking garage?" said David.

"Chang said there was no way in without a door opener or the code," said Larsen. "My guess is Rock climbed up there the old-fashioned way. Even if he had a rope, there's no way he'd leave it dangling."

David shook his head.

"What?" said Larsen.

"Every car in that garage will have one of those door openers. Probably a half-dozen spare keycards to get into the building, too," said David. "If this Rock guy didn't figure that out and toss a few down already, these guys are dumber than dumb."

"He's right," said Howard. "We have to assume they can get up into the parking garage pretty damn fast."

"You're both right. That's the thinnest part of the plan," said Larsen.

"If you get into the lobby fast and manage to get close to the front windows, you should see them respond. I mean, they have to cross the street. Right?" said David. "You get up to the second floor of the garage and— ambush them from above when they access the garage."

"If I get there first," said Larsen. "All they have to do is run up one ramp and they're on the second floor. I don't even know the layout of the apartment building. And we only have one keycard."

"We'll figure that out on the way in," said David. "Leave the doors you need propped open. As long as we communicate effectively, we'll be fine."

"We'll be fine?" said Larsen, smiling. "Sounds like a shitty plan."

"The least shitty," said David.

"You guys are starting to scare me," said Howard.

"You should have been with us at the airfield," said David. "Makes this plan look like a quick stop for a six-pack at the gas station."

"What happened at the airfield?" said Howard. "What airfield?"

"You really don't want to know," said Larsen.

Chapter Fourteen

David had second thoughts about the plan the moment he hung his backside out the window. No way this was going to work. No way three guys climbing down a bunch of knotted sheets tied around a leather couch was a good plan. It felt more like the Three Stooges, except you didn't get up and walk away from a mistake in this episode. He slithered down the sheets, clutching each knot on the way down—convinced that the thousand-count Egyptian sheets pulled right from the package would tear any second.

A few seconds later, his boots touched concrete, and he felt infinitely better. David released the sheet and hid behind the nearest car, aiming his rifle at the ramp descending to the third level. Howard came down next, landing smoothly in the empty parking space. Larsen struggled getting through the window, his injured thigh pressing against the sill inside and outside the apartment. He left a two-foot-long, bright red smear on the tan siding under the window, dropping to his feet from several feet up and kneeling in agony.

"Motherfuuuh," muttered Larsen, forcing himself up.

Howard helped him to the car, where he took a seat next to David and leaned back against the vehicle. He continued to curse under his breath for a few more moments, until finally looking up.

"We need to rethink the plan," said David.

"Already?" said Larsen, winking.

"Yeah. Already," said David. "And I'm not special ops, so keep that in mind."

"Neither am I, anymore," said Larsen.

"I do not have the same close-quarters shooting skills as you," said David.

"True. But you're a solid shot and you don't have a fucked-up leg," said Larsen.

"Not exactly a ringing endorsement."

"Don't sell yourself short," said Larsen. "I'll take out Rock. You'll take out whoever is with him, if anyone is with him."

Howard started to protest. "I thought there was only one guy."

"Ninety percent sure on that," said Larsen. "I wouldn't put two people in the garage, but I'm not Ochoa."

"So you were more than likely going to need my help in the parking garage anyway," said David.

"Pretty much," said Larsen.

"Then what?" said David.

"You'll be the one to grab Dr. Hale. In and out of the apartment within ten seconds. Stay clear of the windows. Howard, I need you down in the lobby, strictly for surveillance. You'll be the early warning system. I'll set up an ambush on the second level of the parking garage."

"You just described a completely different plan," said David.

"Different people are doing different things," said Larsen. "But it's the same concept. We come back to this building the same way. Third-floor parking access door."

"That's the only thing that's the same, by the way," said David. "What if Ochoa and his crew decide to take a shortcut to Chang's place and go through the front door?"

"Then Dan reports their movement and hides out. I ambush them in the stairwell, Dan hits them from behind, and you escort Dr. Hale to this building."

"What if they split up?" said David. "Two in the garage and one through the front door, or the other way around."

"We'll figure it out," said Larsen.

"Maybe you should position yourself at the front of the garage with your camera and take them out when they cross the street," said David.

"Guys, once again, we're assuming they don't have people in Chang's building already," said Howard.

Larsen shook his head. "No. They're waiting for some reason. They must know he isn't there."

"Or they've been told he might be on the way," said David. "Our escape from the airport wasn't exactly covert. Wouldn't take much to put two and two together. We essentially disappeared south of downtown Indy."

"Doesn't change anything," said Larsen, rising to a knee. "Let's get this over with."

They moved quickly and quietly to the other side of the rooftop level, stopping at the top of the ramp leading down.

"How do you want to do this?" said David.

"Normally I'd say crawl partway down the ramp, but I can't do that without passing out at this point," said Larsen.

"Your leg?" said David.

"Yeah. Scraping it across concrete isn't going to work," said Larsen. "The two of us walk down and search for targets. I don't think they'll have anyone on the third level. We know Rock is on the second. That's the access point to the building."

"Or he's patrolling," said Howard.

"He'll be sitting tight by the door, which will make him an easier target," said Larsen.

"Unless there's two of them," said David.

"That's why I'm bringing you along," said Larsen. "And to make you crawl down the next ramp. You'll carry my remote camera, and I'll scan for Rock and any other surprises. If it's just one of them, I'll take the shot."

"How about I crawl down this one, too, just in case?" said David.

Larsen nodded and gave him the camera, telling him how to activate it. David tucked it into a zippered pouch on his vest and low-crawled to the edge of the ramp, thinking this was a great way to get shot in the head. He got a few feet down the concrete ramp and worked his way to the side, staring into the parking lot for several seconds—letting the details soak in. The access door to the building they had just left was directly ahead of him, beyond the ramp's landing. It looked similar to the door in the alley.

Detecting no movement or hidden gunmen, he crawled a few more feet, expanding his view until he could see the far side of the garage. Still nothing. He couldn't visually clear the rest of the level without poking his head beyond the side edge of the ramp—presenting an easy target for anyone hiding in his blind spot.

David dug through the pouch and removed the miniature camera, pressing the button on the bottom for three seconds until a small green LED light appeared. He inched the camera beyond the ramp's edge, pointing the lens toward the unobservable part of the garage.

"Perfect. Hold it right there," said Larsen.

He held it in place until Larsen told him the level looked clear. David turned his body until it faced the other side of the garage, shifting his rifle to do the same. Larsen and Howard joined him, crouching on the ramp.

"I assume the ramp to the second floor is stacked above this one?" said Larsen.

"Why don't you stick your head over the side and look," said David, winking.

"I'll take a pass on that," said Larsen, helping him up.

Together, in a tight formation, the three of them descended to the third level, spreading out when they reached the sparsely crowded parking area. They swung wide of the opening leading to the second level and regrouped behind an SUV three spaces away from the top of the ramp.

"Same procedure," said Larsen. "But you don't go as far this time. Let the camera do the work."

"It's the size of my thumb," said David, holding out the camera. "I'm afraid I'll drop it or get my hand shot off if I stick it too far out."

"You should have said something earlier," said Larsen before removing two objects from his vest.

He expanded a black telescoping stick and screwed a custom clamp to the end of it before taking the camera from David's hand and attaching it to the clamp.

"You had this all the time?" said David.

"It's a simple, but handy piece of gear," said Larsen.

"Would have been even more handy about three minutes ago," said David.

"I'd actually forgotten about it until I saw you sticking your hand out," said Larsen. "Better late than never."

David shook his head and muttered, grabbing the camera and making sure it was secure. Satisfied that it wouldn't drop if he bumped it against the edge of the ramp, he took a few deep breaths and nodded at Larsen.

"Let's do it."

Chapter Fifteen

Larsen crouched next to David, scanning the digital image displayed on his visor's heads-up display (HUD). David was playing it safe, sticking the camera the bare minimum required to get a picture beyond the edge of the ramp. Working carefully, they'd taken close to ten minutes to clear roughly half of the garage. He hadn't expected to find anyone hidden in the areas they'd checked, but he wasn't taking any chances. For all he knew, Rock could be hidden in the backseat of a tinted SUV. It would probably take them three times as long to scan the rest of the garage. Maybe longer.

He tapped David's right calf, indicating he wanted him to move the camera a little to the right. The system they had devised for communicating silently was simple. He tapped his right thigh, asking him to raise the view just a tad. The foot would have lowered the view. Perfect. He studied the image again, zooming in and out on cars and shadows, still not spotting anything suspicious. Another tap to the right thigh got the view closer to the end of the parking lot. Nothing stood out.

A tap to his left calf shifted the view slightly left, followed by a tap to the left thigh, bringing the far wall of the parking level into view. The door to Chang's apartment building was barely visible in the far right edge of the image. He studied the picture for what felt like an eternity, shaking his head. Fifteen minutes later, having digitally scoured the entire parking level, he still had nothing. What was he missing? Or was Rock inside the building, with a motion sensor guarding the door? If that was the case, they had a problem.

He tugged on David's vest, and the police officer retracted the camera, crawling backward until he was back on the third level.

"Nothing?" said David.

Larsen shook his head. "Nada. Fuck."

"Did you record the video?" said David.

"Thirty-three minutes," said Larsen.

"Let me take a look," said David. "Can I skip to the last part?"

He unstrapped his helmet. "Fast-forward. Rewind. Zoom in and out. Everything."

While David leaned against a concrete support, watching the video, Larsen kept a close eye on the bottom of the ramp. If they couldn't locate Rock, the mission was too risky.

"Got him."

Larsen backed up until he stood next to David, who had removed the helmet. Howard took his place at the top of the ramp.

"Where?" said Larsen, taking the helmet.

"Minivan parked facing Virginia Avenue. Second vehicle from the end," said David. "Don't get too excited. We still have a problem."

He knew what it was before examining the paused video. There was a third vehicle from the end, blocking their shot. Well, not exactly blocking it. Complicating it. He took a close look at the video, running it backward and forward a few times. David had a good eye. Larsen had missed the difference in window texture between the minivan's front passenger window and sliding passenger-side door. The front window was lowered. Not only that, the driver's side rear sliding door was open, the only tip-off being a slight indentation visible on the roofline of the van. He still couldn't see Rock, but now they knew where to look.

"Nice catch," said Larsen. "I want you to watch the rest of the video, in case we're dealing with two of them."

David took the helmet and spent the next several minutes examining the tape.

"I think he's alone," said David, exchanging helmets with Larsen.

"Then let's watch a little longer and see if we can pinpoint Rock. If we know where to shoot, we can simultaneously target the same spot."

Howard turned his head and eyed him skeptically.

"Then run like hell. You and Howard get Dr. Hale. I do whatever I can to stop them from getting to you."

"That's by far the worst plan you've come up with yet," said David, patting his shoulder.

"I'll take that as a compliment, coming from you," said Larsen.

"Uh-huh," said David, refastening his helmet. "After you."

Larsen walked to the top of the ramp and lowered himself into a crawling position, acutely aware of the agonizing ordeal ahead. He started to slither down the rough concrete, stopping to let the sharp burning sensation in his thigh subside. When it didn't, he continued to pull the front of his body across the coarse surface, silently screaming the entire time. With David holding the camera in place, Larsen shifted into position just out of the minivan's line of sight. He adjusted the camera position with a series of taps on David's legs and magnified the image, waiting for Rock to move. Fortunately, he didn't have to wait long. The dark outline of a head momentarily appeared through the series of vehicle windows, disappearing a few seconds later.

"He's in the second row, passenger side. Head leaned back," said Larsen, raising the visor. "I can't see the head right now."

"Do you want to wait until we can see it?" said David.

"He leaned forward for a second; that's not enough time."

"So how do we do this?"

"We scoot down far enough to get both of our gun barrels lined up and I count us down. As soon as we fire, Howard yanks me up and we start down the ramp. You stay here for a few seconds in case our bullets missed the mark. Then you haul ass to catch up with Howard."

"This is insane," said David.

Larsen squirmed down the ramp until the minivan came into view, leaving a trail of smeared blood above him. The pain was excruciating, now radiating to his pelvis. He wasn't sure how he was going to do what needed to be done over the next several minutes—but he knew he'd get it done. He always did. David nestled in right next to him and took aim at the minivan.

"You got a shot?" said Larsen.

"Yep."

"This is going to happen fast," said Larsen. "I'm going to mark the point of aim with the laser and count down from two."

"Ready."

He centered the reticle of his rifle on the rear cargo

window of the SUV and triggered the red laser, making a slight adjustment to his point of aim.

"Two. One. Fire," he said, the rifle bucking into his shoulder.

The SUV's window completely crumbled, revealing two tightly spaced holes in the passenger-side cargo compartment window. He had no way of assessing the damage beyond that. Before he could form another thought, he was yanked upward and forward by Howard, who propelled him down the ramp in a controlled enough manner to get his own two feet going. They barreled halfway down the ramp until they had enough clearance to hop over the edge and land on the second level. The landing jolted Larsen's leg and hip, which had locked tight in anticipation of the pain. By the time he got moving, David had pushed himself to his knees.

"Blood splatter on the wall next to the minivan," said David as Larsen passed. "We're clear."

"Get to Chang's apartment," said Larsen. "I'll let you know what happens out here. Stay low. Ochoa may have a line of sight into the garage."

Larsen veered to the left and crouched, sliding between two sedans to reach the four-foot-tall concrete wall facing Virginia Avenue. The suppressed gunshots would undoubtedly draw Ochoa's attention.

Chapter Sixteen

Paul Ochoa straightened up on the couch. "You hear that?"

"Sounded like a suppressed gunshot," said Ripley, lowering the binoculars and settling in behind his rifle.

"Sounded like two," said Ochoa. "Close by."

"I don't have any movement in the target apartment," said Ripley.

Something was up. They couldn't all be imagining gunshots.

"Rock, did you hear another gunshot?"

He waited a few seconds before repeating his question. When Rock failed to reply the second time, he got off the couch and wandered closer to the open balcony, careful not to block Ripley's view of Chang's apartment.

"Stansfield, you hear anything?"

"I heard something, but it was pretty muffled down here. Couldn't tell where it was coming from."

"Any activity on the street?" said Ochoa.

"Nothing to the south," said Stansfield. "You have a better view north than I do."

"I need you to check on Rock," said Ochoa.

"I was afraid you were going to say that," said Stansfield. "On my way."

Ochoa approached the closed side of the balcony slider, peering north up the street through the open side.

A hammer blow to his right shoulder spun him ninety degrees, followed immediately by a shock to the chest that knocked him to the hardwood floor. Unable to speak, he turned onto his bloodied right side and clawed ineffectively for the edge of the couch.

Ripley was on the floor next to him in an instant, grabbing his tactical vest to pull him out of the line of fire. A warm splash hit Ochoa's face, and Ripley crumpled on top of him, hands clutching his throat. He lay flat on his back as bullets snapped into the drywall directly above his head, forming perfect holes. He remained trapped under Ripley, unable to help his teammate or himself while bullet after bullet poured through the open balcony, most of them thumping into the sniper's body.

The maelstrom of projectiles stopped just as quickly as they started, the sound of a suppressed rifle firing on full automatic drifting through the apartment.

"Shooter. Second level. Parking garage," said Stansfield. "He's still up there."

Ochoa managed to slide his left hand along his chest to press the transmit button.

"I'm hit bad. Ripley is KIA," said Ochoa. "Get to Chang's apartment and kill everyone there."

"This has to be one of our teams. Why would they attack us?"

"How the fuck should I know? Nothing about any of this makes sense," said Ochoa. "Just do it."

"Maybe there's a misunderstanding," said Stansfield.

"A misunderstanding? They killed Rock first. Then opened fire on me and Ripley. There's no misunderstanding. Get it done, or we're not getting out of this alive."

"Copy that," said Stansfield, in a very noncommittal voice.

He didn't have time for this. If the shooter was still active, Ochoa needed to get clear of the balcony window. Easier said than done. Ripley's two-hundred-pound corpse resting on top of him complicated the matter. His right shoulder was trashed, making it impossible to pull Ripley off. He could try to push Ripley away with his left hand, but without any leverage or the ability to roll onto his injured right side, he wasn't likely to make much progress. His only real option was to roll to the left, away from the rest of Ripley. Of course, that would probably draw the shooter's attention.

For a brief moment, he considered bringing Stansfield back to his position. It might save both of them. Then again, Stansfield hadn't sounded too enthusiastic about his last order. In fact, he'd sounded mutinous.

No. He'd stay right here and play possum for now, letting Stansfield's fate play out across the street. Lying there motionless, he remembered his CTAB. Maybe he could get a search and rescue mission dispatched to his location—particularly if he reported Chang in his possession.

Chapter Seventeen

David raced down the main second-floor hallway for the stairwell that Chang swore was in the elevator lobby. If Chang had been mistaken about that small detail, they might not reach Dr. Hale first. Even worse, they could run into trouble in the stairwell, when they eventually found it. He didn't want to think about that. The last place on the planet he wanted to get into a gunfight was in a stairwell.

"Talk to me, Larsen," he said, bursting into the elevator lobby and immediately spotting the "STAIRS" sign. "I'm about to hit the stairs."

"You have time," said Larsen. "The shooter just blasted his way through the front door. You'll be on the third floor before he gets to the stairs."

"I hope so. Heading up now."

He yanked the door open and pointed his rifle down the stairs while Howard sprinted past him, headed up the stairs. Following closely behind, he reached the third-floor landing, where he found Howard attaching a fist-sized device to the wall next to the door.

"What are you doing?" said David.

"Just a little surprise," said Howard, pressing a few buttons on the device.

David opened the door and took a quick peek into the hallway, checking both directions. A placard across the hallway indicated that apartment 310 was located to his left.

"We don't have time for this," said David, stepping out of the landing with his rifle pointed down the hallway.

"Trust me," said Howard, joining him. "You'll be happy I took the time."

A metallic bang rattled through the stairwell, spurring them back into action. Howard pulled the door shut while David took off toward Chang's apartment. He reached the plain black door a few seconds later and started entering the code. Howard crouched next to him, aiming his rifle back toward the stairwell just as he pressed enter. A mechanism inside the door whirred before David turned the handle and pushed inward—the door remaining in place.

He entered the code again, with the same result.

"Shit," muttered David.

"Take my place," said Howard. "You think it's a deadbolt?"

"I have no idea," said David. "What did you set in the stairwell?"

"Motion-triggered flash-bang," said Howard, pulling a similar-sized device from the pouch attached to his vest.

"I don't see how that will help us with the door," said David, nodding at the device.

"No. This is a breaching charge," said Howard. "A fairly sizable one, too. Should take out the primary locking mechanism and any deadbolts."

"What about Dr. Hale?"

"We just have to pray she's not standing at the door or anywhere near it," said Howard.

He wedged the charge between the door and the door frame, a few inches above the door handle, before pressing a combination of buttons.

"What if she heard me trying the code?" said David.

"We can't exactly warn her," said Howard. "That would drag her over to the door for sure."

A muffled explosion echoed through the hallway. Howard's flash-bang just bought them a few more seconds.

"Blow the door," said David, clearing the area.

Howard followed him, counting down from two. David never heard zero. The breaching charge detonated with a thunderous crack, shooting splinters onto the dark brown laminate floor. The door swung on its hinges into the apartment, a jagged, two-foot-wide hole missing where the door handle had been.

David hurried through the entrance into the smoky space, relieved to see a figure on the couch—safe at the other end of the apartment.

"Dr. Hale? My name is David Olson. I'm a friend of Dr. Eugene Chang. He sent us to get you out of here."

The doctor backed up toward the balcony slider, grabbing a kitchen knife from the coffee table in front of the couch.

"This doesn't feel like a rescue," she said.

"Dr. Hale, I don't have time to explain," he said, digging through his vest for his badge. "Dr. Chang is at NevoTech. I volunteered to come here with a few other law enforcement officers. I'm a cop with the Westfield PD."

He tossed his badge in her direction, the wallet bouncing off the coffee table and landing near her feet. She picked it up and examined it.

"This isn't Westfield," she said, throwing it back.

Howard's rifle shattered the temporary quiet, barking twice.

"We're running out of time!" yelled Howard.

David's earpiece crackled. "I hear gunfire. What's your status?"

"Howard is keeping that last shooter off our ass. I'm trying to convince Dr. Hale to come with us," said David. "She's not convinced."

"Just grab her and get the hell out of there!" said Larsen.

"She's holding a knife," said David. "And we can't exactly go anywhere with a shooter on the loose."

"Copy that. I'll be right there," said Larsen. "Keep the shooter occupied."

"Be careful entering the stairwell," said David. "The doors make a lot of noise."

"Is that Chang?" said Hale, still holding the knife in front of her.

"Can you move away from the balcony slider?" said David. "It's not safe."

Howard fired again, causing Hale to flinch.

"And this is?" said Hale.

"They sent a team to kill Chang. We spotted them in the apartment building directly across the street," said David. "There might be more. We don't know."

She moved away from the slider, cautiously making her way to the hallway entrance on the right side of the apartment.

"Where are they now?" she said.

"The last one is in the hallway out there, trying to kill us," said David. "The rest are dead."

"I'm not sure what this guy is doing. He hasn't fired a

shot. I think he might be trying to surrender," said Howard.

"What makes you think that?"

"He stuck his hands out of the doorway and yelled something," said Howard. "I can't hear a damn thing after that door charge."

"Pass that along to Larsen," said David. "He should be coming up behind the guy in a few seconds."

"Got it."

While Howard's conversation with Larsen played out over the radio net, David continued his negotiation with Dr. Hale, who still didn't look convinced that they were here to help.

"We need to get you back to NevoTech, a few blocks away. It's completely locked down. Completely safe," said David. "Over two hundred company employees and family members are hiding out on campus. Many of them injured. They really need your help over there. The campus has a fully stocked infirmary, even some surgical equipment. The only thing they don't have is a doctor."

"It all sounds a little too convenient," she said, her skeptical look slightly fading.

"Ma'am," interrupted Howard, "I'm head of security at NevoTech. We're doing everything we can to help the people that made it onto campus, but some of them are severely injured and simply won't survive without the help of a doctor. That's why I volunteered for this mission. An emergency room doctor is exactly what we need."

"I was just doing a rotation through the ER," said Hale.

"Well, in that case…" said David, trying to get her to crack a smile. "Seriously. We need your help. My son is with them. We've put everything on the line to bring you back. You can't stay here."

"Especially now that you blasted the door apart," she said.

"Even if the door was completely intact, it would only be a matter of time before this place wouldn't be safe," said David. "You've seen what's happening out there, right? This is going to get a lot worse before it gets better. It's already near impossible to walk down the streets without getting ripped to pieces. Please come with us. I promise we'll keep you safe."

He could tell she was giving it serious thought.

"Time to make a choice," said David. "Once we leave, that's it. You're on your own."

She lowered the knife, still holding it tight.

"Why would anyone want Dr. Chang dead?" she said. "I can't wrap my head around that part."

"Chang specializes in the kind of virus that was released in Indianapolis," said David. "All over the country, actually."

"Released?" she said. "Wait. This isn't confined to Indianapolis?"

"He thinks this was a bioweapons attack. And yes, at least twenty more cities have been hit with the same thing," said David.

"Who attacked us?" said Hale. "What does that have to do with people wanting to kill Chang?"

"We really don't have time for this, Dr. Hale," said David. "Chang can explain his theories when we get back to NevoTech. He thinks the government is involved. Maybe the military."

She cocked her head slightly, indicating that something he said had resonated with her.

"Are you coming or staying?" he said.

"I'm coming," she said.

"Then I need you to leave the knife behind," said David.

"I'm not giving up my only insurance," said Hale. "Plus I thought you said it was dangerous out there."

"It is, and that knife won't help you much," said David, drawing his pistol and offering it to her. "You'll be much better off with this until we can get you a rifle."

She reluctantly accepted the pistol, still keeping her distance.

"How are we getting out of here, exactly?" she said, nodding at Howard, who was pressed against the shattered door frame, rifle aimed down the hallway.

"We're working on that," said David, pressing his transmit button. "Larsen, what's the status on the guy in the stairwell?"

"Under control," said Larsen. "Give me a second or two. Out."

He turned to Dr. Hale with a raised eyebrow. "I'm told everything is under control."

"You don't look convinced."

"That's because nothing has been under control for the past twenty-four hours."

Chapter Eighteen

Larsen took his hand away from the transmit button, his rifle held perfectly level with the other hand. Stansfield stood against the concrete wall, his hands interlocked over his head. A rifle similar to his own lay on the stairwell floor several feet away, kicked out of reach by the operative a few seconds earlier.

"What's the story, Stan?" said Larsen.

"You tell me. This whole thing is a cluster fuck," said Stansfield. "I just want to go home."

"You nearly took my head off," said Larsen.

"Dude, I recognized the helmet and put three rounds into the concrete wall a few inches below your face. Two more just above your head to keep you from spilling my brains onto the street. You didn't seem to have any hesitation laying waste to the rest of us."

"I figured you gave me a pass. That's the only reason I didn't shoot you on sight," said Larsen, pausing. "I had to take out Ochoa. I knew he'd kill me on sight. Same with Rock. Ripley seemed alright."

"Ripley would have killed you just the same," said Stansfield. "The team was a bit high-strung for my tastes."

"They're all dead," said Larsen.

"Ochoa is still alive," said Stansfield. "Sounds like he's in a bad way, but he's still there."

"Great," said Larsen, transmitting to the team. "Get Hale out of the apartment. We still have one active shooter out there."

"I thought you got them all," said David.

"One of them is wounded, but still in the game. Get her out of there immediately before you take a full mag through the windows."

"What about the shooter in the stairwell?"

"I have him in custody. You're clear to move," said Larsen.

"On our way."

"Dr. Hale is the woman we saw?" said Stansfield. "What does she have to do with this?"

"Nothing. Friend of Chang's," said Larsen.

"Where's Chang?"

"Safe."

"Ochoa says we have orders to capture or kill him. Wasn't that way when we jumped," said Stansfield.

"Wasn't for me either," said Larsen. "The orders changed as soon as I reported that we'd landed. I didn't buy it for a second."

"Neither did I," said Stansfield. "But I would have killed him if it meant I could get the fuck out of here."

"I appreciate your honesty," said Larsen, wondering if keeping Stansfield alive would be more trouble than it was worth.

He couldn't kill the guy in cold blood, but maybe they could tie him up inside Chang's apartment and...that would be the same as killing him.

"Will you help me get Ochoa?" said Larsen.

"If that gets me home," said Stansfield.

"It might," said Larsen. "Unfortunately, there are no guarantees out there. Things are beyond our control."

"I'll do it."

"All right. First things first. I need your pistol," said Larsen.

"Do you want me to lie flat—"

"No time for that," said Larsen. "Turn around, remove the pistol and toss it behind you."

Stansfield faced the wall and unstrapped his holster, flinging the pistol toward Larsen's feet. A knife followed, clattering across the brushed concrete floor.

"Any grenades?" said Larsen.

"Negative."

The soft shuffle of feet outside the propped-open door caught Larsen's attention.

"Larsen?"

"We're good in here," said Larsen. "Subject is disarmed, in the corner of the stairwell to your immediate left. When you enter, hug the wall to your right so you can stay out of my line of fire."

"I can see why Ochoa was jealous of you," said Stansfield. "You're good."

"That's close-quarters battle one-oh-one," said Larsen, motioning for David to bring the rest of the group through.

"He wasn't at the one-oh-one level with a lot of things," said Stansfield, turning his head slightly.

"Keep your eyes on the wall while they pass," said Larsen. "We'll have time for introductions later if you keep your word."

Stansfield nodded, squaring his face with the corner. Dr. Hale stopped next to Larsen.

"You're hurt pretty bad," she said.

"I'm fine for now. I'll take you up on some medical care a little later," said Larsen, glancing at her long enough to give her a quick nod.

"Where do you want us?" said David.

"Stay inside this building on the second floor," said Larsen. "I'm headed across the street to take care of some unfinished business."

"Understood," said David. "Be careful."

"Always," said Larsen.

Larsen waited for the three of them to vanish down the stairs before putting his plan into motion. He removed the magazine from Stansfield's rifle before ejecting the round in the chamber.

"Turn around."

He tossed the rifle to Stansfield, who swiped it out of the air. "I know you have at least twelve magazines within easy reach."

"I can't imagine I'd live long enough to pull one from its pouch," said Stansfield.

"As long as we understand each other," said Larsen. "I need you to radio Ochoa and tell him you neutralized Larsen's bitch—Brennan—but at least one of them made it into the apartment."

"I'd never call her a bitch," said Stansfield.

"Just say something to that effect. Say she winged your leg. Tell him you're approaching the apartment and can hear some yelling inside. Arguing."

"I'll do what I can," said Stansfield.

Larsen listened as Stansfield reported to Ochoa, arguing with him about what to do next. Picking up what he could from the one-sided conversation, he got the distinct impression that Ochoa didn't care what happened to his last remaining teammate.

"Was that good enough?" said Stansfield.

"He's up to something," said Larsen, slinging

Stansfield's rifle around his shoulder. "Let's head to Chang's apartment. If you can lure him into view, I'll take him out for good."

"This is going to get me killed."

"Not if we do it right," said Larsen.

They entered the hazy apartment, Stansfield several feet ahead of Larsen. He took a quick measure of the place, deciding on a rather hasty plan that might get them both killed.

"Stand aside," said Larsen, raising his rifle.

He fired three bullets through the center of the sliding glass door to the balcony, shifting the rifle to Chang's kitchen to his left and firing several times. He repeated the sequence again, capping off the fabricated firefight with at least ten bullets stitched across the slider.

"Tell him you took down Larsen," he said, quickly reloading. "But the woman's still alive. Hit in the thigh and bleeding badly. Ask what you should do."

Stansfield followed his directions, engaging in a heated conversation with Ochoa, while Larsen slipped into the hallway next to the living room.

"He said to kill her and get out of the building," said Stansfield.

"Tell him that Larsen had a rope and that you're coming down the front of the building—instead of going back through it," said Larsen from the other room. "Tell him to cover the ground floor of the apartment building so you don't get capped by whoever is still alive on Larsen's team. I'll pop him when he appears across the street."

"He's not that stupid," said Stansfield.

"He's not that smart, either," said Larsen.

The moment Stansfield started talking, Larsen slipped

into the master bedroom, which had a balcony facing the street. He stayed toward the back of the room, in the shadows, as he took up a concealed position behind the bed. Quickly locating the shattered balcony slider across the street, he centered the rifle reticle on the missing section of glass and waited.

"He said he'll cover me," said Stansfield. "This better not get me killed."

"The second he shows his face, he's dead," said Larsen.

"I'm opening—"

A sharp crack hit his ear, followed by a heavy thump. He didn't bother calling out to Stansfield, who had more than likely taken a bullet to the head, dropping him like a bag of dirt. Instead, he pressed the trigger repeatedly, emptying his thirty-round magazine into the apartment across the street, shifting his aim around during the fusillade to ensure a lethal spread of bullets. When his rifle went silent, he quickly reloaded and fired an entire second magazine. He dropped the empty magazine from the rifle and quickly moved into the hallway leading back to the living room and kitchen area.

"What the fuck is going on up there?" said David in his earpiece. "Sounds like world war three erupted on the street. Those rifles aren't as quiet as you think."

He crouched before peeking into the room. Stansfield lay in a heap next to the coffee table, a glistening pool of blood spreading from his head across the hardwood floor.

"Stansfield is dead," said Larsen. "Ochoa gunned him down before I could react. I'm going to cross the street to make sure Ochoa is done. I'll check his command tablet for any updates."

"Leave all that shit, Larsen," said David. "We need to get out of here."

"We're not going anywhere until Howard's people get the SUV fixed up for another diversion," said Larsen. "I'll be in and out in two minutes."

"We'll move into the parking garage and cover you in case your shooting match drew any attention."

"Stay out of sight until I confirm that Ochoa is dead," said Larsen. "He took Stansfield out with a single shot."

"Understood," said David.

Larsen dashed out the doorway, taking a hard left toward the splintered front entrance. He emerged in the second-floor hallway, immediately detecting someone to his right. He whirled and aimed at a man in his early twenties, wearing glasses, who raised his hands almost instantaneously.

"Get back in your apartment," said Larsen, glancing over his shoulder at the hallway behind him.

"Are you the police?" said the man.

"Not even close," said Larsen. "The best thing you can do for yourself is lock yourself in your apartment."

"I'm running out of food," he said. "And I don't think it's safe to go outside."

"It isn't," said Larsen, motioning toward Chang's apartment with his rifle. "Feel free to take whatever you can find in there."

The man started to move.

"Stop," said Larsen, freezing the man in place. "Stay away from the windows. There's a sniper out there somewhere."

When the man disappeared into the room, Larsen took off for the stairwell. He got halfway there before the man scrambled out of the room and tumbled to the hallway floor.

"There's a dead body in there!"

"There's a lot of dead bodies around," said Larsen before plunging down the stairs.

He passed the second-floor landing, pushing through the excruciating pain in his leg to reach the ground floor as fast as possible. If Ochoa had somehow survived the storm of bullets he'd fired into the apartment, he didn't want to give the former SWAT officer the time to gather enough courage to reengage before Larsen crossed the street.

The ground-floor lobby was littered with broken glass from Stansfield's desperate effort to get off the street and out of Larsen's line of fire. The operative must have crashed through the bullet-peppered door with his body. A trail of glass shards snaked along the slate floor from the entrance to the stairwell door. Larsen approached the front of the lobby cautiously, hugging the left side of the long, narrow space to remain unseen from the third-floor apartment across the street. When he got as close to the front of the lobby as possible without exposing himself to Ochoa's firing position, he took a deep breath and sprinted through the shattered door.

Larsen caught movement to his immediate left. A man wearing frayed boxer shorts and a torn, blood-splattered white T-shirt took a few steps back when he burst onto the street. He ignored the man until he reached the other side of Virginia Avenue and ducked under the apartment building's overhang, safe from Ochoa's rifle. A second figure appeared in the street across from the parking garage, attracted by his movement. He pulled at the door to the apartment, not surprised when it didn't budge.

Shit. He'd been hoping to get off the street without

firing his weapon and alerting Ochoa. If Ochoa hadn't seen him emerge from Chang's building, Larsen might be able to surprise him upstairs. Now he was faced with the choice of shooting both of the crazies or shooting his way into the building. He'd almost settled on a quick shot to each of their heads, the quieter of the two options, when another idea materialized.

"This is a stupid idea," he muttered, unsheathing the serrated combat knife from his vest.

He did the math, concluding that he should be able to pull it off. Of course, that was without the leg injury. By the time he reworked the equation, it was too late. The first crazy was ten feet away, running full speed at him with a pair of kitchen scissors. Given the man's single-minded focus and rage, it wasn't a fair fight on any level. Larsen twisted left at the last moment, deflecting the scissors with his left forearm and jamming the combat knife to the hilt under the guy's rib cage with his right hand. The knife's impact was immediate, the man instantly losing all fight. He jabbed the knife into the crazy's stomach twice in rapid succession before tossing him to the ground to face his second attacker.

A woman dressed in pristine khaki shorts and a purple drop-neck shirt had closed the distance faster than he'd anticipated. She swung a broken wine bottle, scraping it across the rifle magazine pouches attached to his body armor vest. He quickly stepped inside her swing radius before she could bring the bottle back around, and grabbed the back of her neck, yanking her forward onto his knife. Like the other guy, her body slackened with the first blow and came to a near complete standstill after the next two. He let her fall to the sidewalk and scanned the streets, not seeing any immediate threats.

"Did you hear any of that?" whispered Larsen.

"Hear what?" said David.

"Don't worry about it. I'm almost inside the apartment building. Out," he said, opening a pouch on his vest that had remained unopened until now.

Larsen removed a plastic olive drab device the size of a cigarette pack and pulled the cover off the adhesive strip on the back of it before pushing it flush against the edge of the door, directly next to the card reader. He pulled the cotter pin on the device and stepped to the side. The thermite charge ignited, burning in place against the door with an intense light that lasted several seconds. The cloud of smoke produced by the charge drifted mercifully to the right, vanishing around the side of the building. He'd gotten lucky, having forgotten about the large quantity of smoke produced by the burning thermite.

Larsen tugged on the door, which easily came loose, exposing the red-hot area cut straight through the locking mechanism. Careful not to touch the melted steel, which could easily ignite the material on his vest, he slid into the lobby and started searching for the stairs. Less than a minute later, he was on the third floor, standing several feet away from the door to apartment 302. The mess in the hallway around the door indicated he was in the right place. At least a dozen of the bullets he'd fired from Chang's apartment had penetrated the back wall of Ochoa's position, punching jagged holes in the drywall, leaving chunks of the building material strewn across the floor.

He inched closer, careful not to cross one of the holes and possibly give his position away. A few feet from the door, he lowered to the floor and crawled under one of the openings in the wall, rising on the other side next to the door frame. He now faced a second choice. Loud and fast or quiet and slow.

He took two explosive breaching charges from the same pouch, not wanting the thick smoke created by the thermite charge to obscure his immediate view into the apartment. The thermite would certainly mask his entry, making it hard for Ochoa to hit him, but in a situation like this, the odds were overwhelmingly stacked against the entry team. If he didn't neutralize Ochoa within the first few seconds, all bets were off. Within moments, he'd attached the charges to the door, best-guessing the deadbolt's location.

"This is going to suck," he muttered, simultaneously pressing the timer buttons on both devices.

Larsen had enough time to crouch and open his mouth to avoid an overpressure situation, before the small charges detonated, knocking the door partially inward. He shouldered the door the rest of the way and rapidly moved inside the room, sweeping his rifle across the apartment. A figure sat upright in a dining room chair that had been moved behind the couch, head slumped forward and both arms slack at the sides. The stock of a rifle protruded above the top of the couch.

"You lose, Larsen. Or Ragan. Or whoever," croaked Ochoa from the chair, his head rising an inch before falling forward.

"It's Larsen," he said, sidestepping along the edge of the apartment to a point where he could see the side of Ochoa's face.

"I was really hoping it wasn't you," said Ochoa. "I can't stand you."

"The feeling is mutual," said Larsen.

"Just get it over with," said Ochoa, trying to lift his head again.

"I think I'll take a look at your CTAB first."

"Finish it. You fuck!" he hissed, his head coming up a little farther than before.

"Not until I see what you've been up to," said Larsen, moving closer.

"You don't have the guts to kill me, do you?" said Ochoa. "Ha! You're pathetic. Everything you do is pathetic."

Larsen fired a single bullet through the top of Ochoa's right thigh, yielding no response beyond a slightly turned head. A second bullet passed through his right hand, with the same result. He was paralyzed from the neck down—posing no threat.

"Damn, Ochoa," said Larsen.

"What? Feeling bad about this?" said Ochoa.

"Not really," said Larsen, walking past him to recover the CTAB, which lay next to Ripley's dead body. "But I'll do the right thing before I leave."

"What a consolation."

Larsen picked up the CTAB, seeing that the screen was locked. Not a problem. He took the device over to Ochoa and lifted his hand onto the screen, pressing his blood-smeared thumb against the biometric reader. The CTAB activated, the sophisticated software installed into the reader capable of rendering a decision despite the bloody mess on the screen. He scrolled through the message history, selecting the last message received.

"You son of a bitch," he mumbled, looking at Ochoa.

The man grinned, his scarred face twisted in delight.

"You lose."

Without giving the decision any thought, he raised the

barrel of his rifle even with Ochoa's head and pulled the trigger, putting the man out of his misery.

"David, David, it's Larsen," he said.

"Yeah. We're here," said the police officer. "Is that Ochoa guy done?"

"He's done," said Larsen. "But he left us with a serious problem."

"Yeah. You guys have attracted some attention from the local crazy population."

"It's a far bigger problem," said Larsen, tossing the CTAB on the table next to Ochoa's corpse. "Ochoa reported that he had Chang in custody."

"Jesus," said David. "How long do we have?"

"ETA twenty minutes," said Larsen. "And that was four minutes ago."

Chapter Nineteen

David peered over the top of the concrete wall, careful not to expose too much of his head. He spotted at least six people slowly converging on the stretch of Virginia Avenue between the two apartment buildings. He wasn't sure if their infected and damaged brains could piece together enough of the scene to determine that someone had just killed two of their own a few feet from the entrance to the building across the street. If they could, and they got curious, Larsen would have to deal with them inside the lobby, wasting precious time.

They no longer had the option of waiting around for Howard's security crew to patch up the SUV for a second diversion. The people behind Larsen's mysterious agency would descend on them within fifteen minutes, and he couldn't imagine they'd be happy to discover Ochoa's team slaughtered—and Chang missing. They needed to be as far away from here as possible when the pickup team arrived.

He scanned the street again, not liking what he saw.

"Larsen, I have six—make that eight—crazies converging on the front door to your building," said David. "One of them is very interested in the bodies."

"I'm on my way down," said Larsen. "Will look for a rear exit."

"I don't know if that's a great idea," said David. "At

least out here I can lend you a hand if things get out of control."

"Agreed," said Larsen. "Did you send Howard over to the other building?"

Howard answered, "I'm holding the door for you."

"Head on down to the lobby and prep Jeremy for an immediate departure," said Larsen. "We can't leave him behind at this point. They'll see the sheets hanging out of the building and put two and two together. Jeremy won't last two seconds under the kind of pressure they're sure to apply, and he knows you're the head of the tactical team at NevoTech."

"Shit. There's no way we're getting him out of this building," said Howard.

"Tell him he leaves with us or I'll shoot him."

"He won't believe that. You wouldn't shoot him," said Howard.

"Dan, if he doesn't come along, I'll shoot him," said David. "My son is back at NevoTech. We can't have any concrete links back to the campus. These people will turn the place inside out looking for Chang. Everyone back there will be in danger if they suspect he's there."

"What if they head there anyway?" said Howard.

"It's a big campus," said Larsen. "Which you know inside and out. We're better off dealing with this on familiar territory."

"I'm headed down with Dr. Hale," said Howard. "I'll leave the door propped open."

"We'll meet you in the lobby," said Larsen. "David?"

"Still here. I count ten close enough to give you trouble," said David. "Two look like they're about to check out the door."

"I'm in the stairwell on the lobby level. Start thinning

the herd closest to the door."

Thin the herd? They were still human beings. People you might have held the door open for at a coffee shop or said good morning to on the street less than twenty-four hours ago. David still thought of them as people, even though he knew they'd try to kill him on sight. He still hesitated—a problem that didn't appear to plague Larsen. The former SEAL had been trained from day one to eliminate targets with extreme prejudice. It was a black-and-white world with good guys, bad guys and defined rules of engagement. David's job as a police officer couldn't be more different. He drove his police cruiser out of the department lot with the assumption that everyone out there was a good guy until they proved otherwise. He had been conditioned to treat everyone he came across on patrol that way, with few exceptions. It was the cornerstone of the job, and it would be a hard habit to break. He wished he didn't have to, but things were different now. He needed to be more like Larsen to stay alive and keep his son safe. More like David Olson, the infantry Marine. With that thought in mind, he lifted his rifle above the top of the concrete barrier and started *thinning the herd.*

Chapter Twenty

Gary Hoenig leaned forward in his seat, squinting at the curved, panoramic command and control screen mounted to the desk in front of him. One of the cameras with a view of the secure research facility (SRF) had detected movement. He swiped the track pad and sent the video feed to the wall of integrated screens on the front wall of the sunken auditorium-style room.

Four heavily armed figures, wearing streamlined tactical gear and night-vision-equipped helmets, ran across the grassy area between the SRF and one of the lower security research buildings, heading north. He "hooked" one of the figures and activated the "track object" feature. Now all of the security cameras would work together to follow the figure, automatically triangulating its location based on motion-sensor input and choosing the clearest camera feed.

The SRF maintained a separate internal security force hired by the facility director from one of the nation's top security contracting companies. All former FBI, SWAT or Tier One Special Forces types. At first glance, the team on the main screen fit that bill, though he found it odd that they had left the SRF in such a large group. Even if the SRF security team was staffed with far higher numbers than he had previously guessed, sending four out at once had to be an anomaly. Maybe the facility director was headed to the campus?

He shook his head. That would be a disastrous idea. The odds of something going wrong on the way in, even with four seasoned operators covering the approach and the gate transfer. The more he thought about it, the less sense it made. Why wouldn't they use the VIP parking garage access on the west side of the campus? It was perfectly secure. Maybe he should reach out to the SRF and suggest an alternate approach, or offer assistance. Roscoe still had a nice supply of smoke grenades, which could come in handy.

Hoenig dialed the SRF security number, which would put him directly in touch with the on-duty team leader. The screen changed to a front-facing view as he waited for the team leader to answer. Several seconds later, with the call still unanswered, he noticed something unusual. He zoomed in for a closer look. Interesting. All of their rifles were equipped with suppressors, just like the rifle the Homeland Security agent carried. He zoomed in a little further.

"Couldn't be," he mumbled before accessing the feed archive on one of his desktop screens and calling up a video of Larsen's group.

He found a clear shot of Larsen in one of the hallways and zoomed in on the image, comparing it to a still shot taken of the SRF team. Their gear was identical. One of the other teams Larsen mentioned had been on the NevoTech campus all along.

"Dan, this is Gary. I have a heavily armed team of four between buildings five and seven. Headed north in a hurry. They originated from the SRF."

"SRF security?" said Howard.

"I called, and nobody responded," said Hoenig. "Their gear is identical to Larsen's."

"This is Larsen. How identical?"

"Down to the suppressors on your HK416 rifles," said Hoenig.

"They came from the SRF?" said Howard.

"I'm looking at the historical data feed right now," said Hoenig. "They emerged about a minute ago."

"This is related to Ochoa's little stunt," said Larsen. "They're all converging for a pickup."

"Right on top of us. Son of a bitch," said Howard. "Gary, I don't have time to explain, but we need to get back onto campus immediately."

"I can't send Mitch out to recover you right now. The SUV isn't ready," said Hoenig.

"How long?" said Howard.

"Ten to fifteen minutes?"

"We can't wait that long," said Larsen. "Plus it's too risky with that team in the immediate vicinity—and possibly another inbound."

"How many teams are still out there?" said Hoenig.

"Two. Including the one you're watching," said Larsen. "Is there any way you can keep them on campus? Maybe override their keycards?"

"Frankly, I'd rather get them off campus and lock them out," said Hoenig. "Locking them inside might create more problems than we can solve. They'll know we're onto them."

"I agree," said Howard. "We have a responsibility to keep the people who sought refuge there safe. Causing trouble for Homeland might jeopardize that."

"Well, we need to get away from here," said Larsen. "They'll turn this area inside out when they discover

Ochoa's team dead—and Chang missing."

"Without a solid diversion, we won't last very long out there. The streets are too hot," said David.

Hoenig stared at the main screen for a moment. The team of operatives had just cleared the northernmost building and turned east, apparently headed toward the same gate Howard had used to sneak over to Chang's apartment. That put the team directly in the path of their return. Even if the SUV were ready for the trip, it probably wouldn't reach the apartment before the team, and if it managed to get there ahead of them, there was no telling what might transpire. The vehicle was bullet resistant, but not bulletproof. Four skilled shooters could easily knock it out of commission if they managed to concentrate their gunfire. Not a hard task to accomplish on empty streets.

"Any ideas?" said Larsen. "We need to get moving."

"I only have Roscoe up high right now," said Hoenig. "And a few security officers on foot patrol. They wouldn't stand a chance against trained operators, even with Roscoe—"

A devilish idea cut the sentence short.

"Gary, you still there?" said Howard.

"Uhhhh—yes," he said. "I just had an idea."

"Is it the kind of idea you can execute two minutes ago?" said Larsen.

"Sort of. The plan has literally been in motion for—" Hoenig checked the time stamp on the main video feed "—ninety-three seconds."

Chapter Twenty-One

Roscoe had reservations about his role in the plan. These guys would most likely die anyway once they stepped outside the gate, but Gary had asked him to "seal the deal." He wasn't sure how he felt about that. He wasn't opposed to taking the necessary steps to secure the campus and clear the way for Howard, but he didn't know anything about the team rapidly approaching the northeast gate. They might not be anything like the crew Howard had run into at Chang's apartment. Their only goal might be to get to their extraction point alive and get back to their families. Roscoe was one trigger pull away from permanently preventing that—which weighed mightily on his conscience.

"You ready up there?" said Hoenig in his earpiece. "They'll be at the gate in a few seconds. We don't know if they'll wait inside the gate until their extraction is imminent, or if they'll attempt to move to Virginia Avenue immediately."

"I'm ready," said Roscoe. "They'd be fools to step outside those gates without some readily available backup."

"I agree," said Hoenig. "But they don't have access to external security feeds, and the SRF rooftop has no sightlines to the parking lot. They most likely don't understand the full scope of the threat out there."

"They'd have to be stupid," said Roscoe.

"They've been tucked away inside the SRF all night—waiting for Chang," said Hoenig. "Only God knows what they did with the real security team. I can't imagine it was a nonlethal situation. SRF security is hardcore. Don't lose sight of that."

Roscoe knew Hoenig was right. He just wished someone else could pull the trigger.

"I'm good," said Roscoe.

"Heads-up, they just arrived at the gate."

Roscoe stood upright from a crouch and rested his sniper rifle on the rooftop parapet, centering the crosshairs of the Schmidt & Bender sniper scope on the northeast gate. Three of the operators kneeled in a formation surrounding the fourth, who pressed a keycard against the card reader.

"Fucking idiots," muttered Roscoe before swapping his rifle for the multi-canister grenade.

"Looks like they're going for it. Stand by for my mark," said Hoenig.

Roscoe nestled the grenade launcher into his shoulder and pointed it in the general direction of the northeast gate. He didn't have to be precise. Once he had the business end of the launcher roughly lined up with the gate, he raised the barrel to a forty-five-degree angle. Given the approximate distance to the gate, the grenade should either land on East Street or fall short inside the campus fence. Several seconds passed before Hocnig's voice broke onto the tactical net.

"Fire the first grenade."

"Firing," said Roscoe before pressing the trigger.

The launcher barely recoiled, firing a single 40mm grenade in a lazy arc over the pristinely landscaped northern campus gardens. He ducked behind the parapet, confident that the projectile was headed where he intended. A few moments later, the nonlethal grenade detonated—shattering the calm with a cascade of ear-piercing blasts.

The projectile was mostly a noisemaker. Harmless unless it struck you directly or exploded at your feet—until today. Now it was lethal to anyone within a five-hundred-yard radius without a secure place to hide.

"Nice shot," said Hoenig. "Landed on the street. Already attracted some attention. Fire a second into the main parking lot. Let's try to draw as many out of hiding as possible."

"Second round out," said Roscoe, pointing the launcher due north at the same angle and firing another noisemaker.

Moments after the second chain of sharp detonations, the crack of suppressed gunfire started to fill the air. It started off with sporadic shots, quickly transforming into a desperate crescendo punctuated by bursts of automatic fire. The team outside the gate was fighting for its life.

"How is it looking out there?" said Roscoe, not wanting to look.

"They're trying frantically to get the gate open," said Hoenig, pausing for a moment. "Shit. One of them is messing with his vest. They might try to blow the gate open with explosives."

"That would be a disaster," said Roscoe. "Do you want me to put a grenade on the gate?"

"If you don't mind," said Hoenig.

"Stand by," said Roscoe.

He rose to his feet, crouching below the top of the parapet to remain hidden. The less time he spent exposed, the better. The team would be looking for him, in between shooting crazies. With his body pointed toward the gate, he rose quickly and sighted in on the turnstile. The figure crouched immediately behind the gate glanced up in his direction and reached for his rifle. Roscoe fired the grenade and dove to his left as several bullets punched through the rooftop wall above him.

The grenade exploded, temporarily stopping the storm of bullets directed at his position. He grabbed the sniper rifle with his free hand and crawled toward the center of the rooftop, where the angle of fire prevented their bullets from reaching him.

"You still with us?" said Hoenig.

"Barely. They got off those rounds really quick," said Roscoe.

"Well, I don't think you have to worry about them anymore," said Hoenig. "They've got bigger problems. I count at least a hundred hostiles converging on them from every direction. They're moving toward the primary pedestrian entrance off the parking lot."

The rate of suppressed gunfire doubled in the time it took Gary to finish his report.

"Doesn't sound like they're going to make it that far," said Roscoe.

"They're doing a number on the crazies, but it's not sustainable," said Hoenig. "They'll make it to the gate, but it'll be their last stand."

"Unless they try to blow the gate," said Roscoe flatly.

He'd have to poke his head up again and risk taking a bullet through the cranium. Wonderful.

"We can't let them do that," said Hoenig.

Of course not.

"How long until Howard and the rest of them get to

131

the northeast gate?"

"Five minutes maximum," said Hoenig. "They're already on the move."

"And I suppose you'll want me in position to help them, too?"

"I'm sure they'd appreciate a hand if things get dicey," said Hoenig. "We made a lot of noise with the grenades. It's pulling crazies from farther away, which might be a problem."

"I'll reload the launcher with smoke grenades," said Roscoe. "Just let me know what I need to do next."

"You might want to keep a few bangers loaded up," said Hoenig. "In case the team out front tries to blow a hole in the fence."

"I'm done using nonlethal methods," said Roscoe, glancing at the dozen or more holes in the parapet wall.

"Just watch yourself up there," said Hoenig.

"Don't worry. I won't make the same mistake twice," he said before slithering toward one of the raised fan units near the front of the roof.

Chapter Twenty-Two

Dr. Lauren Hale leaned against the cool tile wall, her attention drawn between the heated argument in the lobby and the occasional sight of movement through the apartment building's rear exit door. She wasn't entirely sure which of the two posed the most danger, though her experience over the past forty-eight hours told her the argument was insignificant in the grand scheme of things. The guy called Larsen pointed his finger at the scared-shitless young man they had dragged across the lobby and issued a threat that nearly changed her assessment of the situation.

"Jeremy, I'm only going to say this one more time. You either leave with us right now, or I'm going to shoot you where you stand. Got it?"

"I can't leave," said Jeremy. "What if my girlfriend shows up?"

"She's not showing up," said Larsen. "I'm counting down from five, and then I'm shooting."

"What if the National Guard rolls through and gets this under control!" said Jeremy. "When people call down and I don't answer—goodbye job."

"Five!" said Larsen.

"Hold on, Larsen," said David, the police officer.

"Four!"

"Stop the count for a few seconds," insisted David.

"Shit is going down right now," said Larsen. "We should have been on the move thirty seconds ago."

"He's right," said Howard, the NevoTech security guy. "We don't have a very long window of opportunity to get back. There's only so much my guys can do."

"Jeremy, if you stay here, you're a dead man. These people will kill you after they've extracted everything you know—about us. If you come with us, we'll protect you like one of our own. When the National Guard rolls through and secures this part of the city, you can walk right back and pick up where you left off. Nobody upstairs will be the wiser."

She liked Howard's approach better than Larsen's, though she didn't fully trust any of them. They still hadn't satisfactorily answered her most basic questions about the bigger picture—and their rather murky connection to it.

"You have my word," said Larsen. "We'll get you safely inside the campus. As long as you follow our directions."

A rapid sequence of sharp explosions resonated inside the hallway, turning all of their heads toward the exit behind her.

"Guys," said Howard, "time to make a decision."

"I'll go," said Jeremy. "Do I get a gun?"

"No," said Larsen, turning to Hale and offering her one of the spare rifles. "Can you handle this?"

The question caught her off guard, and she hesitated.

"I need to know right now," said Larsen, moving toward her. "We're going to need all of the help we can get out there."

A figure dashed past the door, startling all of them.

"What the hell was that?" she said.

"That's why I need more shooters. Have you ever

fired something like this?"

"Yes. At an indoor range," she said. "Kind of a weird date night."

"Sounds perfect to me," said Larsen, holding the weapon in front of her. "The safety is disengaged, meaning the rifle will fire if you pull the trigger. Keep your finger away from the trigger unless it's absolutely necessary to shoot. We'll help you with reloading if it comes to that. Hopefully, it won't."

"What do I shoot at?" she said.

Larsen and David shared a worried glance.

"Anyone directly threatening either you or Jeremy. Immediate self-defense only. We'll take care of the rest," said David.

Larsen squeezed past her and crouched at the door, peering through the glass door in both directions before looking over his shoulder. He looked pale, like someone who had lost too much blood, but he was still entirely alert. In fact, he seemed like the most responsive and effective member of the group that had ventured out to rescue her. Still, she'd seen patients go from entirely coherent to unconscious in a matter of seconds. She'd have to keep a close eye on him. His leg wound was probably a lot worse than he let on.

"David, I want you on my left the entire time, covering dead ahead to our left. I have the other side. Jeremy, you tuck in right behind us. Do not touch either of us. Dr. Hale, you fall in right behind Jeremy. Howard brings up the rear. We're going to take this at a slow jog to start and adjust from there. Everyone clear on what we're doing?"

"Got it," she said, backing up to make room for David and Jeremy.

"You okay?" she said to the young man.

"Not really, but I wasn't given much of a choice," said Jeremy.

"It's the only viable choice right now," she said.

"Keep up and listen up," said Larsen. "We'll take care of the rest."

"I hate that guy," said Jeremy.

"That's why we gave her the rifle," said David, winking at her. "Seriously. Stay right behind us—no matter what happens. We're bound to hit a few bumps out there."

"Bumps?" she said. "Define bumps."

"Crazies," said David. "Infected. Hopefully not too many at once."

"How many is too many?" said Jeremy.

"We'll be fine," said David.

A second set of distant blasts vibrated the door.

"We're moving," said Larsen, taking a few steps back and pressing the panel button on the wall.

The door opened, flooding the hallway with the repetitive crackle of distant gunfire. She assumed it was gunfire, even though it sounded distinctly different than the methodic ripsaw bursts she'd listened to all night. Larsen rushed outside before she could protest, followed by the cop. Jeremy hesitated for a few moments, and she shoved him into the humid morning before he could change his mind. She stepped through the door behind him, her attention immediately drawn to rapid movement to her right. Hale opened her stance and raised the rifle; a shirtless man in khaki cargo pants was barreling down the side of the building toward them.

"Contact right," said David, followed by a single gunshot.

The man catapulted forward and smacked headfirst into the concrete sidewalk, his blood-encrusted kitchen knife clattering along the service road pavement next to him. She stood frozen in place, her rifle still aimed at the empty space above the man's twitching corpse. A hand squeezed her left shoulder, startling her.

"You good?" said David.

"I'm fine," she said, slowly lowering the rifle.

"Good instinct coming through the door. I think we're in good hands," said David.

"I don't know," she said. "I froze after that."

"Your finger went right into the trigger well. I think you'll be fine."

"Keep it moving," said Howard, sliding past her with his rifle aimed down the side of the building.

She sprinted behind David to catch up with Larsen and Jeremy, who jogged slowly down the service road passing behind the parking garage. A staggered group of three people appeared in the distance, running toward the continuous gunfire to the west. The ragged, partially dressed trio disappeared behind a building on the road ahead of them without glancing in their direction.

Larsen guided them to the right, toward an unfenced backyard, picking up the pace as they crossed the parking lot behind Chang's building. A third set of tightly spaced explosions rattled in the distance, booming like industrial-grade fireworks.

"Contact right," said Howard, his rifle already snapping rounds toward an unseen threat.

She turned her head in time to see a woman crash down the dilapidated stairs of a paint-chipped deck, followed immediately by a skinny teenager aiming a pistol. Several bullets struck him at once, knocking him backward into a pair of rusted folding chairs. The pistol discharged as he toppled over the chairs, echoing across the neighborhood and momentarily drowning out the distant gun battle at NevoTech.

A man holding an upside-down beer bottle appeared in the doorway attached to the deck, vanishing just as quickly in a hail of bullets from their rifles.

"Contact front," said David.

Larsen and the cop turned their rifles toward a group of several infected that scrambled in their direction from an empty, dirt-covered lot to their left. Behind them, Howard fired twice, hitting an unseen target deep inside one of the yards. They were coming from every direction. Before she could turn her head to check on Larsen and David, she bumped into Jeremy, who had stopped dead in his tracks.

"This is out of control," he hissed, shaking his head. "We need to go back."

Hale pushed him aside and rushed forward into the firing line, pointing her rifle at the bloodstained gang of human ghouls pushing uncomfortably close to their perimeter. She repeatedly pressed the trigger, not sure if she was helping or hurting the situation. It didn't matter. She couldn't sit back and do nothing. Not if these things kept coming out of the woodwork like this.

Chapter Twenty-Three

Larsen stopped firing when the last crazy took a bullet through the forehead, but the doctor continued to pull her trigger until the rifle was empty, drawing another glitchy lunatic off the street visible between the two houses. He let it take several steps down the path before firing a single shot through its head, dropping it like a ragdoll.

"Get Rambo over there squared away," said Larsen. "A little trigger discipline goes a long way."

"A little thank-you might go a long way, too," said Hale.

"Thank you for bringing one more crazy at us," said Larsen. "And you're welcome for the rescue."

"I'll thank you when the rescue is complete."

"You're free to head back," said Larsen, nodding at Chang's apartment building.

"That's no longer an option thanks to you," said Hale.

"It was never an option," said Larsen. "Do I have to explain why?"

"Cut the chatter," said David. "We need to focus."

Another figure appeared on the street, pausing for a second to look at them before moving on—unable to resist the sound of a pitched battle to the west. A few more people ran past the opening, heading in the same direction.

"This might be harder than we thought," said Larsen, changing rifle magazines. "Those pyrotechnic devices caught the attention of every crazy within a two-mile radius."

"We should wait here until the streets clear," said David.

"We don't have that kind of time," said Larsen, checking his watch. "Eight minutes. And you can bet your ass that the team fighting for its life out there has reported its situation. We need to be tucked away inside NevoTech's campus when the recovery mission gets here."

"Agreed," said David.

"I'll make you a deal, Larsen," said Hale.

"Really?" said Larsen.

"You get me to NevoTech in one piece, and I'll patch up your leg," she said, the faintest traces of a grin breaking through her serious façade.

"If you throw in no more full-mag shooting sprees, it's a deal," said Larsen.

"Deal."

While David showed her how to reload the rifle, a large group of infected scrambled past the gap between houses.

"Keep everyone well out of sight until we're ready to move," said Larsen before transmitting over the control net. "Gary, what are we looking at?"

Gary Hoenig's voice crackled in his earpiece. "I was just about to get in touch. The team is trapped outside, moving west along the front fence. They're thirty seconds from being overrun. I've never seen this many crazies converge on the parking lot before. What's your status?"

"Hiding out in a backyard. Maybe fifty feet from

Merrill Street," said Larsen. "I see a lot of foot traffic on Merrill."

"Yeah. And it's not letting up from what I can tell," said Hoenig. "I'd suggest you reroute farther south, but you'll probably run into the same problem, except you'll be on the streets longer."

"Can Roscoe give us a smoke screen?"

"Negative. Roscoe is the only thing keeping that team from punching a hole in the fence with explosives. I can redirect his attention when I know for sure that the team is dead."

"Then I guess we'll have to run and gun this," said Larsen.

"Godspeed," said Hoenig.

Larsen shook his head. "This is going to suck."

"Run and gun?" said Hale.

"It's exactly what it sounds like. We run and gun our way to the northeast gate," said Larsen, drawing his suppressed pistol and offering it to Jeremy.

"What about the other rifle?" said Jeremy, pointing at the weapon slung across David's back. "Wouldn't that be more effective? I know how to shoot one of those. I mean, I've seen it done a lot. And I used to play *Battlefield 4.*"

Larsen stared at him for a second, wondering if he should rescind the pistol offer.

"Suppressed weapons only," said Larsen. "Unless you want to become the center of attention on Merrill Street."

Jeremy accepted the pistol, gingerly handling it like something plucked from a toilet.

"No safety. You just point and pull the trigger," said Larsen.

The young man nodded, still looking nervous.

"What's the plan?" said David.

"You're not going to like it," said Larsen.

"Tell me something I don't know."

"We'll switch up the order," said Larsen. "You and Dan up front. Me in the back. They'll be coming up behind us pretty quick."

"We have a few smoke grenades," said Howard, patting the pouch attached to his vest. "How do you want to use them?"

"I don't want to be messing with those while we're on the run," said Larsen. "We'll toss them east on Merrill before we take off."

"How far are we running?" said Hale.

"Maybe two football fields," said Howard. "It's not very far. We can be at the gate in less than a minute."

"If we don't hit any bumps along the way," said Hale, looking at David.

"I expect a bumpy ride," said the cop.

"Or we might sail right through the gate without a problem," said Larsen, pausing to scan their faces. "Nobody's buying that one?"

Nobody said a word.

"Only one way to find out," said Larsen.

Chapter Twenty-Four

David cautiously approached the front corner of the house on Merrill Street, leading with his rifle. If another swarm passed by, there was no chance he would go unnoticed. Their survival would depend on an immediate reaction to the threat—and a lot of bullets. The suppressor attached to Howard's rifle was visible in his peripheral vision, aiming in the same direction. If a large swarm materialized, the rest of the group would swing out and form a tight firing line. That was the extent of the plan. It was simply assumed that *run like hell* would follow.

He tucked his elbow in and inched the rifle around the corner, relieved to find the street mostly empty. Three disheveled crazies ran in their direction, one of them spotting him immediately.

"Three headed our way," said David. "Get the smoke ready. Need an assist, Howard."

Howard swung around to his right, both of their rifles firing simultaneously. David took the third one down before the other two hit the street.

"Pop the smoke!" said David. "Time to move!"

They took off jogging, slowly building speed as they angled across the street. Two hollow metallic *thunks* echoed somewhere behind him, followed by a loud hissing sound. A quick glance over his shoulder confirmed that the smoke grenades had been satisfactorily deployed. It also confirmed that the stream of infected into the area hadn't really slowed. Beyond the thickening white screen, at least a half-dozen people shambled in their direction from the intersection of Merrill Street and Virginia Avenue.

"You got that, Larsen?" said David.

A dozen evenly spaced shots initially answered his question.

"Don't worry about me," said Larsen. "I'll let you know if I need help."

David started to form a smart-ass response, but a broken screen door flew open two houses down from them, disgorging a neatly dressed man, who stumbled down the concrete stoop and fell to his hands and knees. The guy looked up at them, and for a brief moment, he thought the man was normal. Someone who had been holed up inside, waiting for the perfect moment to escape or the right group of people to follow out of the city. His hope was short-lived. The man held a kitchen knife tightly in one of his hands, seemingly oblivious to the fact that he'd ripped half of the skin on his knuckles away when he hit the street.

Howard's rifle cracked twice, knocking him flat to the pavement. Up ahead, at the intersection of Merrill and East Street, a small gaggle of crazies headed toward the NevoTech parking lot slowed to a walk, searching for the new source of the gunfire. He considered stopping on the street to take an aimed shot, but decided against it. Time would decide whether they lived or died on these streets. The less time they spent on this side of the gate, the better their odds of surviving. He picked up the pace, steadying his rifle the best he could manage—while firing repeatedly.

A second group replaced the first, eating up the rest of his rifle magazine. He reloaded on the fly and put the rifle back into action against individual targets streaming into the intersection they were rapidly approaching. There was no doubt that the infected population of Indianapolis would hotly contest their entry, requiring a temporary perimeter around the gate. His earpiece came to life.

"Dan, this is Gary. The team along the front fence line has been completely overrun. They're tearing them to pieces. Won't be long until they shift their attention in your direction."

"Can you give us another pyro?" said Howard. "And some smoke?"

"Forget the smoke," said Larsen. "Fire off the rest of the pyro grenades at the western side of the parking lot. We just need a diversion to keep the main swarm off us."

"A lot of them are already headed in your direction," said Hoenig.

"Then get Roscoe on his sniper rifle," said Larsen. "Have him focus on the area around our gate."

"Consider it done," said Hoenig. "Dan, do you want me to green-light the gate?"

"Yes. Open it now," said Howard. "We're almost there."

"What the fuck does green-light mean?" yelled David, firing at hostiles on East Street.

"It means he's going to open the gate remotely," said Howard.

"Why didn't he do that on the way out?"

"Because we've had problems with the remote system in the past," said Howard.

"What kind of problems?"

"The turnstile occasionally remains open," said

Howard before firing several bullets at various targets approaching from the parking lot.

"Then what?"

"Then we have to reset the gate, which takes time."

David took a knee in the middle of the intersection, waving the rest of the group toward the gate. He reloaded and shifted his fire to the crazies arriving from the parking lot. Larsen squatted next to him, firing at fast movers coming from both directions on East Street.

"Move closer to the gate, or we'll get cut off," said Larsen, patting his shoulder.

He sprinted toward the group approaching the gate, taking a new position between the parking lot and the northeast corner of the fence. Larsen kneeled to the right of him, his rifle barking a relentless torrent of semiautomatic fire. Out of the corner of his eye, he could see that part of their group had disappeared through the turnstile.

Larsen slapped his shoulder. "Empty your mag and get through the gate!"

Working his rifle back and forth across the leading crazies, he barely made a dent in the surging horde. When the rifle's slide locked in the open position, he turned and ran, spotting Howard crouched next to the turnstile—waving him through. When he got to the other side, David reloaded and took a position next to Dr. Hale along the fence next to the gate.

They fired bullet after bullet into the asynchronous mob spilling out of the parking lot as Larsen passed through. Howard slid into the gate a fraction of a second before the first wave of crazies slammed headlong into the turnstile with a sickening thud. He managed to push the rotating security bars far enough to separate himself from the wave of crashing bodies, but not far enough to be released inside the campus. A tangle of flesh jammed the rotating mechanism, bones snapping as Howard frantically rammed his shoulder into the thick cylindrical bars in front of him.

David pulled Dr. Hale back just in time to keep her rifle from being snatched through the fence. He joined Larsen at the turnstile, grabbing one of the bars with both hands and pulling with all of his weight. The substantial metal cage didn't budge.

"Shoot at the body parts jammed in the gate!" said Larsen. "Maybe we can get this to move."

Howard shook his head. "It won't make a difference! The gate mechanism automatically locks in place when it detects a jam—to prevent further injury. The only way I'm getting out of this is by going back out!"

His earpiece crackled.

"Dan, this is Gary. We can cut you out of that. We have a hydraulic cutter for this precise scenario. I can have Mitch and Sean at the gate with the cutter in five minutes."

"What about the helos?" said Howard, directing the question at Larsen.

"I'm not leaving you out here," said Larsen. "David, get Dr. Hale and Jeremy inside. I'll stay with Dan. It'll take the extraction team some time to piece things together back at Chang's apartment."

"Gary, send Mitch and Scan," said Howard.

"Once they get the compressor running, they'll have you out of there in less than a minute," said Hoenig.

"Sounds good right about now," said Howard, pressing his body tightly against the bars. "This is the creepiest fucking—"

His comment was cut short by gunshots from the other side of the gate. David crouched instinctively and scooted behind one of the thick metal pillars anchoring the gate in place.

"We need to thin this out!" said Larsen.

"How? It's one giant mass of people on the other side," said David.

"Don't waste the bullets," said Howard.

A bullet struck the turnstile bars, ricocheting back into the crazies.

"I should be safe enough in here until they cut me out," said Howard.

Before either of them could respond, Howard shrieked in agony, clutching at the back of his neck. His body slammed violently backward, the tip of a knife punching through the left side of his neck. Bright red arterial spray pulsed through the bars, splattering David's face. Unable to immediately conjure any solution to Howard's desperate plight, David defaulted to his rifle, methodically emptying a thirty-round magazine into the murderous herd of crazies on the other side of the turnstile. When he dropped the magazine from the rifle and reached for another, Larsen grabbed his wrist.

"It's over. There's absolutely nothing we can do for him."

Howard slumped to his knees against the turnstile wall, a weak stream of blood rhythmically pumping onto his shoulder. He groaned, trying to speak words that had no chance of forming. David pressed his forehead against the blood-washed metal and gripped Howard's hand through the bars.

"You saved a lot of lives going on this mission. Nobody will forget this."

Howard gurgled an unintelligible sound, a look of desperation washing over his face. He was trying to communicate. David locked eyes with Howard, momentarily blocking out the insane chaos a few feet away.

"Do you need to tell me something?"

Howard nodded and tried to speak. He understood.

"Your family?"

Another nod.

"Where are they?"

He shook his head.

"Are they safe?"

No response.

"You want me to find them? Make sure they're safe?"

Another shake.

"His family is here," said Hoenig over the tactical net.

Howard grunted once and sank a little closer to the concrete underneath him.

"We'll make sure they get through this okay," said Hoenig. "I'm locking down this gate. Go in peace, my friend."

Howard nodded, tears streaming down his cheeks. Larsen reached through the bars and clasped both of their hands.

"It was an honor fighting by your side," said Larsen. "Don't worry about your family. They're my family now."

"And mine," said David.

A faint smile crossed his face before his eyes closed and the smile disappeared. David tightened his grip on Howard's hand, once again blocking out the sheer madness of it all.

"David," said Larsen, urgently shaking his arm.

He heard it over the inhuman discordance beyond the

gate. The deep, rhythmic thumping of helicopter blades. Out of the frying pan—into the microwave.

"You okay?" said Larsen, pulling him to his feet. "We need to go!"

He shook his head, tears in his eyes. "I'm alive."

"That's all that counts in a situation like this," said Larsen. "Trust me."

"I guess," said David, not at all comforted by his words.

Chapter Twenty-Five

Dr. Lauren Hale hurried inside the NevoTech building as the sound of helicopters grew louder. She still didn't understand the full scope of Larsen's urgency, but given the bizarre, nearly inexplicable circumstances surrounding her rescue, and the fact that the head of security at NevoTech had given his life to bring her back, she wasn't about to argue. She held the door open for their return, taking note of Larsen's condition.

"You're going with me to medical," said Hale.

"I'll meet you there after these helicopters leave," said Larsen.

"You need more than another wad of hemostatic powder and a compress."

"This isn't the first time I've been shot," said Larsen.

"You want it to be your last?"

"Actually, yes, I do," said Larsen, grinning.

"You know what I meant," said Hale, turning to David. "Can you help me out here?"

"You look like shit," said David.

"That's it?" said Hale. "Every time his right foot hits the ground, blood spills over the top of his boot. You need plasma and a blood transfusion."

"If those helicopters decide to get nosy—" started Larsen.

"If the helicopters get nosy, there's not much we can do other than hide," said David before tapping his transmitter. "Gary, you should get Roscoe down from the rooftop. Helicopters might spot him."

"He's already down, and I've pulled the foot patrols inside," said Hoenig. "I have a few of the eastern-exposed cameras pointed toward Chang's apartment. If they head this way, we can start moving people deeper into the building. One of the larger auditoriums. I doubt they'll spend too much time rummaging around."

"Don't make any assumptions," said Larsen. "You might want to order that evacuation sooner than later. Moving a few hundred people will take time—and make a lot of noise."

"I can't believe you have that many people here," said Hale.

"That's why we risked everything to bring you back," said David. "They have everything they need here for now, except a doctor to treat the seriously wounded."

She nodded. "Then I guess I should get to work—starting with Larsen. While I'm taking care of him, we need to find a way to triage the rest of the wounded and screen for any infected."

"That's already done, from what I understand," said David.

"Perfect. Where's the infirmary?"

Larsen and David looked at each other and shook their heads. Jeremy just leaned against the wall next to them, seemingly oblivious to their conversation.

"Nobody knows?" she said.

"We're kind of new here," said David.

"Gary, this is Larsen. Can you send someone to escort us to medical?"

"Sean and Mitch should be arriving any second," said Hoenig. "David, if you don't mind, I could use your help observing the helicopters. I'm sending the rest of the security team to help move the people out of the cafeteria."

"I need to see my son," said David.

"You actually have a son here?"

David nodded at her before responding to whoever was talking to him over his headset. "I'll head right over."

"I thought you made that up," muttered Hale.

"I wish I had, but it's true. I'm stuck here with my son—just like everybody else," said David.

Larsen gave him a quick look, which David strained to avoid. They were holding something back from her, and she wasn't in any mood to play games.

"What is it?" she said, taking a step toward Larsen.

"What's what?" he said.

"The look you gave David," she said. "Just when I start to trust the two of you, you're still keeping some bullshit secret."

David held both of his palms out in symbolic surrender. "Sorry. I didn't want to complicate things, but our situation here is a little different. We arrived with Chang early this morning, in an airplane."

"He landed it on Interstate 70, less than a mile from here," said Larsen.

She shrugged her shoulders. "What are you telling me?"

"I guess I'm telling you that we're not stuck here like everyone else," said David.

"Right after you told me you were," she said.

"I guess so," said David. "We're supposed to leave with Dr. Chang tonight. Hopefully slip away undetected.

That was the deal."

"Still is the deal," said Larsen. "Someone wants Chang dead. Someone with enough pull to change my team's orders at the last minute."

"I'm not following any of this. Exactly what do you do?" she said.

"I'm a special agent with the Department of Homeland Security. Part of their CHASE program."

She stared at him without saying a word.

"Critical Human Asset Security," said Larsen. "We're trained to protect and transport people the government deems critical during a specific crisis. In this case, we were sent for Dr. Chang, a scientist who specializes in the kind of rare viruses that may be related to whatever is happening out there. Basically, my orders went from protect to neutralize within the span of fifteen minutes."

"He was working on some kind of vaccine that could have prevented all of this," added David.

"Why would they want him dead for that?" said Hale.

"That's the million-dollar question," said Larsen, shifting uncomfortably on his leg.

"I need to look at your leg," she said. "We can worry about all of this conspiracy stuff later, unless you're hiding something else from me."

Larsen started to laugh.

"What?" she said.

"The plane is full," he said. "In case you're wondering."

"I'd be lying if I said I hadn't thought about it," said Hale. "But my place is here now."

Two men dressed in the same body armor and helmets worn by Howard burst through a nearby door with exasperated faces.

"Jesus. Is he really gone?" said one of the security officers.

"It happened too fast. There was nothing any of us could do," said Larsen.

"He insisted on being the last through the turnstile," said David. "A hero right until the very end."

"His family is going to be devastated," said the guard.

"Do they know he went out there?" said Hale.

"No. They're in the cafeteria with the rest of the people. He stops in when he can to spend some time with them, but we've been busy since they arrived."

"Don't say anything to them right away," said Hale. "Let me get things organized at medical, and I'll send for them when we can all be there. I have a little experience breaking this kind of news. The last thing we want to do is approach them in front of everyone. They'll need time to process this as a family."

The guard held out a hand. "I'm Sean. This is Mitch. We'd really appreciate you doing that."

"It's the very least I can do for a man that sacrificed his life to bring me here," said Hale. "I owe all of you."

"Just doing my job," said Larsen, nodding at David. "Not sure what his excuse is."

David winked. "This guy can be very convincing."

She slid an arm under Larsen's right shoulder, lifting him off his wounded leg.

"How long have you known each other?" she said.

Larsen checked his watch. "I'd say about six hours? Maybe seven?"

Hale took a moment to process what he'd said. Two nearly complete strangers—one leaving behind a son— had embarked on a suicide mission to bring her back to the NevoTech campus so she could treat injured people neither of them had ever met.

"What?" said David.

She realized she had been staring at them for a little too long.

"I'm just trying to wrap my head around this," said Hale, shaking her head. "I mean, who are you people?"

"How long did you work in the ER before finally making your way to Chang's?" said David.

"I don't know. Maybe seventy-two hours?" she said.

"On how much sleep?"

"A few hours here and there."

"Why did you leave?"

"I was ordered to leave by Dr. Owens, the acting head of the ER. I wanted to stay, but the National Guard showed up with some bizarre plan that he seemed to think would be a problem."

"You're just like any of us," said David. "Don't sell yourself short."

For the first time in over three days, she felt slightly buoyed, once again ready to tackle anything.

Chapter Twenty-Six

David rushed past Mitch to get into the security hub, where his son, Joshua, had remained during Dr. Hale's rescue. The overwhelming reality of his son's recent torment hadn't fully sunk in until the moment they reached the door to the hub. Joshua had helplessly experienced the entire ordeal from this room, watching and listening to his father under repeated attack.

"Joshua!" he said, searching the room for his son.

His son stood up from one of the computer stations in front of Gary Hoenig. He tore his headphones off and ran to his dad. They hugged for several seconds, David finally grabbing him by his shoulders and looking into his watery eyes.

"You okay?" said David.

Joshua nodded. "I don't want to be apart ever again."

"We won't. I promise," said David. "I had to go out there this time, but that's it. We lie low until dark. Then get out of here."

"I tried to keep him distracted. Your son has been a big help in here. Took over all of the remote monitoring while I focused on you and—" Hoenig paused, unable to speak.

"Dan will not be forgotten," said David. "Dr. Hale wants to—"

"Mitch already briefed me," said Hoenig. "I'm

grateful. I don't think I could face his wife. Certainly not alone."

"You won't be alone," said David. "When the helicopters leave and things quiet down, we'll go out there and cut him out of the turnstile. Bury him properly and bring the family over. Something like that. They can't see him like this."

"I'm glad someone's thinking," said Hoenig. "I can barely function after that."

"You've been functioning just fine," said David, turning to the screens. "What do we have so far? I heard helicopters. Black Hawks by the sound of it."

Hoenig selected one of the smaller peripheral screens and sent it to the center of the screen bank. The tops of several buildings appeared.

"I have this camera set to panoramic mode, centered on Chang's apartment building. Nothing has arrived so far," said Hoenig. "But I can hear helicopters."

"You have audio?" said David.

"Yes," he said, clicking his desktop mouse and filling the room with the unmistakable beat of helicopter rotors.

"They're here somewhere," said David.

"How wide are the streets?" said Hoenig.

"Not wide enough for helicopters, and it's crisscrossed with power lines," said David, squeezing his son's arm as he moved closer to the screen. "They're probably hovering nearby, trying to contact the team. Assess the situation. My guess is they'll fast rope a team down onto one of the rooftops. What's the closest open area they could use for landing?"

Hoenig split the screen, displaying the satellite filtered Google Map overlay of the area next to the live feed of the building tops.

"Our parking lot," he said.

"They won't land here and travel there by foot," said David. "They should have enough intel from their ground teams to avoid that kind of mistake. They might be able to land a bird on one of the nearby rooftops."

"The top of the parking garage could work," said Joshua. "Tight squeeze but guaranteed to be solid."

Hoenig cast Joshua an admiring look.

"Thousands of hours playing *Call of Duty* and *Battlefield*," said David. "He probably knows more than either of us."

"My son is fifteen, and I wouldn't dispute his knowledge of modern or historical equipment," said Hoenig, zooming in on the top of the parking garage. "You were there. What's your impression?"

"A little tight, but they could use it as an insert and extract point," said David, nodding at his son.

"If they don't draw the entire city to their location," said Hoenig.

A sharp, prolonged buzz saw sound cut through the rotor noise.

"They have ways of rapidly dispersing crowds," said David.

"More like disintegrating," said Joshua.

"What the hell is that?" said Hoenig.

David and Joshua responded at the same time. "Miniguns."

"Oh, shit," said Hoenig, sitting back in his scat. "Look on the bright side. They might do us a favor and clear the streets."

"Let's just hope they don't do it anywhere close to NevoTech," said David. "They could skip a few hundred 7.62mm bullets off the parking lot pavement and into this

159

facility with one of those bursts."

Hoenig pointed at the screen. "There!"

Two Black Hawk helicopters cruised into view from the right side of the screen, flying at rooftop level. One slowed and hovered over Chang's apartment building for a few seconds before drifting forward and stopping over the parking garage. The helicopter turned ninety degrees until it nearly faced the camera.

"What are they doing?" said Hoenig.

Long bursts from the miniguns mounted on each side of the aircraft answered the question.

"Sweeping the street," said David.

The second helicopter hung back for several bursts before moving forward and hovering over Chang's building. Still appearing to be lined up with Virginia Avenue, the helicopter slowly descended until it vanished behind the building.

"They're going after Ochoa's last reported location," said David. "The other team leader."

"And what happens when they find him, you know—"

"Dead?" said David. "I don't know, but my guess is it won't be pretty."

Chapter Twenty-Seven

When Frank Ecker's boots hit the hard asphalt surface, he released the thick rope and quickly moved away, making room for the next member of his team. He removed the heat-absorbing gloves used specifically for fast roping and tossed them to the deck. By the time he'd reached the rooftop access door a few seconds later, the rest of his team was on the deck, forming a tight perimeter around him.

"Team deployed," he said over the tactical net. "All clear below."

There was no reply. With a heavy thud, the rope struck the rooftop and the helicopter drifted away into a nearby over-watch position.

"Valkyrie, this is Ajax. Leave your sniper team on the rooftop, covering the VIP's apartment. We're seeing broken windows on both sides of the street, corresponding to both target apartments."

"Copy," he said, turning to the sniper team crouched next to him. "Any questions?"

They shook their heads and took off for the street-facing side of the roof.

"Let's get this over with," said Ecker.

D-Bird, their breacher, slid his short-barreled M500A2 shotgun out of its over-the-shoulder scabbard and placed the tip of the barrel against the doorknob. Ecker stepped away and nodded, the shotgun booming simultaneously.

The frangible metal-powder slug penetrated the doorknob, obliterating the lock mechanism. Ecker kicked the hollow steel door, which flew inward and banged against the stairwell wall. He triggered his rifle-mounted light and scanned the interior. Nothing waiting for them below except concrete stairs. He'd been briefed about the situation on the ground—though the briefing had been complete bullshit.

You didn't clear civilians from the streets with miniguns in any biological warfare scenario he'd war-gamed in his career, or any scenario for that matter. This was something different, and he didn't want to get caught up in it. He'd been told to shoot first, then shoot again—and that was exactly what he intended to do.

Ecker descended the stairs, reaching another locked door. Shit. They'd made enough noise already. He signaled for D-Bird. It didn't really matter. In and out of here in sixty seconds. That was the plan. The shotgun blast left his ears slightly ringing, the concrete stairwell intensifying the already harsh sound waves. D-Bird sheathed the shotgun and produced a compact crowbar, hitting the doorknob sharply with the curved chisel end and punching through the door. He pulled sharply on the tool, swinging the door inward.

The four operators slipped into the third-floor hallway, Ecker immediately identifying their target location by the door, which had been blasted open, and the dozen or more bullet holes in the wall around it. He lowered his helmet visor for a quick skim of his heads-up display, finding no change to the missing team leader's status. MIA/HIGHPROB-MISSIONINTERCEPT. Missing in action with a high probability of a mission intercept. By who? Nobody seemed to have that answer, so he wasn't taking any chances.

A series of hand signals set his team in motion. Weatherman and Horton, his primary shooters, stacked up on the door, ready to enter the room. After each of them nodded, D-Bird pulled the pin on a flash-bang grenade and released the safety lever, waiting far too long for Ecker's comfort to toss it inside. The two shooters poured into the room a fraction of a second after the detonation, clearing their sectors. Ecker and D-Bird followed, and they all pushed farther inside the hazy, bullet-shredded room.

"I have two KIA," said Weatherman, crouching near the couch. "Living area and kitchen clear."

"Concur. Visible areas clear," said Horton.

"Secure the rest of the apartment," said Ecker.

When the team vanished into the bedroom hallway, he took a close look at the grisly scene, not sure what to make of it. He immediately recognized the dead men as Paul Ochoa and Dan Ripley. Both of the men had been shot multiple times, in various locations, but Ochoa had a bullet hole right in the center of the forehead—surrounded by the blackened powder tattooing associated with near-contact gunshot wounds. This guy had been executed, possibly while seated in the dining room chair that had been moved behind the couch. None of it made sense, and it didn't matter. He was here to confirm the missing team leader's status and look for signs of that team's VIP.

"The rest of the apartment is clear," said Weatherman. "Nothing unusual. No signs of struggle or recent occupancy."

"Copy that," said Ecker. "Let's get out of here."

He picked up the CTAB lying next to the murdered team leader and stuffed it inside a secure pouch attached to his vest. A final look around the room led to a discovery he'd surprisingly missed until now. One of their rifles was missing. A suppressed, longer-barreled HK416 lay on the couch, like it had been discarded. Another piece of a puzzle he had no interest in solving. He transmitted over the net, "Ajax, this is Valkyrie. Ochoa and Ripley KIA in apartment. CTAB recovered. No sign of VIP. Moving to primary extract point."

He slapped Horton on the back and the team slid out of the apartment, the piercing buzz of the helicopters' miniguns leaving him with an uneasy feeling. Who the hell was still pushing their luck against guns that fire a hundred rounds per second? Something had gone really fucking wrong in this city, and he couldn't wait to get as far away from it as possible.

Chapter Twenty-Eight

Karyn Archer, call sign Ajax, kept a stone face as she listened to Ecker's report, even though she wanted to scream and throw someone out the open helicopter door. How the hell could Chang have vanished? Ochoa had reported everything under control, with the scientist in custody—less than fifteen fucking minutes ago! Nobody was going anywhere until they had some answers.

"This is Ajax. What is your immediate assessment of what happened in that apartment?"

"Something doesn't add up. The apartment door was breached with compact charges from the hallway, but the apartment is riddled with bullets that came through the balcony sliders. Ochoa and Ripley both had several gunshot wounds. Whoever fired into the apartment couldn't have been worried about the VIP."

"Or they didn't care," said Archer.

"Someone cared enough to shoot Ochoa in the forehead at extremely close range. Powder burn pattern suggests an execution. It'll take an FBI forensics team to make sense of the rest of this mess."

"No sign of the VIP?"

"Nothing," said Ecker. "I'd be surprised if he was ever here."

She thought about the situation for a few moments. Ecker was right. Little to none of what she'd just heard

165

made sense. Ochoa had been sitting on Chang's apartment for several hours, with no sign of the scientist, then suddenly reports Chang in custody—only to be found executed less than fifteen minutes later. This whole thing was a massive cluster fuck. None of the teams had located Chang prior to Ochoa's report.

Actually, nothing she'd heard all night made sense. Larsen's team had suddenly gone offline shortly after landing at Chang's residence northwest of the city. She had sent Ragan's nearby team to investigate Larsen's silence, only to divert her to the city when Archer received a bizarre tip regarding Chang's whereabouts.

A 10th Mountain Division emergency broadcast bulletin had been flagged by the CHASE system, detailing a gun battle at a regional airport northwest of Indianapolis. A small group of civilians had somehow managed to blow up a forward refueling point to cover their escape—in an aircraft registered to Dr. Eugene Chang.

The aircraft had been forced south, mysteriously vanishing somewhere near the downtown area. The coincidence couldn't be ignored. Chang had piloted the aircraft and was now in the city. She figured he'd take refuge in a familiar location, either his apartment or his research space. Now she had no idea. They'd head over to NevoTech next and take a quick look around from the air. The team originally situated in the Secure Research Facility hadn't reported in several minutes.

"Ajax, this is Valkyrie. Did you copy my last?"

"Affirmative. Head across the street to Chang's apartment and conduct a search of the premises," said Archer. "We're missing something."

"Copy. On my way. Keep the streets clear for us."

Archer glanced at the intersection next to Chang's building as one of the miniguns fired a long burst into a mob of infected that had just appeared. The stream of tightly spaced bullets cut a bright red swath through the crowd, dropping most of them in a snarled tangle of punctured bodies and twisted limbs. She wished the idiots behind this mess could be here to see what they'd created. There was no way they could have envisioned things getting this bad when they set it all in motion. She simply couldn't believe it. A second, shorter burst knocked the remaining survivors on the street under a red mist.

"The streets are clear."

Chapter Twenty-Nine

David stared at the massive screen, nervously rubbing his unshaven face. The helicopters slowly rose above the buildings and turned toward NevoTech.

"Did Roscoe shoot at the team along the fence?" he said.

Hoenig shook his head. "No. Not with a rifle. He fired one of the pyrotechnic grenades at the gate while they were setting an explosive charge—to get them away from the gate."

"So it could easily be interpreted as a nonlethal response to a clearly unauthorized and potentially dangerous breach of the campus security fence," said David.

"Well, I'm not sure I'd call it nonlethal under the circumstances—" started Hoenig.

"I'm just hoping that the team reported themselves locked out, with the NevoTech security taking steps to keep them from getting back in. That's very different than taking them under direct fire with rifles."

"I guess we'll find out if it's different enough," said Hoenig.

"I think we'll be fine," said David. "They barely stayed on Virginia Avenue for three minutes, and they don't have enough people on those helicopters to effectively search this facility."

"They might go for the SRF," said Hoenig.

"Let them," said David. "They won't find what they're looking for over there."

"Yeah. That's kind of what I'm worried about."

"They'll be in and out if they stop," said David.

"And if they stick around for more than a quick look?" said Hoenig.

"Then we have the tactical advantage. You have a heavily armed security team that knows the campus inside and out. Plus you can see every nook and cranny of the campus—both inside and outside. That puts us at a significant advantage."

Hoenig just stared at him for a few seconds, his face giving no indication that he was buying into David's optimistic musings.

"Let's just hope they move along," said David.

"If you're any indication of the quality of operators on those helicopters, then hoping they move along is a much better strategy."

"Joshua, can you keep a close eye on the southern and eastern arrays while we focus on this?" said Hoenig.

"Sure," said Joshua.

His son slid into his previous seat behind a trio of oversized monitors and started shifting through camera feeds.

"I have a job for him when this is over. Part time of course," said Hoenig.

"I'm not entirely convinced this will ever be over in the traditional sense of the word," said David. "But I'm sure he'll take you up on the offer if it does."

The two unmarked Black Hawks arrived over the parking lot, immediately drawing several crazies out of the trees and brush surrounding the field of pavement.

Small-arms fire from the helicopters' open doors stopped them in their tracks.

"They must be running low on minigun ammo," said David.

"Or that wasn't a big enough crowd to warrant their use," said Hoenig. "Who knows what they were dealing with over on Virginia Avenue."

"Good point," said David.

One of the helicopters drifted toward the fence, descending as it edged sideways. A few feet above the ground, two heavily armed, body-armor-clad figures jumped to the pavement and sprinted toward the fence where the ill-fated CHASE team had made its last stand just minutes ago.

"I don't like this," said Hoenig.

"Neither do I."

The two operators dug through the pile of bodies pushed up against the fence, separating the CHASE team from the infected.

"This is not good," said Hoenig. "Crazies approaching from the east, along the fence line. They just crossed East Street."

The screen split, one side focused on the helicopters hovering over the parking lot, and the other side tracking a fast-moving mob passing in front of the gate that still held Howard's body. The two CHASE operators continued searching through the bodies.

"What the hell are you doing?" said David, yelling at the screen like it was a Colts game. "Get the hell out of there!"

The front of the horde made it halfway down the fence line before one of the miniguns fired, cutting down half of the group at once. A long pause ensued as the higher of the two helicopters spun in place to unmask its remaining loaded gun. The second burst of concentrated gunfire raked the other half of the approaching mob, knocking them against the swaying fence.

"Did you see that?" said David.

"I did," said Hoenig. "One more—"

Before he could finish, another burst of automatic gunfire tore into the few crazies still running toward the exposed CHASE operators, most of the bullets striking the already weakened fence. A section of the wrought-iron barrier separated from its supporting post, warping inward under the near simultaneous impact of a few hundred bullets travelling at least twice the speed of sound. The section stayed upright, but an easily passable gap in the perimeter of the fence opened.

"They'll be all over that," said David.

"Not right away," said Hoenig. "But we'll need to plug that hole. There's no way we can retrieve Dan without drawing them inside the perimeter."

"We can't bend that steel back in place," said David.

"No. But we can push the armored SUV against the gap," said Hoenig.

"They can still squirm under the vehicle," said David. "Or climb over the top."

"We'll have to post a team out there with suppressed weapons to keep any of the more curious types from slipping through," said Hoenig. "After we get Dan."

"After we get Dan," repeated David.

The two-man team finished digging through the pile of bodies a few seconds later, one of them pocketing something before they sprinted toward the nearest helicopter. They hopped onboard with little time to spare, the helicopter quickly rising above a sizable group of crazies that had converged from every direction. With the miniguns out of ammunition, the operators packed inside each helicopter's cargo compartment fired their rifles and light machine guns at the expanding mob. Before the shooters could make a dent in the swarm, the helicopters tilted east and picked up speed. Hoenig tracked the helicopters with the cameras until they disappeared beyond the low-rise buildings near Chang's apartment.

"How long until the SUV is ready to roll?" said David.

"If it's not going back out in the parking lot, it's ready now," said Hoenig. "No sense in putting a new tire on a doorstop."

"The sooner we get that gap filled, the better," said David, nodding at the screen.

The crowd of infected in the parking lot had started to disperse, some of them headed in the general direction of the gap.

"The miniguns didn't finish everyone off," said David. "The wounded will draw some of them close to the hole. I'll head up to the roof and keep them out."

"I'll send Roscoe with you."

"Dad, I can help," said Joshua, standing up.

"Josh, do me a huge favor and help Mr. Hoenig here," said David.

"That's not fair, Dad. You know I can handle myself. I helped get us here from the plane."

"I know you're not going to believe me when I say this, but I'm not asking you to stay behind because I don't think you're capable," said David.

"Then what—"

"Let me finish," said David.

"Sounded like you were done."

"Are you done?"

Joshua shrugged his shoulders.

"I want to protect you—"

"That's the same thing!" said his son.

"Are you going to let me finish or what?" yelled David.

His son shook his head and sighed.

"I'm trying to protect what's in here," said David, poking his own head. "We're shooting people out there. It may not feel like it when you're running for your life, but up on the roof, shooting people over and over again? That'll stick around and fuck with your head. Trust me. That's why I don't want you up there. It's a bad deal for anyone unlucky enough to be doing it."

"I think I'd be fine," said Joshua, the confidence drained from his voice.

"Nobody is ever fine with it. No matter what they say," said David.

"I just want to help."

"You are helping," said Hoenig. "More than you realize."

"And if they break through in numbers that can't be handled from the rooftop, Mr. Hoenig will send you with the first team that responds," said David.

"Really?" said Hoenig.

"Why not? He can handle himself," said David, eliciting a partial smile from Joshua.

"Shit," said Hoenig, grimacing at the screen.

David shifted his attention to the live feed on the wall, immediately seeing the problem. Several infected seemed headed for the gap in the fence.

"This is going to be a long day, isn't it?"

"And every day after that," said Hoenig.

He absorbed the heaviness of Gary's statement, feeling

guilty that he had a way out of this. Then again, David's "way out" could just as easily break apart in midair, scattering his son and him across one of the endless cornfields surrounding Indianapolis. He hadn't forgotten Chang's concern about one of the wings. Or they could be blown right out of the sky by a patrolling Apache helicopter—resulting in the same, cheery cornfield ending. Anything was possible once that plane lifted off the highway.

Despite these possible outcomes, he was willing to take the risk to get his son out of here. The situation inside the city would worsen, inevitably spilling over into NevoTech. He could see that. Anybody could see that. The feds had zero capacity to adequately and humanely respond to a crisis of this magnitude—in dozens of cities across the country. A single hurricane was enough to tip FEMA over. And then there was Chang's theory about the government somehow being behind this. He really didn't want to think about that, and it didn't matter. Either way, the city of Indianapolis, and everyone that remained inside the quarantine boundary, was doomed. Everything they did now to keep this place safe was a temporary solution.

"We'll have to skip the rooftop for now. Send Roscoe to the same door we used before. I'm pretty sure I know how to get back to it," said David before nodding at Joshua. "Ready?"

"For what?"

"To hold the line until they can get the SUV in place."

"Grab my kit," said Hoenig. "It's hanging on the wall behind you."

"This is for real?" said Joshua.

"It's what you wanted, right?" said David, moving

toward the body armor and rifle hanging from coat hooks next to the door.

When his son didn't respond immediately, David grinned.

"Careful what you ask for."

Chapter Thirty

Joshua ran with his dad down a long, wide hallway, loaded down with a loose, ill-fitted tactical vest and oversized ballistic helmet. Mr. Hoenig was a big guy, and not in the overweight sense of the word. He was tall and stocky, the exact opposite of Joshua. His dad hesitated at one of the four-way junctures before continuing forward.

"Are you sure this is the right way?" he said.

"It's the right way," said Hoenig in his earpiece.

"Thanks, Gary," said David. "The old man still has a few marbles left."

"I wasn't saying that," said Joshua. "How did he hear me?"

"I'm just messing with you," said David. "I set my radio to voice activate, since we're only on one net right now."

"Should I be on that?"

"No. You talk too much," said David.

"He's messing with you again," said Hoenig.

"Want to head back yet?" said David.

"Nice try," said Joshua.

"How far away is Roscoe?" said David.

"Thirty seconds behind you."

"How many are through the fence?"

"Three. And they're pretty scattered. You'll have to go hunting for one of them," said Hoenig. "The other two are in sight of the door, but not an immediate threat."

"What's the situation outside the fence?"

"Not bad. A few looky-loos but no large groups," said Hoenig.

"Let me know if anything develops," said David.

"Will do. You're coming up on the door. Be careful."

They slowed a little, a green exit sign sticking out of the wall indicating their destination. His dad stopped several feet in front of the sign, crouching next to a window. Joshua mimicked his stance, edging close enough to his father to see outside the building.

"We have one dead ahead of us. Halfway between here and the fence," said David, making more room by the window. "Where's the other one?"

"To your two o'clock when you open the door," said Hoenig. "Maybe a hundred feet out."

Seemed straightforward enough.

"So we take them down at the same time?" said Joshua, tightening his grip on the M4.

"Not with that thing," said David, looking at Joshua's rifle. "Suppressed shots only. We're waiting for Roscoe."

"What?" said Joshua. "Then what am I here for?"

"You're *here* in case something goes really wrong out *there*."

"Can you switch out of voice-activation mode?" said Hoenig. "I feel like I'm seated between a bickering couple."

"Funny," said David, flipping a switch on the radio velcroed to his vest.

Joshua didn't think it was funny at all. His dad seemed to be mocking him.

"Why did you bring me along if I can't shoot?" said Joshua.

"I didn't say you can't shoot. I said we need to do this as quietly as possible, or we'll drag the entire neighborhood into the campus," said David.

"You didn't say that."

"Did I have to?" said David.

He shrugged his shoulders and frowned.

"Don't be so eager to shoot people," said David.

"I'm not eager to shoot people," he grumbled. "I just don't like to be coddled."

"Nobody is coddling you," said David, his face softening. "There's just a limited supply of suppressed weapons, some of which we've redistributed to the tactical security team. Unless there's a good reason, all shots fired outside the building need to be suppressed. Even from the rooftop."

"What if I swap rifles with Roscoe?"

His dad raised a skeptical eyebrow.

"All right," said Joshua. "So what exactly is my job out there?"

"Situational awareness," said David. "When we have to range away from the door to find the third wanderer, you'll watch our back."

"Mr. Hoenig can do that from the security hub."

"Good point," blurted David before shaking his head. "Sorry. A video screen is not the same as being there. You can read the subtle signs Hoenig can't, and better coordinate our attention."

Joshua still wasn't altogether buying the importance of his role, but he decided to keep his mouth shut about it. His dad must have read his face.

"Hey, we've all been tail-end Charlie before. It feels

really unimportant, until everything changes—and it becomes the most important position on the team," said David, taking a moment to read his face. "Still not buying it?"

"A little more than before," said Joshua.

The sound of thumping boots echoed through the hallway, drawing closer until Roscoe burst into the open. The stout security guard stopped next to them, putting his hands on his knees to catch his breath.

"I really need to shift some of my gym time from weights to cardio," he said, huffing for a few seconds. "Damn! Okay. I'm ready."

"Are you sure?" said David.

"One hundred percent," said Roscoe. "As long as we aren't running."

"I wasn't planning on it," said David. "But you know how things can go out there."

"Yeah. Sideways. Real quick."

"I think you've met my son, Joshua?"

"Briefly. When you guys arrived," he said, extending a hand. "You ready to go out there?"

Joshua accepted Roscoe's firm grip and shook hands. His arm felt like a twig that might snap. The guy must spend all of his time in the weight room. Before he could answer Roscoe's question, his dad cut in.

"He thinks he's the third wheel," said David.

"Because his rifle isn't suppressed?"

"Was everyone listening to the conversation?" said Joshua.

"Shit. Ain't no third wheels around here," said Roscoe, peeking through the window. "How do you want to do this?"

"We ease out the door and stay low. Use the shrubs

framing the walkway for concealment, then take simultaneous shots," said David. "We'll have to hunt for the third."

"I'm sure Gary will lead us right to him," said Roscoe.

"I will," replied Hoenig. "You guys going to talk about this all day or actually take care of business?"

"That's my Gary," said Roscoe. "Ready when you're ready."

"Let's get this over with."

His dad crept up to the door and carefully pushed the crash bar with the top of his left shoulder until it was fully depressed. With the locking mechanism disabled, he slowly leaned into the door, opening it far enough to fit through. Roscoe followed, quietly dropping himself to his hands and knees on the brick walkway outside the building and disappearing to the left.

Joshua held the door open with one hand and lowered himself to the tile floor with the other, clanging one of his rifle magazines against the metal door as he squeezed through. Great. He'd be grounded to the security hub for sure after this. When he finished squirming through, he held the door with one of his feet, easing it shut before crawling next to his dad.

"Sorry about that," he whispered.

"About what?" said David.

"Making noise."

"I didn't hear anything," said David. "Nice job closing the door with your foot."

"You saw that?"

"I saw you fighting to get that vest through the door, too," said David, winking. "Roscoe, status?"

"Tracking my target," said Roscoe.

The security guard lay several feet to their left, aiming

his rifle through a break in the thick green shrubs lining the other side of the brick walkway. His father lay against the right side, his rifle in a similar position.

"Joshua, count us down from three. Slowly but evenly," said David.

"Me?"

"I can have Gary do it," said David.

"No. I'm good," said Joshua. "Ready?"

"Do it," said Roscoe.

"Three. Two. One," he said, almost pausing. "Fire."

Despite knowing exactly when to expect the suppressed gunshots—they startled him.

"Targets down," said Hoenig. "I see a few turned heads outside the fence, but that's about it. Stay put for a minute. I'll let you know when it's safe to move."

"Staying put," said David.

Roscoe turned his head to them. "I'm not gonna lie. I hate being out here. I saw what they did to the team from the SRF."

"We'll be fine," said David.

"You're starting to sound like Larsen," said Joshua.

"That's when you know things are really bad," said David, and they both laughed quietly.

"Who's Larsen? That other dude?" said Roscoe.

"Yeah. He says that every time we're about to do something really jacked up," said David. "Kind of a running joke that's not really funny."

The distant sound of a vehicle engine caused them all to turn their heads back toward the building.

"Gary, tell me that's the SUV."

"It's on the way," said Hoenig. "Bad news is we have to drive it around the front of the campus. We can't squeeze it through anywhere else unless we take it into the parking lot and jam it against the fence from the outside."

"That's too risky for the guys driving," said David. "We're fine with a little extra attention here."

"Speak for yourself," said Roscoe, laughing.

The engine noise grew louder.

"They're driving across the lawn in front right now," said Hoenig.

"We can hear them," said David.

Joshua lifted his head, catching movement to their right. The third crazy must have heard the gunshots or engine noise—and backtracked.

"Contact. Right," he said, without thinking.

His dad rose to a kneeling position and fired a single shot that spun the cleanly dressed woman to the left. A second shot knocked her to the grass. She lay motionless over her crumpled legs for a few moments, until one of her arms started to drift slowly to her blood-splattered chest. Joshua stared at the dying woman, confused by his reaction. He didn't want her to die. She looked too normal to die. Too much like his mother.

He heard someone call his name, but his gaze was fixed on the woman's fading movements.

"Joshua," said his father, squeezing his shoulder.

"What?" he said, hesitating to take his eyes off the woman.

"I need you at the door, watching our eastern flank," said David. "This could blow up in our faces if they attract a large enough swarm. If that happens, we can't waste time swiping cards."

Joshua nodded, still confused by his emotions. "Are you sure you don't need me on the fence?"

"It's up to you," said David. "This is going to make a

lot of noise either way."

Joshua looked at the fence and the crazies beyond, feeling no pull in that direction.

"I got the door."

His father patted his shoulder. "We're gonna be fine."

Joshua cracked a grin. "Are you sure that's not just your inner Larsen shining through?"

"I sure as hell hope not," said David.

While his dad and the others defended the breach in the fence, cutting down any of the infected trying to squeeze past the oversized vehicle, Joshua crouched in the open doorway—watching their backs. His eyes kept darting to the right, to the woman lying in a heap near the corner of the building. She'd stopped moving. He backed up a few inches, the door frame blocking his view of her bloodied corpse. He'd seen enough for a lifetime. Unfortunately, this was very likely just the beginning.

Chapter Thirty-One

Larsen gritted his teeth as Dr. Hale pulled the stitches in his thigh tight and tied a knot, her fingers pressed against the wound. She'd applied the last of the topical anesthetic from the infirmary, which did nothing to dull the deeper pain. The limited medical supplies in NevoTech's small infirmary must have been gutted by the initial rush of injured employees. Not that any of it could have made much of a difference. The labels on the mostly empty shelves implied that the infirmary focused on treating minor injuries and routine illnesses. Small cuts, scrapes, fever and diarrhea—the kind of things that might distract an employee from work.

On top of that, the employees that had sought shelter on campus had stretched the infirmary's already limited supplies very thin. Hale had used the rudimentary stitch kit from his IFAK (individual first aid kit) to sew the wound shut, along with the rest of his antibiotic ointment. In hindsight, he should have grabbed Ochoa's and Ripley's IFAKs. The kits were basic, but they would give Hale the ability to stabilize and treat some of the more serious wounds that might arise.

"Sorry about that," said Hale, looking around. "Do you have anything in your kit to wrap this properly? I don't see any larger bandages. No butterflies either."

"We can reuse the Israeli," said Larsen, grabbing the

blood-soaked compression bandage.

"I really hate to do that," she said.

"You can wrap a layer of sterile gauze under it if that makes you feel better," he said.

"It does," said Hale. "Sort of."

Chang stepped into the room with a packed tray of food, closing the door behind him. The smell of French fries hit Larsen first, followed by overcooked hamburger.

"Breakfast of champions," said Larsen.

"Apparently, they have no shortage of fast-food items in the freezer," said Chang.

"That smells so good," said Hale.

"I can finish this on my own," said Larsen.

Hale didn't need additional convincing. She scrubbed her hands and joined Chang at the nurse's desk, barely pausing long enough to swallow between bites. By the time Larsen had reaffixed the blood-soaked Israeli bandage and washed his hands, Chang and Hale were hovering over his food like vultures. He approached them, shaking his head.

"If I didn't know any better, I'd say 'welcome to the 77th annual Hunger Games,'" said Larsen.

Chang and Hale laughed, easing into their seats.

"Literally," said Chang. "I didn't realize how hungry I was. I haven't had much of an appetite over the past twenty-four hours. Kind of hit me all at once."

"The two of you can split mine," said Larsen. "I'll hit up one of the vending machines."

"I think most of those are empty," said Chang.

"You need to eat," said Hale. "You lost too much blood."

"I feel fine."

"The adrenaline hasn't worn off yet," said Hale. "Trust

me. You're about to crash hard. Eat up."

Larsen didn't argue, wolfing down the greasy burger and overcooked fries before either of them changed their minds. He was accustomed to going for long periods of time without eating more than a protein bar or drinking the water he carried on his back—even under the harshest physical conditions. It was all part of the rigorous training that had defined his professional career as a SEAL. He knew his limits, having repeatedly pushed himself physically and mentally to the very brink of falling apart. But he also knew it was easy to miscalculate, which he had nearly done a few moments ago. He'd lost enough blood to throw everything out of whack. Hale was right. It would have caught up with him, probably at the worst possible moment.

He leaned against the wall next to the desk, letting the food somewhat settle into a nervous stomach.

"Is everything under control out there?" said Chang. "They started to evacuate everyone, then stopped. That's how I managed to sneak a few burgers away."

"The helicopters are gone for now," said Larsen. "But they unintentionally blasted a section of the perimeter fencing out of place. Security managed to block the gap with their SUV, but it's not an airtight fix. They'll need to keep at least one person at the nearest door. Hoenig can keep an eye on the gap from the security hub and let them know if they need to go outside to stop any intruders from getting past the SUV. They really should post two armed guards to be one hundred percent safe."

"Doesn't sound too bad," said Hale.

"It's not, but it adds another layer of difficulty to an already tenuous situation," said Larsen. "Even one crazy poking around can set off a chain reaction. Guard fires one or two shots, which attracts more attention, requiring more shots. If the shots are fired with a roving mob nearby, things could go from bad to worse faster than the security team can react. Someone can crawl under or climb over the SUV in a matter of seconds."

"The building's exterior doors would still be locked tight," said Chang. "And security can compartmentalize any of the building areas that are breached."

"True. But what happens when the power is cut to the city," said Larsen. "They probably have some sort of backup generator system to run the security features, but I can't imagine they have more than a three- or four-day supply of fuel for the generators. This NevoTech haven is a very temporary solution to a long-term problem. There's only so much food here. Medical supplies are nearly nonexistent. The disaster outside these gates isn't going away any time soon. Staying here is a guaranteed death sentence."

"What can we do about it?" said Hale.

"Nothing from here," said Larsen. "Tonight, when we fly clear of this mess, I'll do what I can to notify the right people about the situation here. Maybe the National Guard can mount a rescue operation."

"And take everyone to one of the quarantine camps?" she said. "Or wherever they're taking people."

"It has to be better than staying here," said Larsen. "Chang, you said it earlier. What we're seeing outside right now is just the tip of the iceberg."

"Statistically. Yes. Dr. Hale, when did you first start seeing violent patients?" said Chang.

"It was around ten or eleven p.m. on Thursday night. One of the patients waiting in the ER went haywire. Nearly killed me. He put another patient in a coma. We hadn't seen anything like it prior to then. The police removed several patients earlier in the day for excessive verbal abuse or outbreaks, but we just assumed that was due to frustration. People were waiting hours to get into the ER, and it was hot outside. I didn't like it, but I couldn't really blame them. I had no idea it was related to the virus. None of us did. We had a few more violent outbursts that night, all preceded by verbal abuse—then we started to see it in the patients already admitted to the ER. We had to start handcuffing people to their beds."

Hale zoned out for a few moments, staring at the wall while she whispered, "I can still see that guy. Must have been two hundred and fifty pounds of pure muscle and rage. He was so angry. Just furious."

"He hit you?" said Larsen.

"A few times," she said, lifting her T-shirt to expose a fist-sized black and blue mark.

"Jesus. I assume you had that checked out?" said Larsen.

She nodded. "Bruised rib. Still hurts like hell when I think about it."

"I bet," said Larsen, turning to Chang, who squinted his eyes like he was running numbers in his head. "So. What does it mean?"

"Sounds like you saw an early outlier. Possibly someone already prone to violent behavior," said Chang, shaking his head and sighing. "And that was thirty-six hours ago."

"A lot has changed in thirty-six hours," said Larsen. "It's like *The Walking Dead* out there, except they're not walking. They're running and shooting guns."

"This is bad. Based on my research and some very trusted secondhand information, we're looking at a ninety-five percent neurological impairment rate."

"All of them will get like this?" said Hale.

Larsen had heard this prediction already.

"We don't know the exact rates. If this were a normal strain of herpes simplex encephalitis, I'd say less than five percent of the cases. In a population just under a million, maybe fifty thousand spread across the entire city?"

"That's a lot of people," said Hale. "But this isn't a normal strain, is it?"

"No. From what I could tell from the sample you delivered, this is an intentionally modified strain. Weaponized. There's no doubt about that," said Chang. "I just can't determine the impact of those modifications on the virus behavior using the equipment here at NevoTech. My guess is that the designers of this virus have increased its affinity for the temporal lobes and its specificity for attacking the areas that govern behavior. The anecdotal evidence I mentioned suggested something in the fifty to seventy percent range for severe, violent symptom presentation."

"That's fucking insane," said Hale. "You're saying that half of the city could go homicidal?"

"Not actively and aggressively homicidal, but easily pushed to that point," said Chang.

"Same thing," said Larsen.

"And the rest of the population?" said Hale.

"Varying degrees of brain damage."

"My god. Who the hell would release something like this?" said Hale. "How could our government let something like this happen? How could this slip under the radar?"

Larsen glanced at Chang, who took a deep breath, his face betraying the theory in play.

Before he could begin, Hale shook her head. "Bullshit. This administration has some serious problems, but releasing a biological weapon against your own population is something entirely different. I'm not buying it."

"I'm not here to sell you on any theories," said Chang. "But my colleagues outside of NevoTech—scientists who have dedicated their lives to preventing this kind of attack—agree that the complexity of a simultaneous attack on dozens of cities suggests a state-sponsored effort."

"Or a well-organized terrorist organization," insisted Hale. "It wouldn't be the first time."

"I was ordered to capture or kill Dr. Chang," said Larsen. "Don't forget that. Someone in our government wanted him dead or in custody."

"I haven't," said Hale. "Trust me. I just don't know where to go with that right now. Not sure if I need to go anywhere with it, since you're both leaving tonight."

"We'd take you if we had room," said Larsen. "But we're already well over the weight limit for the airplane."

"My place is here for now," said Hale. "I'm good with that. Seriously. Whatever is going on out there, I'm way better off here. Thank you for getting me here. I just wish I had some real medical supplies. I'm not sure what I can do for the people trapped here."

"You'll figure out something," said Larsen. "And we'll do everything in our power to get you some help."

"Something tells me the two of you might not be in the position to ask for help once you get out of here."

Chang laughed. "She has a good point. I hadn't thought about that."

"I haven't had the time to think about it," said Larsen.

190

"I don't think I've stopped moving since I landed at your house."

Hale checked her watch. "Well, unless the helicopters come back, you've got about twelve hours to put some thought into it."

"I'm planning on sleeping for half of that," said Larsen. "All of it, if I could."

Chang's satellite phone chimed, the scientist fumbling to retrieve it from one of his cargo pockets. He glanced at the caller ID.

"It's the friend I told you about."

"Something tells me I may not be getting that nap," said Larsen.

Chapter Thirty-Two

Chang pressed the green button and placed the Iridium satellite phone against his ear.

"This is Chang."

"Gene, it's good to hear your voice," said Stan Greenberg. "You had me worried. I tried to call earlier."

"I've been a little busy," said Chang.

"That's what I figured—hoped, actually," he said. "The farther away the better. Preferably Canada. Where did you end up?"

"Indianapolis," said Chang.

"Gene, that's really not funny. Seriously," said Greenberg. "Did you manage to get out in the plane?"

"I'm not kidding, Stan. I tried to drive to the airport, but the 10th Mountain Division had already set up a quarantine block just a few miles north of my house," said Chang.

"So you drove into the city?"

"I flew into the city."

"What?" said Greenberg, sounding exasperated.

"It's a long story," said Chang. "The bottom line is that I'm safe for now."

"Where are you?"

"Is this connection secure?" said Chang. "You didn't seem so sure about that last night."

"I've been assured that my end is secure," said

Greenberg before mumbling something outside of the receiver that Chang couldn't understand.

"I've just been told we should be fine right now," said Greenberg. "But they don't want you using the phone again from the same location."

"How far away do I have to move to use it safely?" said Chang.

"Hold on," said Greenberg, followed by a long pause. "At least a mile. Preferably another state. That's what they told me. And you should remove the battery when we're done with this call. They suggest you reinsert the battery at four o'clock p.m. to check for messages. Unless you think you'll be far enough away to make a call."

"I'm not going anywhere. The streets are too dangerous," said Chang.

"Please tell me you're not at your apartment," said Greenberg. "That's the first place they'll look for you."

"It turns out there's no first, second or third place they'll look for me," said Chang. "They'll look for me everywhere. A team was sent to my house, my apartment and NevoTech labs. I'm standing next to the only surviving member of all three of those teams."

"Gene," said Greenberg, "what are you saying?"

"I'm saying that I've had a long night, Stan. These teams were initially deployed to keep me safe. Part of some Department of Homeland Security-sponsored critical human asset protection unit. At least that's what they thought they were. Their orders changed to 'capture or kill' as soon as they hit the ground. The guy with me now refused to follow his orders. He's the only reason I've survived this long."

"What happened to the other teams?" said a deep voice in the background of the call.

"Who is this?" said Chang.

"Mr. Greenberg's new friends. Your new friends," said the voice.

"I fully trust them," said Greenberg. "They've been trying to prevent an attack like this for years. They're the source of all firsthand information from Monchegorsk."

"Jesus," said Chang, shocked by Greenberg's implication.

"Not exactly. But it has a nice ring," said the voice. "Do you mind if we put this on speaker? I think it will facilitate a more effective conversation."

"That's fine. I'll do the same on my end. I'm with some people you may want to speak with," said Chang, pressing a button on the phone before placing it on the desk. "You're now on the line with the DHS agent I mentioned and a local emergency room physician."

"Perfect," said the man. "You can call me Terrence. What is your current location?"

"We're at the main NevoTech campus," said Chang.

"I was really hoping you wouldn't say that," said Greenberg.

"Trust me. It wasn't my first choice either," said Larsen. "I'm the DHS guy, by the way."

"Welcome to the big top," said Terrence. "What happened to the other team sent to NevoTech?"

"Only one team was sent here. They got themselves killed trying to move from here to Chang's apartment about thirty minutes ago," said Larsen. "My team was sent to Chang's house north of the city, but we had an internal issue that left the other three dead. One of the agents under my command discovered the change to our orders and turned on the rest of us," said Larsen.

Hale shifted away from Larsen, casting him a confused

and distrustful look.

"I can attest to this," said Chang. "Unfortunately, I heard and watched it play out live on the security feed. He did everything he could to defuse the situation."

"Did you see these orders?" said Terrence.

"Yes. Larsen, I mean Eric—shit," said Chang. "Sorry."

"Eric Larsen in case you missed it," said Larsen, shaking his head.

"Larsen showed me his command tablet and all of the information it contained—including all of his orders. Initially, they were supposed to protect and escort me to safety. That turned to a capture-kill mission within the span of fifteen minutes," said Chang.

"Sadly, this is all starting to make sense," said Terrence. "You mentioned a third team? At your apartment."

"We neutralized that team in place," said Larsen.

"Who did?"

"I did. With some help," said Larsen.

"Gene, why did you risk going to your apartment?" said Greenberg.

"Critical personnel recovery," said Larsen, hoping to streamline the conversation.

"Understood," said Terrence. "Girlfriend? Boyfriend?"

"No!" said Hale. "I'm a local ER doctor. It's complicated, but not that kind of complicated."

"Good enough for me," said Terrence. "Larsen, what's your background?"

"Naval Special Warfare. Ten years."

"Are all of these teams similarly talented?"

"No. It's a mixed bag. Mostly regular military and police. Some Special Forces. Some SWAT," said Larsen.

"Dr. Chang, can we go back to something you said

earlier? Regarding the roadblock," said Terrence.

"Sure. They stopped me a few miles north of my house," said Chang.

Larsen wasn't sure how he felt about the trajectory of their conversation. This Terrence guy had rather quickly and effortlessly taken complete control, turning it into a one-sided intelligence-gathering session.

"Are you sure they weren't National Guard?" said Greenberg.

"The staff sergeant at the roadblock identified himself as 10th Mountain Division. From what I now understand, there are two quarantine boundary lines around Indianapolis. The inner boundary is under National Guard control. The outer zone is controlled by regular military units. 10th Mountain Division in this case."

"It makes sense," said Greenberg. "They can establish the initial quarantine zones faster using locally mobilized units. Then transport regular ground units from major bases around the country to start a secondary line. Probably use those to reinforce the National Guard where necessary."

"Right," said Terrence. "But the 10th Mountain Division got there pretty damn fast. Too fast."

"I agree," said Greenberg. "And I'm not aware of any rapid response military protocols designed to move U.S. troops to domestic hot zones that rapidly. We usually have a hand in those."

"The soldiers were not equipped with biohazard suits," said Chang. "I found that a bit odd."

"Neither were the National Guard soldiers that arrived at the hospital," said Hale.

"That's because this virus isn't contagious in the traditional sense," said Greenberg.

"And they knew exactly what they were dealing with," said Terrence.

"Gentlemen, sorry to rush this conversation, but here's the bottom line. The city of Indianapolis is like a scene out of a horror movie, with mobs of crazy people attacking anything that moves on the streets. I'm guessing you knew that already, and you have a good idea of what happened."

"Essentially," said Terrence.

"Then what can you tell us that we don't already know or haven't seen firsthand?"

"It'll get worse. At some point the government will run out of options. They'll either completely cordon off the city and let it die out on its own, or they'll expedite the process."

"We already guessed that much," said Larsen. "What else?"

"Don't trust the government?"

"Funny," said Larsen.

"I wish I had more for you, Mr. Larsen, but I don't," said Terrence. "We're still reacting to the crisis. Investigating. Frankly, it took us by complete surprise. I thought we had completely eliminated this threat. Obviously, I was wrong."

He shrugged his shoulders, looking at Chang, who took his cue to continue the conversation. Larsen didn't have anything else to say.

"Stan, we're going to wait here until it gets dark and leave. I hid my plane a quarter of a mile or so away on the interstate."

"You landed on the interstate?" said Greenberg.

"Why didn't you just keep flying?" added Terrence.

"That's an even longer story," said Chang. "The short

version is we didn't have a choice."

"It was either that or eat a Hellfire missile," said Larsen.

"Among other things," said Chang. "The aircraft was overloaded. I had five passengers, including Larsen. The sun was coming up, and we couldn't risk another round of aerial maneuvers."

"I'm speechless," said Terrence.

"Finally," said Larsen.

An uncomfortable pause ensued.

"Wait. Passengers?" said Greenberg. "Wait. Did I miss something? I thought Larsen was the only survivor from his team?"

"We landed with a police officer, his son, and a married couple," said Larsen. "Are we having fun yet?"

"What the hell happened last night?" said Greenberg.

"Like I said. It's a very long story," said Chang. "Things got weird after our phone call."

"That's an understatement," said Larsen.

"Dr. Chang, in the interest of full disclosure, and moving this conversation to a close, I need your help."

"I have samples of the virus, along with my initial DNA analysis, hidden in my lab," said Chang. "I can grab that in a few minutes. I'd be happy to deliver that when I get out of here."

"I was thinking more along the lines of temporary employment, working alongside Dr. Greenberg. My guess is that the two of you can determine the source of this virus, pointing me in the right direction. I can't stop this catastrophe, but I can sure as hell punish those responsible."

"Can you use a slightly worn-out former SEAL on the team?" said Larsen. "I'm a little sarcastic."

"A little? I'm sure we can find room for you," said Terrence. "What do you say, Dr. Chang?"

"I'll do whatever it takes to punish the people responsible for this," said Chang.

"All right. I'm sending a team to escort you and Larsen out of there. They are my absolute best people," said Terrence. "They'll parachute onto the NevoTech campus after dark and get you through the quarantine lines."

"No. I promised the people we came with that I'd fly them out," said Chang, glaring at Larsen. "We wouldn't have made it here without their help."

"I'm not arguing with you," said Larsen, raising his hands.

"Dr. Chang, getting you and that data out safely is critical to our country."

"You can take the data and escort me to the aircraft," said Chang. "I'm flying those people out of here."

"Flying is far too risky," said Terrence. "My people can protect you on the ground. They'll give their lives to keep you safe. You have my word on that. Up in the air, they can't help you. You'll be at the mercy of an alert radar controller or a sharp squad leader on the ground."

"I won't leave them here," said Chang. "If you want my help, you have to abide by that. I'm happy to give you the data if your people escort us to the aircraft, but I can't turn my back on a promise."

"It's a deal," said Terrence. "Check your messages at 4 p.m. I'll send you an update regarding the team's ETA and drop zone. You can text a few words to let me know you got the information. That won't be enough for them to triangulate your position electronically."

"Make sure the drop zone is inside the NevoTech campus," said Larsen. "The parking lot may look like it's enclosed, but it isn't. You'll want to find a DZ tucked away between the buildings."

"There's a decent size park in the southwest part of the campus," said Chang. "It's circular, so it should be easy to see from the sky."

"We can guide the team in," said Larsen, "if they need the help."

"Sounds like a plan," said Terrence. "Is there anything else?"

Dr. Hale pointed at herself. "This is Dr. Hale. I need a favor."

"My team will gladly escort you out, too," said Terrence. "Anything to keep Dr. Chang happy, though it sounds like you'll have to walk out with the team. Unless my math is wrong and the plane has more room."

"No. I'm staying. I have over two hundred patients counting on me here," said Hale. "I'm asking for supplies. Antibiotics. Hemostatic powder. Compresses. Morphine. Trauma stuff. This place has been wiped clean."

"I'll put together something," said Terrence. "They won't be able to jump in with a lot, but every spare pound they can manage will go toward medical supplies. Biggest-bang-for-your-buck-level stuff."

"Thank you," said Hale. "I'll take whatever you can give me."

"Then that's it," said Terrence. "We'll be in touch. Call if something game changing happens. Stan? Final words?"

"Gene, all of you, stay safe and don't let your guard down," said Greenberg. "The situation inside the city will undoubtedly get worse as the day progresses."

"Fantastic," said Larsen. "Because it wasn't a complete shit show already."

"You're going to fit in nicely around here, Eric," said Terrence.

After Chang ended the call, they stood around the desk for a minute before Chang broke the silence.

"Do you trust this Terrence guy?"

"My gut says *maybe,* but logic and experience says *not at all,*" said Larsen. "I'm worried that his team will grab you and disappear the first chance they get."

"How do we prevent that?" said Chang.

"I'll think of something," said Larsen, not at all sure what that might be.

Chapter Thirty-Three

Jack Harper held Emma's hand as they shuffled back to the cafeteria with the rest of the refugees that had sought shelter on campus. They'd decided to hang out among fellow NevoTech employees and their families instead of spending the day alone in one of the evacuated sections of the building. The group they had arrived with broke apart on arrival, each going in a different direction. The thought of sitting by themselves in a quiet boardroom or employee lounge held little appeal after the crazy night they had endured. They needed to be with other people, at least for now.

"What do you think happened?" said Emma.

"I don't know," said Jack. "I thought I heard helicopters."

"Shouldn't we be going to the rooftops instead? Waving flags around?"

"You'd think," he said. "But who knows at this point."

He meant that earnestly. He truly didn't know what to think anymore. Their world had been turned upside down and shaken like a martini—with no warning. Nothing would ever be the same again, on any level. He tried to process that, but couldn't wrap his head around it. His brain continuously defaulted to a single focus. Keeping Emma safe. There was only one problem. He couldn't translate that focus into a solution. Since arriving at

NevoTech, he'd felt strangely helpless, left to wonder if they might have been better off trying to slip through the outer quarantine boundary on foot.

"Either way, I feel safer here," she said. "I can't imagine going back out there if we don't have to. Helicopters have to be a good thing. Right?"

"I honestly don't know," said Jack.

She didn't say anything else until they took a seat at one of the tables on the fringes of the bright, two-story glass and steel cafeteria.

"What's wrong?" she said. "Other than the obvious."

He glanced around, still not sure this was the answer to his problem. Families returned to their tables, clutching backpacks and the few other belongings they'd managed to carry onto campus. Cushions from the lounges lay scattered on the floor among the tables, serving as makeshift beds for the injured, so they could stay close to family and friends. From what he could tell, at least half of the wounded had remained behind when security rushed everyone out of here. Maybe the plan was to get all of the kids settled in the auditorium before coming back to ferry the injured. He had no idea. The whole scene was surreal.

"Jack," she whispered insistently, "are you okay?"

He snapped out of it. "Sorry. I was just thinking."

"Thinking about what?"

"This," he said, shaking his head. "Us. Getting you out of here."

"Maybe we're better off here," she said.

"Are you saying that because you don't want to go back out to the plane?" said Jack. "And I don't mean that to sound snippy. I'd prefer not to get chased by a mob again if I can avoid it."

"That's part of it," said Emma, taking his hand from across the table. "I'm also worried about the actual flying part. Chang said the wing looked bent."

"I couldn't tell the difference between the two wings," said Jack. "But I'm not a pilot."

"You don't have to be a pilot to know he put a ton of strain on the airframe," said Emma.

"No. You don't," he said. "Then there's the military quarantine thing. What are the chances of slipping through undetected—and staying undetected?"

"We barely got away from those helicopters," said Emma. "What if they have jets in the air tonight? We can't outrun an F-16 in Chang's Cessna."

"If he flies low enough—I don't know," said Jack. "If we stay here? I don't know. I guess that's the problem. I just don't know. Part of me thinks we're better off in that plane. We'd know our fate within minutes instead of sitting around here, hoping for the best."

"This can't last that long," she said. "If the military has the area surrounded, it's only a matter of time before they start clearing the city. I heard someone saying that there's enough food on campus for another week. Longer if they start rationing."

"It won't be that easy," said Jack.

"What won't?"

"Clearing the city. You saw what's out there. How do they clear a city full of crazy people?"

"I don't know," she said. "Maybe we should talk with the others about it. I'd be interested to hear David's take on the overall situation. He has to be thinking the same thing about his son. I'd trust his opinion."

"That's a great idea," said Jack, standing up slowly.

His entire body ached, especially his legs. Casually

running four or five miles a few times a week hadn't come close to preparing him for last night's ordeal. Halfway up, he detected the start of a cramp in his right hamstring.

"Cramp," he announced, extending the leg and leaning into a tight stretch.

His quick reaction settled the muscle spasm, but left him with a lingering doubt about leaving the campus. If something like this happened out there—it could mean the difference between life and death. He didn't want to think about it.

"You all right?" said Emma, grabbing his arm to keep him steady.

"Yeah. I'm fine. But I'm taking up cross fit when this is over," said Jack. "I didn't realize the apocalypse would be this demanding."

Chapter Thirty-Four

Emma Harper followed the security guard up the dimly lit concrete staircase. She slowed her pace to let Jack catch up. The cramp in his thigh wouldn't go away, forcing him to stop and stretch every thirty seconds to keep the muscle spasm at bay. Climbing stairs would probably push his leg over the edge.

"Keep going," said Jack. "I'll catch up. This leg won't leave me alone."

"Are you sure?" she said.

"It's straight up, right? Hard to get lost," said Jack, stretching against the wall. "And I don't want to hold up any of the security team."

"Take your time," said the guard. "It's not like anyone's going anywhere."

"It sounds so depressing put like that," said Emma.

"It wasn't meant to be cheery," said the guard. "I'm Sean, by the way. Sean Fitzgerald."

"Emma and Jack," she said, shaking his hand. "You were in the security hub when we arrived. Part of the tactical team."

"That's me."

"It's hard to recognize you guys right away with all of that gear," said Emma. "Not to mention the fact that I was still scared out of my mind. I probably wouldn't have remembered meeting my own mother."

"And you're not scared now?" he said.

"I'm scared," said Jack, easing out of his stretch.

"I'd be lying if I said I wasn't still scared," said Emma.

"Me too," said Sean. "Things are getting worse out there."

"We thought we heard helicopters," said Emma. "Did anyone try to contact them?"

The security officer stared at her for a second before responding. "The helicopters had a different agenda. That's all I can say for now."

Emma wasn't sure what to make of his response. Why would he hold back information from them? She wasn't going to push the issue with Sean, but she'd bring it up with David. The security team shouldn't be keeping secrets or withholding information from the people that had sought refuge here.

"No problem," said Emma, unable to resist a small jab. "I'm sure Howard has his reasons."

"Howard's gone," said Sean. "He was killed bringing the ER doctor back."

"I'm so sorry," she said. "I didn't know. Obviously. We've been a little cut off since we got back. I don't know what to say."

"Sorry, Sean," said Jack. "I could tell all of you were tight."

Sean took a deep breath and sighed, clearly fighting back tears. "He was a good boss. An even better friend," said Sean, wiping his eyes. "You ready?"

"We're ready," she said, pulling her husband away from the wall.

Humid air washed around them when Sean opened the door to the roof. Emma stepped onto the asphalt roof and took in the clear blue sky. A bird zipped overhead, chased by another. The echo of a nearby gunshot shattered any illusion of normalcy conveyed by the two birds.

"Over there," said Sean, pointing toward the far side of the rooftop. "Northeast corner. They know you're coming."

"Thank you," she said. "I'm very sorry about Howard."

The man nodded. "Keep that leg stretched out. You might have to leave the rooftop in a hurry."

She raised an eyebrow. "Helicopters?"

"They aren't here to help," said Sean. "They made that obvious."

They made their way to the other side of the rooftop, surprised to find nearly everyone from Chang's plane gathered in the corner. David and one of the security guards pointed rifles away from the building while Larsen and Chang leaned against an air-conditioning fan unit several feet away. David's suppressed rifle barked, snapping into his shoulder, the shot sounding a lot louder than this morning. Larsen noticed them first, rising to greet them.

"Looks like we're getting the band back together," said Larsen. "What brings the Harpers up to the penthouse level? Miss us already?"

"We didn't expect to find everyone together," said Emma.

Emma and Jack shook his hand, while Chang scribbled on a map of the city pressed against the air-conditioning unit.

"Actually, this works out great," said Jack. "We wanted to run something by everyone."

"David might be a little busy," said Larsen.

The police officer's rifle cracked again, the security officer next to him nodding. David left the rifle on the ledge and joined them.

"What's up?" said David.

Emma didn't hesitate. "We're thinking about staying here instead of flying out tonight, but we wanted to get your—David's opinion. We know the two of you are flying out no matter what."

"I knew you guys didn't come up here to see me," said Larsen, looking rejected.

"Sorry. I didn't mean—"

Larsen grinned. "Just fucking with you. You'll have to try harder than that to hurt my feelings. Not sure about Dr. Chang, here, though. He's kind of sensitive."

Chang ignored them, continuing to mark the map with his pencil.

"We just figured that David might be the better person to ask," said Emma, not sure how to explain.

"I'm getting my son out of here," said David. "As a police officer, I feel a duty to stay and help the people here, but as a parent—I have to get my son out of here. Plus we're going to have some help. They're sending a team to make sure Chang gets to the plane."

"Really?" said Jack. "How?"

"They're going to parachute in tonight and escort us to the aircraft," said Larsen.

"I didn't think we had the room for more passengers," said Emma.

"We don't," said Chang, continuing to work.

"They're going to depart on foot once we get off the ground," said Larsen. "I get the feeling that this is a highly professional and capable team."

"I'm worried about the plane," said Emma. "Every

aspect of it. They could have a pair of F-16s on station overhead. Catch us on radar. Then it's over."

"I haven't heard any jets," said Larsen.

"What if we do?" said David. "Chang?"

"I hadn't thought of that," said Chang, looking up from his map. "We should make sure the rooftop and ground teams listen for jets."

"Even if they put up some kind of combat air patrol, that doesn't mean they'll spot Chang's plane," said Larsen. "He'll be flying away from any known airport radars, at treetop level."

"We can't stay here," said Chang, pointing north, toward the downtown area. "Take a look."

Emma saw it immediately. Several pillars of smoke rose above the city skyline. One of them looked as thick as one of the skyscrapers to the northwest. She turned slowly, checking every direction. They were surrounded by smoke columns, the closest appearing to be several blocks away, in the direction of Chang's apartment.

"I'm mapping the fires by direction and estimated distance," said Chang. "No matter which way the wind blows, we're screwed."

"I guess that's it, then," said Emma, glancing at Jack, who nodded.

"What about all these people?" said her husband.

"The best we can do is get a warning out to the authorities. Let them know that the facility is secure and the people inside are not infected," said Larsen.

"How do we do that?" said Jack. "I'm not exactly keen on the idea of approaching the military."

"None of us are," said David. "I could probably do it once we get clear of here. Pass it along through a sheriff's office."

"That'll never get through," muttered Emma.

"Staying here won't help," said Larsen. "Not if the city burns down around us."

"The fires will be the least of our problems," said Chang.

"What do you mean?" said Jack.

"The fires will drive everyone onto the streets," said Chang. "A half million infected."

"That's why I'm willing to risk the slightly broken wing," said David. "Worst-case scenario, we hightail it out of here with the team sent to escort Chang. The man sending them didn't sound like the type to underestimate the situation."

"He hasn't seen this," said Jack.

"No. But the team he's sending has," said Chang. "I trust they'll be competent."

"An entirely new level of competent," said Larsen. "Way above my skillset."

"All right," said Emma, looking at her husband. "We leave with the rest of you."

Jack nodded. "I think we're in good hands."

"I've seen you in action with that revolver," said Larsen. "We're all in good hands."

"I can't imagine the hell this guy's wife puts up with," said David, thumb pointing to Larsen.

They all laughed.

"She's a trooper. No doubt about that," said Larsen, his voice trailing off.

"She's lucky to have you," said Emma. "And I know you want to get back to them more than anything. You will. I can feel it."

Larsen beamed, his stoic face finally cracking.

"Brother, if you're going to cry, I suggest you take it behind the air conditioner," said David, winking at Emma. "You have a reputation to uphold."

"Fuck you," said Larsen, laughing.

"Sorry to change the subject," said Emma. "But what happened with the helicopters? We heard helicopters, and Sean said something kind of cryptic about them."

"Not sure why he was being cryptic," said David, motioning for them to follow. "Take a look at this."

David led them to the corner of the rooftop, where the security guard leaned forward against the concrete parapet, scanning the parking lot with binoculars. The police officer pointed to an SUV parked against a gap in the fence. A few dozen bodies lay sprawled on the sidewalk just beyond the SUV.

"The helicopters were sent to grab Dr. Chang. Long story short—they came this way looking for Chang and ended up shooting a hole in the fence. One more reason why—"

David stopped, glancing furtively at the security officer.

"Dude, I'm a grown-ass man," said the guard, turning around to face the group. "I can handle the bad news. The name's Roscoe, by the way. Nice to see you all again. Carry on, David."

"I was about to say—this is one more reason why I think NevoTech is fucked," said David. "From one grown-ass man or woman to another."

"Thank you," said Roscoe, shifting his binoculars. "Hey, we got another one. Damn if they don't get curious about that SUV."

"I think it's the fact that your rifle's suppressor has seen better days," said Larsen. "We should probably swap that out for one of the rifles we grabbed near Chang's place."

"Fuck. I hate the naked ones," said David, looking toward the parking lot.

"Naked?" said Larsen.

"Yeah. That seems to be the new thing for some reason," said David, heading back to the corner of the rooftop. "That, and they're starting to fight each other a lot more."

Emma held Jack's hand tightly as David nestled the rifle into his shoulder. A naked man staggered across the parking lot from East Street, headed directly for the gap in the fence. She looked at one of the buildings beyond the man, keeping him in her peripheral vision. Everyone on the rooftop became perfectly still for several moments until the rifle kicked into David's shoulder. She saw the man drop out of the corner of her eye, but that was all she allowed before turning to Jack.

"He's down," said Roscoe. "I don't think a second shot is necessary."

"Good," said David.

Emma focused on Jack, neither of them needing to say a word. The sooner they got out of here, the better.

Chapter Thirty-Five

Chang led Larsen across the campus to the eastern side of the Secure Research Facility, where they met two of NevoTech's security guards. They were equipped with full body armor and M4-style rifles, but they weren't part of Howard's elite tactical response team. He needed them at critical points along the perimeter.

Larsen nodded at the two guards. "Thank you for helping out with this. Hoenig briefed you?"

"He did," said one of them. "Sounds pretty straightforward—assuming there was only one team in the building."

"That's the key here. Don't assume," said Larsen. "That said, I'm almost one hundred percent sure it was only one team."

"We'll let you lead the way," said the guard, "until that's confirmed."

"Smart man," said Larsen, turning to Chang.

The scientist stared at his keycard, looking lost in thought. Probably nervous, which was completely understandable.

"Dr. Chang? You ready?"

"I think we might have a problem," said Chang.

Larsen instinctively glanced around, assuming the "problem" was something Chang had noticed about the surroundings. He still hadn't stopped staring at his ID.

"Talk to me, Chang," said Larsen. "You're making me nervous."

The two guards crouched, backing up against the concrete wall behind them.

"No. It's nothing like that," said Chang. "I don't think this ID will get me into my laboratory area. SRF security is handled in a silo. I remember picking up my ID at the SRF."

"You just thought of this?" said Larsen.

"Sorry," said Chang.

"No. That's fine. We've all been a little preoccupied," said Larsen, activating his radio. "Gary, you there?"

"At your service."

"We had a question about Chang's ID card," said Larsen. "What kind of access can you authorize from the security hub?"

"Any level of access specific to Chang's employment at NevoTech," said Hoenig. "The only thing we can customize here is general access to employee public areas and buildings. Everything else uploads to the ID card through his secure profile."

"Chang remembers picking up his ID card at the SRF," said Larsen.

"That might have been a courtesy," said Hoenig.

"So he should have access?" said Larsen.

"Yes. Unless the team barred his entry," said Hoenig.

"They can do that?"

"Absolutely. It's a security feature designed to immediately prevent an employee from gaining further access."

"Why the hell would you need that?" said Larsen.

"Active-shooter scenario, mainly," said Hoenig. "Viral containment. In the eight years that system has been active, I've seen it used twice."

"And they can activate it from inside the SRF?"

"Right. They have a security hub like mine, only smaller. They can activate it from there, or remotely by logging in to one of the facility's computers."

"How do we get in if his card has been spiked?" said Larsen.

"How much explosives did you bring?"

"Enough to blow one of the windows," said Larsen. "I assume it's all ballistic glass?"

"You guessed right," said Hoenig.

"Well, there's only one way to find out," said Larsen. "Dr. Chang? If you'll follow me."

They walked up the wide limestone stairs to the glass-paneled entrance, homing in on the single door to the right. A featureless glass second door sat about twenty feet to the left, which had to be the exit. It was situated far enough apart from the entry to prevent crossover. Chang approached the door to the right and pressed his card against the card reader, triggering a small red light at the top of the black, rectangular box. Shit.

"Try it again," said Larsen.

Another swipe resulted in the same underwhelming indication that the card didn't work. Larsen pulled on the door, which predictably didn't budge. Not even a click.

"Now what?" said Chang, shrugging his shoulders.

Hoenig replied, having watched their progress on one of the hundreds of cameras spread out around the campus. "There's another option, but you're not going to like it."

He'd already figured it out.

"I'm going to need everybody on deck for this one," said Larsen.

"That's what I figured," said Hoenig. "Are you thinking about a smoke screen?"

"No. They seem to be attracted by sound just as much as sight," said Larsen. "The smoke will just cut down on our situational awareness."

"I'll start getting everyone together," said Hoenig.

"I thought this wasn't mission essential?" said Larsen.

"Do you want the help?"

"See you in a few minutes," said Larsen. "We should brief everyone at the same time. Not that this will be too complicated."

"We'll be waiting."

Chang shook his head slowly. "Please tell me you're not going to do what I think you're going to do."

"You need to get in there, right?"

He didn't answer right away, which was the same as answering the question.

"Then it looks like I'm taking a very short trip outside the fence."

Chapter Thirty-Six

David tightened his grip on the rifle, glancing around nervously. Larsen's plan was a bad idea. It wasn't the mechanics of the plan that bothered him. Overall, it was really quite simple. Larsen and Mitch, one of the tactical security officers, would scurry over the top of the SUV and jump down onto the sidewalk outside the fence. One of them would carry a knotted rope over the SUV and drop that on the other side.

They would then hustle over to the mangled Homeland team about twenty yards away and locate one or more of their security IDs that had been stolen from the SRF's real security team. With the IDs in hand, they'd return to the SUV and use the knotted rope to quickly climb over the steep tailgate while the security team provided covering fire.

Sounded easy until you looked at the bigger picture. Given all of the recent commotion in the area, the bushes and trees lining the parking lot could be packed with infected. Even more could be lurking in nearby alleys, homes and streets. Any delay on the ground out there would increase the number of fast-moving targets the security team would have to neutralize—and he didn't have a ton of faith in the majority of the shooters assembled to protect Larsen and Mitch.

Most of them were regular campus security guards that hadn't carried a firearm until yesterday, when Howard had equipped them with rifles. Half of them didn't remember how to change a rifle magazine until about ten minutes ago. God help them if a rifle jammed.

"How are we looking?" said David.

"Looks clear to me," said Roscoe, panning the parking lot with binoculars. "But you and I know they're just waiting."

"Yeah. This'll get Pavlov's dog busy, really quick," said David, pressing his radio button. "Gary, what are you seeing?"

"Nothing unusual on the streets around the parking lot. A few wanderers."

"All right," said David, taking another look at the men and women positioned on the rooftop and ground.

Roscoe, the best shooter on campus next to Larsen, was in his usual position at the northeast corner of the rooftop. Eight regular security guards armed with M4s had been spread out along the front of the roof, six of them directly facing the parking lot. The remaining two covered the approach from East Street. All of them had orders to engage well beyond the fence. Under no circumstances were they to fire at targets close to the fence line.

Eight more security guards, led by Sean, one of the tactical officers, were spread out behind the fence, ready to provide point-blank fire against anything that got too close. Including Mitch and Larsen, twenty shooters stood ready to beat back anything the city threw at them. It should be enough as long as Larsen didn't get held up outside the fence for too long.

"Everyone up here ready?" said David.

"Yep," said Roscoe before the others responded with enthusiastic nods.

"Sean, this is David," he said over the tactical net. "You guys ready?"

"We're ready."

"Make sure the crew pulling the rope doesn't panic," said David.

Sean had handpicked four volunteers from the cafeteria to pull the knotted rope, in a controlled manner, once Larsen and Mitch started climbing over the back of the SUV. If done right, the two of them should be up and over in a few seconds. Done wrong, they could pull the rope away, leaving them stranded.

"They got it," said Sean.

"Gary? Any changes?" said David.

"None. This is as good as it gets," said Hoenig.

"Larsen?" he said, looking down at the two men crouched behind the SUV's front bumper.

"Can we get this over with already?" said Larsen, holding his hands palms up.

"Go for it," said David.

"About time," said Larsen. "We're on the move."

Larsen and Mitch hopped onto the hood and ran up the windshield simultaneously, pounding their way across the vehicle's roof. Mitch jumped from the back of the SUV, landing in a deep squat on the pavement, while Larsen quickly sat on the back of the vehicle and slid down to the bumper. A sensible move considering his leg injury. They were both on the run within moments of hitting the sidewalk. So were the crazies.

"Contact. Northeast corner," said Roscoe.

"Hold your fire," said David, scanning the vast parking lot over his rifle.

A woman wearing a bloodied nightgown raced toward the fence.

"Northwest corner. Two targets," announced a guard to David's left.

Two equally blood-soaked men ran diagonally across the lot, pushing each other as they dodged parked cars.

"Due north," said another.

"Southeast corner."

There was no point to holding back any longer. Word on the street was out.

"All positions. Fire. I say again. Fire," said David. "Single shots. Knock them down. Move on to the next."

A crackle of small-arms fire erupted as the first volley of shots snapped across the corpse-littered expanse of asphalt. Half of the infected plummeted to the ground, the rest still coming. David tracked one of the survivors rushing in from the west, pressing the trigger once. The ragged figure toppled, piling headfirst into the curb next to the sidewalk.

A quick scan across the lot confirmed his initial fears. The initial wave of crazies had been replaced by a number twice as large—all converging rapidly on the fence. The rate of gunfire had increased dramatically—but fewer of the infected were falling. The inexperienced shooters couldn't keep up. He picked a target closest to Larsen and fired, knocking it down. A slight shift in his aim sent another spinning. David looked over his rifle and didn't like what he saw.

"Larsen, you have like ten seconds before you need to head back," said David over the net.

"We're picking through fucking body parts down here. Feel free to come down and help."

David fired again, hitting a woman within fifty feet of

the fence, a meat cleaver skidding across the pavement.

"Ten seconds. Not fucking kidding," said David. "Sean, I need you all over the situation down there."

"It's under control!" said Sean.

A quick peek downward confirmed it. Four of the security guards formed a tight line behind Larsen and Mitch, firing rapidly at the increasing number of crazies that were managing to elude his rooftop shooters. The rest focused their efforts on the flanks, preventing the infected from sneaking up the sidewalk on either side. David fired a few more times before stopping to fully make a final assessment of the situation.

Their wall of protective fire was collapsing fast. Too many of them were getting past the rooftop shooters, and it was only a matter of seconds before the ground-level firing line was overwhelmed.

"Larsen, time's up," said David. "Get back now."

"Without the card?"

"Without the—"

"I got one!" yelled Mitch, holding it up to show him.

"We're on our way back!" said Larsen, grabbing him and pulling him toward the SUV.

David shifted his rifle toward the SUV, preparing to fire at the closest targets.

"Roscoe, it's you and me," he said.

Roscoe didn't respond. He changed magazines and fired repeatedly—in a steady, controlled manner. David guarded Larsen and Mitch as they sprinted toward the gap in the fence. A fast mover broke past the gauntlet of security guards defending the far right flank, headed straight toward them with a hand ax. He centered the green reticle a hair above the crazy's head and pressed the trigger, snapping the man's head forward and toppling him to the sidewalk.

Larsen reached the back of the SUV first and kneeled, covering Mitch's escape. The tactical security officer let his rifle hang by its sling and grabbed the rope as high as he could with both hands. Sean jumped onto the hood and frantically signaled for the rope crew to start pulling. At least a dozen crazies had closed to within thirty feet of the SUV. Larsen was cutting this too close. They'd never get the rope back in time.

"Get the fuck out of there!" said David.

The former SEAL fired a few more times before turning to leave. David's brain instantly did the math. Larsen wasn't going to make it. They'd pull him off the rope before he could get out of there. Moments before the crazies reached him, Mitch grabbed his hand and yanked Larsen upward.

Three or four infected slammed into the back of the SUV, one of them grabbing Larsen's boot. A hard, two-handed tug nearly pulled him into the mob's clutches, but Sean wrapped his arms around Mitch's waist and kept them from tumbling over the back. Before the tug-of-war could be joined by more crazies, Larsen drew his pistol and emptied the magazine into the faces below. The hand released, sending the three of them tumbling backward onto the roof of the SUV.

David snapped off a shot at a crazy that tried to climb up the back bumper, knocking him sideways onto the cement path. Another tried to follow Larsen, but fell to one of Roscoe's bullets.

"Sean, get everyone inside. They'll just keep coming if they see you on the ground," said David. "We'll clear the deck from here."

"I'm moving everyone out," said Sean. "We'll be

inside the door—just in case."

He watched Larsen and Mitch hop down next to Sean on the lawn inside the fence, and motion for the rest of the guards to follow. When the last of the security team had cleared the fence, he ordered the rooftop shooters to engage any infected near the SUV. As the gunfire rose to a crescendo, he broadcast over the tactical net.

"I sure hope that card works, Eric," said David, drawing a quick laugh from Roscoe.

A few moments passed before Larsen responded.

"I'll strangle someone if it doesn't."

Chapter Thirty-Seven

Chang pressed the bloodstained card against the reader next to the door and waited. For a brief moment, nothing happened, and Larsen started to shake his head. Before Larsen could utter what was guaranteed to be a sarcastic, foul-mouthed comment, the small LED turned green, and the door clicked.

"Open fucking sesame," said Larsen, pulling the solid, pneumatically assisted door open as far as it would go. "After you."

Chang stepped inside the spacious lobby, walking tentatively across the dark slate floor. Something smelled off, but that was all he could tell. The reception area was silent except for their discreet footsteps crossing the hard tile. He looked over his shoulder to see Larsen and the two guards communicating with hand signals before fanning out to clear the room. Larsen spent a considerable amount of time examining the floor and walls near the reception desk, eventually turning to Chang.

"Someone died in here. You can smell it," said Larsen. "They cleaned up the mess pretty well. I only found a few specks of blood on the back of this chair."

A comfortable office chair rolled out from behind the desk, coming to a stop in front of one of the security guards, who looked like he'd rather be outside the gate than in this building.

"We should probably locate the bodies first," said Larsen. "Then head to your lab."

"You think they're all dead?" said Chang.

"If the security team working here was comprised of former Special Forces types, I don't see how the Homeland crew could take any of them alive without raising some kind of alarm. They obviously shot the officer manning the desk and moved him—or her."

Chang had a hard time accepting Larsen's logic, and not because he thought Larsen was wrong. It was something else.

"I don't get it," said Chang. "Your team would never have done something like this. Right? I mean—I know you wouldn't do this, but the rest of your team? I can't see them obeying these orders."

"Dix and Brennan, not a chance," said Larsen. "Peck? I'm not so sure about Peck."

"What are the chances that all four members of a team would be on the same page about something like this?" said Chang. "Even one of the guys on Ochoa's team turned out to be skeptical."

"What are you saying?" said Larsen.

"I wonder if this team might have been something else altogether," said Chang.

"How? I trained with them at Grissom facility," said Larsen. "They've been in the program as long as I have."

"Think about it. Your orders changed when you hit the ground. It's probably fair to say the same thing happened to Ochoa. He was just a lot more enthusiastic about following his new orders than you were."

"That's one way to put it," said Larsen.

"But this team had to be different," said Chang. "Irrespective of their final orders regarding me, they were sent into a specific situation requiring them to kill four security guards, and they apparently didn't hesitate. That suggests a different breed altogether. Your team would never have been given this assignment."

Larsen looked conflicted by Chang's suggestion, like he didn't want to believe it.

"Fuck," muttered Larsen. "A secret program within a secret program, and none of us the wiser. Brilliant."

"There's still one more team out there," said Chang.

"Ragan's team," said Larsen. "She's hardcore, but not a killer."

"What did you think of this team back at your base?"

"Same thing," said Larsen.

"Let's get the data and get back to the security hub," said Chang. "This is creeping me out."

"Everything you've been through today, and *this* is what's creeping you out?"

"Oddly enough, yes," said Chang. "The part of me that still refuses to believe that the government is behind this outbreak is rapidly dying. This revelation may have put the final nail in its coffin."

"I wish I could say that I disagreed," said Larsen before turning to the security guards. "Do the two of you feel comfortable hanging out here while we're gone?"

"I think we can manage," said one of the guards, patting his rifle.

"Keep yourselves out of sight," said Larsen. "Just to be safe. Report anything."

"The building is under surveillance on all sides," said the guard. "And the door is locked."

"Then how did the other team get inside?" said Larsen.

The two guards glanced at each other, putting a little distance between them.

"They were probably here before all of this went down," said the other guard.

"I jumped out of an airplane with one of those guys at about two in the morning," said Larsen. "Don't make any assumptions."

"Then how did they get in?" said the guard.

"They parachuted onto the roof," said Chang, doubting his own response. "Can they really do that?"

"My team could do it," said Larsen. "Shall we?"

As Chang walked over to the door leading deeper into the facility, the two guards split up, settling into the shadowy recesses of the lobby, where they would presumably be harder targets. Larsen joined him at the door.

"Let's do this differently," said Larsen, holding out a gloved hand. "I'll swipe and you open it when I say. I'll lead with the rifle."

"Sounds good to me," said Chang, handing him the card.

He stood behind the door and grabbed the handle, waiting for the signal. When the light turned green, Larsen quickly pocketed the card and raised his rifle.

"Do it."

Chang pulled the heavy, featureless door open far enough for Larsen to slide through. Moments after he disappeared into the hallway on the other side of the door, Chang heard a meaty thud, followed by mumbled curses.

"Larsen?" said Chang, not daring to stick his head out

from behind the reinforced metal door. "You all right?"

"I'm fine," said Larsen. "Apparently the cleanup didn't extend past the lobby."

Chang opened the door a few more inches and peeked inside. Larsen lay on his back in a wall-to-wall pool of dark, semi-slick-looking blood. Two thick trails of gore traced a path from the pool to a closed door halfway down the fluorescent-lit hallway.

"Holy mother," said Chang, clinging to the handle, ready to slam the door shut at the slightest provocation.

"You want to give me hand?" said Larsen, reaching upward. "They must have piled the lobby security here while they hunted down the rest of the team. This is a lot of blood."

Chang opened the door all the way, eliciting a few murmured obscenities from the security guards. He gripped Larsen's sticky, gloved hand and braced against the door frame, pulling him to his feet.

"Watch your step," said Larsen, walking carefully out of the mess.

He followed Larsen's footsteps as closely as possible, keeping one hand on the wall to keep himself stable. While he traversed the blood slick, Larsen removed his gloves and tossed them aside, leaving smudges of red where they hit the wall. Chang's feet squished across the tile floor, leaving bloody footprints all the way to the door labeled SECURITY.

"This isn't going to be pretty," said Larsen, drawing his pistol and offering it to Chang. "You can stay out here. I won't be long."

"I think I can handle it at this point," said Chang. "But I'll take the pistol."

"You know the deal," said Larsen. "There's no safety.

Slip and fall, and you might shoot yourself—or me."

"How do you not let any of this bother you?" said Chang.

"I wasn't being funny. I really don't want you to accidentally shoot me," said Larsen, winking at him. "Sorry. It's my way of dealing with shit. The worse things get, the more I joke. I can try to stop if it bothers you."

"No," said Chang. "I'd be more unnerved at this point if you stopped."

It was true. Larsen's seemingly inappropriate sense of humor was strangely comforting in the face of this nightmare. He wished he could project the same unaffected appearance—a sort of false bravado—but he couldn't. He was scared out of his mind.

"Brace yourself," said Larsen, pushing the door inward.

Chang started to gag immediately, turning his head slightly. One of the security guards slouched over the armrest of an institutional-looking navy-blue fabric couch, an expansive mosaic of splattered blood and darkened clumps plastered against the off-white wall where his head had once rested. The other two had been dumped on the floor in front of the couch, their bodies twisted in a grotesque heap. Even Larsen seemed to be frozen in place by the scene.

Chang dropped the pistol and put his hands on his knees, dry heaving twice before throwing up in the hallway. He coughed a few times and spit, trying to clear his mouth before speaking.

"This. This is—"

His stomach heaved again, but nothing came out. Larsen closed the door and kneeled next to him, putting a hand on Chang's shoulder.

"I'm going to get you through this, Dr. Chang," said Larsen. "The CHASE program is the work of monsters. This whole thing out there is the work of monsters."

Chang looked up at him, seeing an even wider crack in his normally calm, stoic face. Larsen looked enraged. His eyes were squinted and his lips pressed together.

"Will you get angry if I kind of throw something back in your face?" said Chang.

Larsen shrugged his shoulders. "Go for it."

"After everything you've seen and been through today, why did *this* push you over the top?"

"Fair question," said Larsen, a faint grin breaking across half of his face.

When Larsen didn't answer right away, appearing to have drifted away in thought, Chang almost told him to forget about it.

"I knew something was fucked up as soon as they changed my orders," said Larsen. "But I thought we were being co-opted by another agency to do their dirty work. Some kind of last-ditch effort to cover their tracks. I mean, they had to know most of us wouldn't play along. Right? I figured they were just throwing us at the problem, seeing what would stick. Why not?

"Chang, it wasn't until right now that I truly realized that the whole CHASE program was a sham from the beginning. Created specifically for this scenario. Shit like this is going down all across the country. It's really quite brilliant when you think about it."

"What is?"

"The whole thing. They create this massive program that can be deployed anywhere and everywhere. All under the guise of safeguarding the nation's best and brightest. Critical human assets. All a bunch of bullshit. They spike the program with loyal zealots to handle the sticky jobs—no pun intended—and throw the rest of us at the problem. That's probably how they took your colleagues out of circulation, along with anyone else they deemed a threat."

"It's diabolical," said Chang. "Though it would have been a hell of a lot easier just to send someone out to my house earlier in the day to kill me."

"True. But this gives them plausible deniability," said Larsen. "All mission interaction flows through the CTAB. There's no human-to-human interface. Nothing that can be independently recorded. I'm sure they can scrub and manipulate the CTAB data. I can't believe I didn't see this coming."

"How could you?" said Chang. "How could you possibly imagine a conspiracy this sick. It's unfathomable on every level."

Larsen shook his head, looking tired and defeated. Two words Chang would never have used to describe him before they opened this door.

"Let's get this over with," said Larsen. "I could use a long nap."

"Hey, if it wasn't for you, I'd be dead or sitting in some black site prison cell," said Chang. "They made a huge mistake hiring you."

Larsen's face softened, his lips relaxing. It wasn't a smile, but it was a start. "I'm not a very good employee—am I?"

"Not at all," said Chang. "Can you imagine what they're saying about you right now?"

"Nothing good—I hope."

"Nothing good at all," said Chang. "That's your CHASE program legacy."

"I can live with that," whispered Larsen.

"Keep that locked away in your head. It's important," said Chang.

Larsen stared at him until it became a little uncomfortable.

"We're going to be fine, aren't we?" said Larsen.

"I have no idea," said Chang. "I thought that was your department."

Larsen laughed, finally smiling.

Chapter Thirty-Eight

Dr. Hale washed her hands and sat on the stool in front of her last patient, a fifteen-year-old girl with a deep four-inch slash down her left bicep. She'd been attacked in her backyard last night by a hatchet-swinging neighbor. The father sat by her side, holding her right hand and pressing his forehead against hers. He'd barely said a word since they'd walked into the infirmary. According to a NevoTech employee that knew them well, the mother had been killed in the same attack. Hale wasn't about to press either of them for details. That wasn't her job. She was here to treat physical wounds. The rest would have to wait.

"Ashley, this is going to sting. Like a—you know what," she said, dipping a sponge into a stainless steel tray filled with a chunky liquid.

The girl's arm stiffened. "What is that? It smells funky."

"It's a little concoction we put together in the kitchen," she said. "Lemon juice. Minced garlic. Chopped onions. They're all natural antiseptics."

"There's no iodine?" said her father.

"Unfortunately, all of the medical supplies were used up before the two of you arrived last night. There wasn't much here in the first place."

He nodded and then kissed his daughter's temple. "It'll be fine."

"This is a potent antiseptic brew. Something I learned from a naturopath seminar," said Hale. "Plus, it'll keep the vampires away. Along with everyone else."

Ashley smiled. Almost laughed.

"Ready?"

After she nodded, Hale ran the sponge along the inflamed wound, eliciting a hiss from Ashley.

"It really hurts," said Ashley.

Her father cast a distrustful look.

"Trust me. This is actually better than iodine or any of the other chemicals they use to disinfect wounds," said Hale.

She finished sponging the wound before wrapping it in a thin layer of gauze. With the gauze in place, she poured a liberal amount of extra virgin olive oil on the cloth before wrapping the forearm in a second, thicker layer of gauze.

"Shouldn't the wound be able to breathe?" said the father.

"Olive oil contains a significant amount of phenolic compounds, which have been shown to be effective against strains of bacteria that are immune to antibiotics. It's been used for thousands of years to treat wounds."

"You're like some kind of hippie doctor," said Ashley.

"Far from it," said Hale. "I have a serious shoe addiction. That's why I became a doctor. Shoes can get ridiculously expensive."

They both laughed, the father finally opening up. "Sometimes I think that's the only reason I'm working. To buy them new shoes."

Hale knew where this conversation was headed before

he finished his sentence. Mom. She immediately shifted topics.

"Ashley, Dad, I need both of you to do something for me," she said.

"Okaaaaay," said Ashley, taken aback by the shift.

Her dad nodded abruptly, his eyes conveying that he understood what she had just done for them. Hale spun her stool and grabbed two small plastic cups from the counter behind her, returning just as quickly.

"Round two," said Hale, offering each of them one of the cups. "You're not going to like the hippie doctor after this. Three cloves of smashed garlic and chopped onions, lightly sautéed in olive oil. A very potent antibiotic."

"What do we do with this?" said the father.

"You eat it," said Hale, turning her head to the bowl of crackers next to them. "With the crackers. I want to attack the bacteria from the outside—and inside."

"Does she have an infection?" said the dad.

"She has external inflammation consistent with an improperly cleaned wound. Same as every other cut or scrape I've seen today," said Hale. "But I don't want to take any chances. This is a deep cut. If I had access to antibiotics, oral or IV, she'd be one of my top candidates."

"I see," he said, furrowing his brow.

"Smells raw," said Ashley.

"I didn't want to cook out all of the good properties. It's best taken raw—but I know that's a really tough sell. That's why I had them cook it down a little. Like a cracker spread? It'll keep the boys away. And the vampires. Whichever is the bigger threat."

"The boys," said her father.

"Dad!" said Ashley, taking one of the cups.

A knock on the door distracted all of them. Larsen barged in, followed by Chang.

"What the hell?" said the father, standing up and moving in front of his daughter.

Larsen glanced at Ashley's dad for a second before shrugging his shoulders. "What's the problem?"

"I'm seeing patients. As in this is fucking private?" said Hale, turning to Ashley. "Sorry for the language."

"Not a problem," said the teenager.

"I have a problem with this," said her dad.

"We'll be out of your way in a second," said Larsen.

"We can come back," said Chang, clearly uncomfortable with the situation.

"Sure. We'll just wait outside," said Larsen. "With the vaccine that can prevent all of this shit from happening."

"It's experimental," said Chang.

"Sounds pretty far along in the experimental stage," said Larsen.

"He's in like extra-special asshole mode right now," said Chang. "Thank god. You should have seen him earlier."

"I'm not judging anyone," said Hale. "What's this vaccine?"

"NT-HSE893. An experimental, once-monthly pill taken to prevent HSV1 and HSV2 infection, which I believe is the key to stopping the virus that has been unleashed out there," said Chang.

"But nobody here is showing symptoms," said Hale.

"Yet," said Chang. "Some of these people arrived less than twelve hours ago. My guess is that the virus was delivered through the water supply over a week ago. Maximum infection occurred within a few days of its release, but there's a remote possibility for the virus in question to survive longer. This vaccine should kill anything brewing within your patient population."

"We'll take it," said Ashley's father.

"Side effects?" said Hale.

"GI upset in a small percentage. Maybe headaches," said Chang. "It's a relatively clean drug."

"How many doses do you have?"

"Enough for everyone here," said Chang, handing her a Ziploc bag filled with yellow pills. "The sooner you get this out there, the better."

"Howard's funeral is in forty minutes," said Hale. "They're doing it in the circular park. We're all heading over in about twenty minutes. I'll make an announcement when everyone returns."

"Do they need any help with Howard?" said Larsen.

"Everything is taken care of from what I understand," said Hale.

"All right. We'll see you there," said Larsen, nodding at Ashley and her dad before sniffing the air. "Are you marinating them for dinner? Smells like garlic."

"Don't let the door hit you on the way out," said Hale.

Chang followed Larsen out, glancing over his shoulder. "He's in rare form. Sorry."

"We're all in rare form," said Hale, holding up the bag of pills. "Thank you for these. Life's work?"

"Yeah. All in a Ziploc bag," said Chang. "Not exactly how I imagined it."

"I'm just glad you imagined it," she said.

When they closed the door, she opened the plastic bag and removed two pills, setting them on the edge of the desk next to Ashley and her father. She spun in her chair and slid back to the medical supplies counter, pausing with the bag in her hand. Keeping her back to them, she took out two additional pills, quickly placing them in her mouth. She forced them down with a quick sip from a water bottle she kept on the counter.

Two pills. She hoped it would make a difference. The last time she'd checked, her temperature had reached one hundred point five degrees. Based on what she knew from the past two days in the ER, she had another twelve hours before they'd need to strongly consider locking her up—or kicking her off campus.

Chapter Thirty-Nine

A young woman, clutching a young boy, held the door open and nodded directly at David, leaving him no opportunity to continue lingering. He'd arrived in the atrium, a massive glass enclosure adjacent to the outdoor garden, where at least half of the funeral attendees had paid their respects to Dan's wife and kids. No matter how hard he tried, he couldn't walk through the door on his own. He kept edging toward it and backing away as the people trickled past him on their way back to the cafeteria.

David wasn't sure why he was having such a hard time with this. He'd been to several funerals for officers killed in the line of duty before. Never an easy thing to do, but he'd always opened the door to the funeral home and fearlessly walked inside. It was part of the job, and it was expected. Just like this. Then why was he having so much trouble? He knew the answer. Guilt.

Guilt for having made it through the fence. Guilt for not having taken Howard's position by the gate and insisting that he go through first. Guilt for not having been able to keep him safe inside the turnstile. Guilt. And it didn't end there. It fed on itself, getting stronger by the minute. If he didn't do this now, he'd probably never do it. Guilt had a way of putting your life on hold.

He smiled at the mother and put a hand on the door.

"Thank you. I've been standing in here for five minutes, hoping this wasn't real."

"I only saw him once," she said. "When we first arrived. He took our temperatures and told us everything would be okay here. I never even knew his name. He could have sent us away. My husband was the one that worked for NevoTech."

David knew he should politely nod and walk through the door, but he couldn't. She wouldn't have brought it up if she didn't want to talk to someone about it.

"Is your husband here?" he said, mouthing it quietly.

"He's on a business trip," she said, her eyes indicating something very different.

"Well, I'm sure he'll find you guys soon enough," said David. "My wife's on a business trip, too. Kind of glad she was out of town for this. Shouldn't be long until everyone can go home."

She smiled, her eyes watering. "Did you hear that, Ben? This man is a police officer. He knows things."

Her son looked up at him with an exhausted, frightened face. The faintest sparkle of hope crossed his face when David smiled at him. He'd forgotten that he'd pinned his badge to the outside of his tactical vest. Howard had suggested he do this, to give people a sense of law and order when they saw him in the building.

"You take good care of Mommy," said David. "All right? The two of you have to look out for each other."

"But what about Daddy?" he said, glancing up at his mother.

David kneeled next to the boy and put a hand on his shoulder. "Until Daddy gets back, I'm deputizing the two of you. Do you know what that means?"

The boy nodded. "Do I get a badge?"

"Unfortunately, I don't carry spare badges," said David. "Or guns. Don't get any ideas."

The boy finally cracked a smile.

"Uh-huh," said David, winking at him. "I had you figured out the moment I saw you. No. I'm deputizing the two of you to keep an eye on each other. I'll carry the gun for you."

"Thank you," said the mother, trying hard not to openly cry.

"Stay safe, you guys," he said, and with that, he walked outside.

As soon as he stepped into the mid-afternoon heat, he wanted to turn around. Larsen and Hoenig stood close to Howard's family, almost as if they were waiting for him. Jesus. He just wanted to float through the line with everyone else. Like that was even an option. He wore full tactical gear and carried a rifle. He could no sooner pass through with a "sorry for your loss" than Hoenig. Damn it! Why was this so hard?

Larsen must have noticed him hesitate. He was already on the way over. David willed his feet forward, every step across the grass feeling like a slog through thick mud. He was about to apologize for taking so long to get here. Roscoe had left here at least fifteen minutes ago. An eternity for the family, he imagined. The enclosed garden space was mostly deserted at this point.

"Brother, you look like shit. What's the deal?" said Larsen.

"I'm having trouble with this."

"We're all having trouble with this," said Larsen, searching his face for a few seconds before nodding. "Okay. I know. Forget all of that. She doesn't know any of the specifics. Hoenig insisted on that."

David shrugged his shoulders. "What do you mean?"

"All she knows is that her husband died outside the fence alongside you and me, on a mission to escort a doctor to the campus," said Larsen. "We carried him back. That's it. That's the script. That's all you need to know. You can drop that weird guilt-trip pack you're carrying. It gets really heavy, really quick. I've already talked to her. She's not interested in details. She just wants to hear you say something honorable about Dan. For her and the kids. Crying is absolutely acceptable."

"You're bizarre," said David. "In a good way."

"Just trying to keep you from face-planting," said Larsen. "I've seen that look before. Quite a few times, actually. It never gets easier. That's a big part of why I got out. Been to one too many of these."

David patted his shoulder. "Thank you. I needed the pep talk."

"I'm sure it won't be the last," said Larsen. "Chang talked me off a cliff earlier."

"I heard it was pretty bad in there," said David.

"I don't want to think about it," said Larsen. "I just want to get as far the fuck away from here as possible."

David liked the sound of that initially, but his mind quickly pictured the young mother and her son, Ben. What would happen to them?

"Jesus, man. Are you with me?" said Larsen. "I feel like you're miles from here."

"Actually, it's the other way around," said David, looking over Larsen's shoulder at Dan Howard's widow.

How in the hell could they leave? They'd made a promise. Larsen understood immediately.

"There's no other way. I can't go to the authorities. Neither can Chang. The Harpers mean well, but who the hell is going to listen to them?" said Larsen, tapping his badge lightly. "You're the only one here with a chance in hell of getting anyone to listen. This is not some kind of weak Jedi mind trick, David. You need to get out of here, for everyone's sake. Help isn't coming otherwise."

"I don't know," said David.

"I do," said Larsen, stepping out of his way and putting a hand on his shoulder. "Let me introduce you to Dan's family."

With nothing in his way, real or imagined, David took a deep breath and forced his legs to move.

Chapter Forty

Major Nick Smith scanned the city skyline to the south, disturbed by the volume of smoke rising from the low-lying buildings separating his location at the hospital from the downtown district. He could barely see the skyscrapers through the thick haze at this point. He raised his binoculars and took a closer look. Tall flames poured out of several blackened structures, a number of smaller fires evident in adjacent buildings.

The fires had spread faster and wider than he'd anticipated, steadily advancing on Interstate 65, their primary route out of the city. He didn't think the fire could damage the eight-lane, raised highway, but if it managed to pass underneath and ignite structures north of the interstate, they'd have to reroute the final convoy. Not a huge problem, but the remaining routes would take them through heavily populated residential areas—and most of his higher volume passenger-carrying vehicles were unarmored. The current run from the hospital to the interstate was sketchy enough.

If he succeeded in rescuing the people from the hospital, they needed to do it before the whole place went up in flames. Of course, sneaking a hundred or so people through a militarized quarantine zone wouldn't be easy.

"Major, Dr. Owens is looking for you," announced the

sentry guarding the rooftop access. "Shall I send him up?"

"Yes," said Smith. "I'm at the southeast corner."

"Copy that. He's on his way."

Smith tucked the binoculars in a case attached to his vest and turned away from the burning city. Dr. Owens, dressed in jeans and a deep scarlet ER scrub shirt, walked out of an open doorway set in the cinder-block access enclosure. Owens, a veteran emergency room doctor, was the de facto head of the hospital right now. None of the hospital administration could be found, and most of the physicians had either succumbed to the virus or vanished days ago with the majority of the staff. Owens somehow found himself the spokesperson for one hundred and eighteen souls. One hundred and eighteen people Smith was going to ferry out of here around dark, to make it just a little harder for the drones and surveillance planes.

"Dr. Owens!" said Smith, waving him over.

A crackle of gunfire caused the doctor to duck into a crouch and stop halfway to the edge of the roof. Smith barely registered the noise. Sporadic fits of gunfire were part of the mission's background noise at this point. Nothing to be worried about. Outside of the barrage of gunfire aimed at his convoys, they'd been pretty lucky. The mobs had mostly ignored the hospital and the soldiers guarding it.

They'd had one serious incident during the middle of the morning, when a major gun battle north of the downtown area had drawn hundreds of the infected onto the streets. One of the two-forty gunners got nervous and cut loose a long burst of fire—which attracted dozens of them to the ER parking lot. Instead of applying the military concept of overwhelming firepower superiority against the crowd, and possibly drawing a few hundred to the hospital, he'd gone with a subtler strategy. Distraction.

He'd sent one of the HUMVEEs toward the interstate, guns blazing at the sky. The gimmick managed to draw most of the infected away, where the fireworks to the north proved more tempting than the hospital. His soldiers still had to shoot five civilians who didn't take the bait. They did it with single shots spaced as far apart as possible to cut down on the chance of drawing unwanted attention. The shootings were more like executions than heat-of-the-battle kills. Sergeant Major Riddle and Smith had essentially pulled each trigger, standing next to each soldier when it was their turn to fire.

Smith had originally wanted to do all of the shooting himself, to take that burden off his soldiers' shoulders, but Riddle told him it was a bad idea—that it sent the wrong message. As usual, the sergeant major had been right. The two of them might not be there the next time one of their soldiers faced the same situation. Hesitation in a moment like that could prove fatal for the soldier, and Smith's entire command. He couldn't wait to get the last convoy moving. He was done soldiering for now.

Owens arrived with the same calm expression he'd worn when Smith first met him. He had to give the doctor credit. The guy had stuck around through the worst of it and somehow still managed to look unfazed and under control. Smith could only hope he looked half as measured and competent around his soldiers.

"Major," said Owens, "how goes the war?"

Smith couldn't help laughing. *How goes the war?* Owens was a character—no doubt about that.

"Half the city's on fire," said Smith. "Other than that,

everything's under control."

Owens squinted, looking past Smith. "It'll burn out when it hits the interstate. We have the White River to our west. I hate to say it, but this could be a good thing. The fires will take the infected with it."

Smith had thought of that, too. He just didn't want to admit it.

"We should be gone before the fire becomes an issue, either way," said Smith.

A single gunshot zipped overhead, and Smith stepped away from the parapet, pulling Owens with him. Someone was shooting at them. Unbelievable. A second bullet hit the top of the concrete wall a few seconds after they had left. Not a bad shot, either.

"Contact. Third floor of the building one street over from the hospital annex building. "You want us to respond, Major?"

Smith made eye contact with the lookout situated in the northeast corner, and pointed emphatically due east, in the direction of the gunfire. Another bullet snapped through the air above Smith and Owens.

"Negative," said Smith. "We'll switch to remote surveillance."

They had handheld drones for this kind of thing. It was almost time to put them up again, anyway. The sun was going down, and the convoy was still forty minutes out. The drone teams would run a thorough reconnaissance of the final convoy's primary route out of the downtown area, in addition to scouting some of the alternative routes.

"Hold on a second," he said to Owens before switching to the command and control net. "Riddle, this is Smith."

"Go ahead, sir."

"Overwatch is taking accurate fire. I'd rather not respond and draw any infected to the hospital. Let's get a Raven up to keep an eye on the streets," said Smith.

"Understood. I'll get Vaughn on it right away."

"I'll be down in a few minutes," said Smith, turning back to Owens. "What's up? Everyone ready to roll?"

"They're as ready as they can be," said Owens. "Are we safe up here?"

"Completely. The shooter is in a third-story window a few streets over in that direction," said Smith, pointing toward the ledge they had just been standing beside. "Even if the bullets managed to pass through two feet of concrete, they wouldn't have the angle to hit us."

A gunshot echoed across the rooftop, and the soldier in the nearby corner of the rooftop ducked below the parapet.

"Looks like the shooter lost interest in us," said Smith, motioning for the soldier to stay down.

"Seems pretty accurate—and deliberate," said Owens.

"Yeah. This isn't one of the infected," said Smith. "Probably some antigovernment type who thinks the military is behind all of this."

"What a crazy theory," said Owens, raising an eyebrow.

Smith just shook his head and feigned a thin smile. Part of him still clung to the hope that his government wasn't in any way responsible for the outbreak and that the quarantine effort was genuine. Based on what he'd witnessed inside and outside the city, he knew it wasn't true, which was why he'd decided to help Owens and the remaining hospital staff. Instead of going back down that rabbit hole, he decided not to take the doctor's bait.

"When the convoy returns, we'll load up and wait for dark," said Smith. "It'll make it a little harder for the drones to figure out what's going on."

Owens stared at him for a moment. "This is going to mess things up for you with your command, isn't it?"

"To some degree," said Smith. "Hopefully they'll be too damn busy with this mess they've created to bother with us right away."

"Eventually it'll catch up," said Owens. "When the dust settles, they'll sweep it under the rug, along with anyone that didn't play along."

"Are you saying I should cancel the plan?" said Smith, a little concerned. "Leave you all here to fend for yourselves?"

"No. No. Sorry. That didn't come out right," said Owens. "I'm a little tired. What I meant to say is thank you. Should have started with that."

"Might have been a better start," said Smith.

"Seriously. Everyone down there appreciates what you're risking," said Owens. "And they probably don't know the half of it. I think half of them are in some kind of low-grade shock. The past few days have been unreal."

"I wish we could do more for them," said Smith. "I can't imagine what some of them are dealing with."

"Getting them out of the city and keeping them away from the quarantine camps is like winning the lottery," said Owens.

"Strange lottery," said Smith. "Stay here and die, or get dropped off in the middle of nowhere, with the clothes on your back and a few MREs. Make sure you go over everything again—with everyone," said Smith. "If just one of them fucks up, the whole group will be hunted down and rounded up."

"I've been through it a dozen times with them," said Owens. "They wait until sunrise before placing the first call. We stagger the calls. Stagger the pickups. Spread out. Stay hidden. No calls to law enforcement. No variations from the plan."

Smith was about to speak, when Owens continued. "We've already labeled and collected the phones. The whole plan is on paper, copied multiple times and distributed to group leaders. Everybody is on board and understands the risks of messing this up."

"That won't stop some of them from trying," said Smith.

"We chose the group leaders carefully," said Owens. "And I've recruited a few enforcers."

"Enforcers?" said Smith.

"One's a hospital security guard. Big dude. We actually used to call him the enforcer. He'd show up in the ER when there was an issue and everything calmed down on its own."

Smith laughed. "Sounds like the sergeant major."

"Pretty much," said Owens. "I have a few more on the job. They're already floating back and forth listening for signs of trouble."

"That's all you can do," said Smith.

"What about your soldiers?" said Owens.

"We've brought about a dozen or so into the fold," said Smith. "The rest won't suspect anything is off until we stop and unload your group. Even then, we've come up with a cover story. We'll say we got ordered back into the city immediately to support a trapped unit and had to dump your group. We'll head toward Indianapolis for ten minutes and then learn that the other National Guard unit managed to break out on their own. Something like that."

"Something like that?" said Owens.

"That's about as good as it gets on my end," said Smith. "Once we get back to our forward operating base, the soldiers will be dismissed to get some sleep. They won't be up and mingling with the rest of the battalion until mid-morning—if the rest of the battalion is even there. I'll go right into some kind of after-action briefing, give a basic account of what happened, then be sent to get some rest. I just don't see anyone piecing it together anytime soon."

Owens stared at him with a puzzled look.

"What?" said Smith.

"I can't imagine any scenario that doesn't involve your soldiers going into a temporary quarantine," said Owens. "They'll want to know about everything. Where they've been. What they've seen. I think you're underestimating the full scope of what's going on here—and the government's interest in keeping the street-level details secret."

Smith shook his head. "Damn. I hadn't thought of that. I just assumed since they owned us, they wouldn't worry about us."

"Seriously. You're witness to ground zero. I mean—I don't want to sound like a conspiracy theory nut, which I am, but I wouldn't be surprised if they sprayed you down and hauled you away for *observation*," he said, using air quotes. "Somewhere in the middle of a fifty-mile-by-fifty-mile cornfield—never to be seen again."

"Damn you, Owens," hissed Smith.

"Sorry. I've always been a glass half empty kind of guy."

"Fuck. This is more than a half-empty glass," said Smith. "More like smashed over my head."

"Good thing you're wearing that helmet."

"Funny," said Smith, catching some chatter in his headset. "Raven's up."

Owens looked around as a faint buzzing washed over the rooftop.

"Headed east," said Smith, scanning the sky over the rooftop wall. "There."

A delicate-looking gray aircraft rose skyward at a steep angle.

"Looks like a toy," said Owens.

"Its wingspan isn't much bigger than your arm span," said Smith. "But it's rugged enough, and it's all we have watching over us at this point."

"Godspeed, Mr. Raven," said Owens, saluting the drone.

"More like God help us."

Chapter Forty-One

Laura Ragan wiped the sweat from her face before taking a long sip from her lukewarm, nearly empty CamelBak. She leaned her perspiration-soaked head against the inside of the ambulance and closed her eyes, willing the sun to go down. When she opened them, the deep orange orb was no farther along its downward trajectory than it had been a few seconds ago.

A quick glance at her watch told her they had another thirty-three minutes until it sank below the horizon. They should wait at least another hour before venturing out of the ambulance, but she knew it would be a tough sell. Without even looking at them, she could tell that her team was on the verge of mutiny. They had been trapped in the sweltering, cramped patient-care compartment for most of the afternoon, waiting for dark, when it should be possible for them to move safely on foot to Chang's apartment. It was definitely not safe for them to transit in the daylight. They'd learned that lesson the hard way, and it had cost them a member of their team.

Ragan didn't want to think about it. Not that she had the option. She'd hear Boyd's screams for the rest of her days. They all would. His death had been completely unexpected, and entirely avoidable—if Control had bothered to give them any indication of the true problem inside the quarantine zone. But they hadn't.

She had been warned to avoid contact with law enforcement or military patrols, and to steer clear of quarantine boundary checkpoints. Control clearly didn't want anyone questioning their purpose or mission inside the quarantine zone. Maybe that should have been enough of a warning. Then again, how could she have guessed what was truly happening in the city? Even now Ragan barely believed it, and she'd witnessed something unthinkable.

Their mission had proceeded relatively well despite being rerouted twice. They had driven to the recommended point along Interstate 465, where her team crossed on foot with little difficulty. National Guard vehicle patrols were surprisingly predictable and sparse. After hiking several blocks into the northern outskirts of the city, they hotwired a pickup truck parked on the street and carefully made their way south.

A few tense encounters with bands of desperate civilians left them spooked by the time they reached Interstate 65, but they still hadn't seen anything the team couldn't handle with the firepower at their disposal. Their brief trip along the deserted highway compounded that false sense of security. When they reached an impassible traffic jam less than a mile from Chang's apartment, Ragan led them off the interstate on foot. All hell broke loose a few minutes into their trek.

It started with a small group of hecklers in an apartment building, yelling and throwing bottles down at them. Ragan ignored the racket and moved the team down the sidewalk in a staggered column formation, with Boyd walking point. The first real indication of trouble came a few seconds later, when a shirtless man bolted out of the same apartment building, carrying a shovel. Several feet behind Boyd, Ragan quickly halted her team with hand signals and engaged the hostile target.

By the time she had pressed the trigger, Boyd had wandered dangerously far away from the team, unaware that the team had been halted—until he heard that first shot. If he'd sprinted back to the team immediately at that point, he'd be sweating it out in the ambulance. Instead, he crouched and methodically fired at a cluster of lunatics that had sprinted around the corner of the apartment building on the other side of the street, ignoring her frantic order to retreat.

Dozens of frenzied people, many of them armed with household weapons, flooded the team from every direction, leaving her no choice but to fall back to their vehicle on the interstate. When Boyd finally realized his predicament, it was too late. She'd kept the rest of the team in a tight formation for as long as she could, until it was clear that they couldn't stay in place another moment longer without being overrun.

Unable to divert any of their frantic gunfire to help Boyd, the father of three was knocked down within seconds, vanishing under a mound of bloodthirsty lunatics. His screams distracted the crazies long enough for Ragan's team to gain some ground and get back to the interstate, where they expended much of their remaining ammunition to cut their pursuers down.

Instead of driving away from Chang's apartment, they used the long rows of vehicles to channel the few remaining crazies into their gunfire before they took refuge in an abandoned ambulance. The more she thought about it, the less she wanted to step outside this protective metal shell. She wasn't sure if night would be any different out there. The city's power grid was still working, from what she could tell, which nullified any advantage their state-of-the-art night-vision gear offered.

Her eyes drifted shut; a light kick to the shin snapped her back in focus.

"Now you're tired?" said McDermott, her second in command. "You should have racked out all afternoon."

"Someone had to keep an eye out with all of your snoring," said Ragan.

"It's not that bad," said McDermott.

Pablo Cordova, a former Marine Raider, stretched his arms and yawned. "You were shaking the whole fucking ambulance, hoss."

"Yeah. I was worried you'd attract some of our new friends," said Ragan.

When neither of them reacted to her comment, she quickly realized they weren't ready for jokes about any of the insanity they had witnessed off the interstate. She took another sip of her water, the pressure required to draw another mouthful from the CamelBak increasing. One more swig and she'd be empty. She looked up at McDermott, who spit his water bladder hose out, shaking his head.

"Empty," he said.

"I have one more sip," she said. "You're welcome to it."

He shook his head. "We'll grab some water on the way over."

Cordova pinched the bridge of his nose before running his hand along his shaved head and wiping the accumulated sweat on his pants.

"So what's our move?" said Cordova.

"We wait until the sun goes down and then follow the interstate to the closest point of approach to Chang's apartment. The southbound side of the highway is a parking lot as far as I can see. We'll move between vehicles, watching and listening for signs of trouble."

"We didn't get much warning last time," said Cordova.

"No. We didn't," she said. "And they still haven't said shit. Nothing new on the tablet."

McDermott used his rifle to lift himself off the ambulance floor. "I say we follow the yellow brick road right out of fucking town and skip round two of *don't get eaten by your neighbor.*"

"They weren't eating him," said Ragan.

"Well, they weren't giving him a neck and shoulder massage."

"We've been given a midnight extract at the top of the parking garage next to Chang's apartment building," said Ragan. "That's a little more than a mile away. Following the yellow brick road out of here, as you so colorfully stated, puts us on Interstate 70 for several miles— through heavily populated areas."

"At least we'd be on the highway," said McDermott. "Better than the city streets."

"I don't disagree with that, but they know exactly where we are at all times," she said, removing her CTAB from the pouch on her vest.

"That fucking thing. A lot of good it's done us," said McDermott. "This whole thing has been a shit show since we landed."

"We have a job to do," said Ragan, firming her tone.

"I know," said McDermott. "I just don't get the impression that Control has a good handle on the overall situation."

"They probably don't," said Ragan. "And they probably don't care. They just want Chang."

"That's the kind of myopic vision that gets people killed."

"It's in our hands to keep that from happening," said Ragan. "We'll approach cautiously. If we can't get near Chang's apartment, I'll pull the plug on this."

McDermott still looked skeptical. "We're low on ammo. Keep that in mind."

"It's right next to finding us some water," said Ragan, checking her watch. "Thirty minutes and we'll recon the area. If all goes well, we'll be at the target inside of an hour."

"Or eaten alive," said McDermott, with a deadpan face.

"Nobody is getting eaten," said Ragan.

Cordova chuckled, followed quickly by McDermott.

"I'm just fucking with you," said McDermott. "But the first sign of trouble, and I'm hauling ass, with or without you."

"You're forgetting something," said Ragan, drawing a puzzled look from McDermott. "I'm faster than you."

"Shit. Then you don't have anything to worry about," said McDermott.

They all laughed quietly before settling in to wait for the sun to trace its final path below the horizon. It would be a long thirty minutes—spent worrying.

Chapter Forty-Two

Larsen and Chang cracked dozens of glow sticks, arranging them on the ground in the shape of an arrow. The ten-foot-long multicolor beacon had been placed in the grass at the center of the flower garden area, pointing east in the direction of the night's prevailing wind. The air had been relatively calm until about seven, when it kicked up to a steady five to seven knots. Normally nothing to worry about, but they were working with a hundred-and-fifty-foot-diameter drop zone, which didn't leave a lot of room for error.

They had turned off all of the lights casting illumination on the enclosed common area so the arrow would be visible with night vision from high above. If Terrence's people were as good as the man claimed, the impromptu beacon should be all they needed to execute a precision landing. Larsen had landed in far tighter spaces, with no ground markers. He snapped the last glow stick, which engulfed his hand in a bright red light, and placed it next to a pale green stick at the tip of the arrow.

He glanced at Chang, who stared up at the dark blue sky. "Any updates from Greenberg?"

"Nothing since the late afternoon," said Chang. "No news is good news. Right?"

"I guess," said Larsen, looking east over the one-story

structure surrounding the common garden area.

The lighter blue sky blended less and less with the deepening shades of night closing in on the horizon, the scattered clouds no longer reflecting orange or yellow colors. Any remaining vestige of day would be erased within the next twenty minutes. He really had hoped to be on his way to the plane by now, but at this point they had no choice but to wait for their new friends. It was too dangerous to leave on their own.

Not only had Chang grabbed the data he'd hidden in his lab, but he'd also downloaded all of the NT-HSE893 vaccine research, which he intended to deliver to Greenberg, along with his analysis of the virus samples. Even Larsen understood the significance of getting this information into the right hands—and it wouldn't hurt to have four experienced shooters escort them to Chang's aircraft. If his limited experience on these mean streets had taught him anything, it was that anything could happen.

A gust of warm, smoky air swept through the garden, momentarily obscuring the illuminated beacon. Anything could happen.

"David, this is Larsen."

"Go ahead," replied David, who was situated with the rooftop sniper guarding the fence breach.

"We just had a thick blanket of smoke roll over the drop zone," said Larsen. "What's happening out there?"

"Other than fires everywhere?"

"Yes. Other than fires everywhere," said Larsen, shaking his head. "Unless it's that simple."

"I think the wind shifted about fifteen degrees, coming a little more out of the northwest. There are some big fires out that way," said David.

"Do you think it'll be a problem for the drop?"

"I don't think so. It's a variable wind," said David. "I'll let you know if it steadies from the northwest."

"All right," said Larsen. "Chang hasn't received an update, so we'll hang out here and wait."

"Are you sure you don't want backup down there?" said David.

"If we can't trust these guys, we're really screwed," said Larsen.

"I suppose if this was some kind of setup, they'd have flown those helicopters in already."

"It's truly out of our hands."

Larsen sensed a shift in the ambient lighting outside the enclosed garden area. The sky somehow got a little crisper. Almost brighter.

"Did something just happen out there?" said Larsen.

"The city just lost power," said David. "But NevoTech is fine."

"All stations, this is Hoenig. The campus is running on auxiliary power from battery and generator backup. Security systems are unaffected."

"Gary, this is David. You might want to figure out how to kill the external campus lights. My guess is that this blackout will empty out every apartment and house in the city. Those fancy Central Park-looking lamps inside the fence will attract a lot of unwanted attention."

"Shit. I don't know the first thing about the auxiliary or emergency lighting," said Hoenig.

"Then you might want to consider dispatching teams to shoot out the lights," said David. "We can take care of about two dozen from our rooftop perch."

"I don't think that's a good idea with our new friends arriving any minute," said Larsen.

"This is a matter of life or death for the campus in the long run," said David. "Not to mention our little escapade out of here."

"I agree," said Larsen.

"What's happening?" said Chang, from a nearby stone bench.

Larsen took his hand off the transmit button. "Power grid failed in the city. We're trying to figure out how to shut down the external campus lights."

"Jesus. They'll be all over this place," said Chang.

"My sentiments exactly. Maybe we should just head to the plane right now. You can leave the thumb drives and stuff with Hoenig."

His earpiece crackled. "This is Fitzgerald. I'm down in the cafeteria. One of the women here works in facilities maintenance. She doesn't deal with the power, but she knows where we might be able to figure something out."

Hoenig answered before Larsen could comment. "Mitch is on his way. When he arrives, I want the two of you to figure this out."

"Understood," said Fitzgerald. "She seems to think this is going to take a while, so you might want to go with David's plan for now."

"Roscoe, David, hit as many lights as possible from your position. When you're done, I'll send out a team with one of the suppressed rifles to clear the eastern lights. Give you guys a break when you make your run for the plane."

"Thanks, Gary," said David.

A string of gunshots echoed through the common area.

"If Chang's friends don't hurry the fuck up, we're leaving without them," said Larsen. "Lights or no lights.

Things are about to get busy out there."

"Does anyone else hear that?" said David, over the net.

"Hear what?" said Larsen.

"Sounds like an airplane," said a voice that Larsen was pretty sure belonged to Roscoe.

"Definitely an airplane," said David. "Coming in fast."

Larsen cocked his head, finally hearing the deep buzz of an approaching aircraft. If this was the team sent to escort Chang, they were flying way too low for a parachute jump. He flipped his night-vision goggles into place and ran toward the luminescent beacon in the center of the garden, craning his head skyward.

"Son of a bitch!" he yelled.

"What?" said Chang, jumping to his feet.

The night-vision goggles caught the silhouette of a uniquely designed aircraft, which streaked directly overhead before pulling into a steep climb.

"Hot damn!" said Larsen. "Where the fuck did they find one of those?"

"One of what?" yelled Chang, sliding into place next to him.

"It's hard to explain. Ever hear of the OV-10 Bronco?"

"I've had a private pilot's license for more than twenty years," said Chang. "Civilian OV-10s are pretty fucking rare."

"Well, that's what you're hearing right now. An OV-10 Bronco in a steep climb," said Larsen. "Powerful fucking aircraft. I saw the twin boom and stabilizers. Unmistakable."

"So much for the corporate jet."

"No way they could have pulled off a high-altitude

jump from a civilian jet without hijacking it," said Larsen.

"I got the impression that was part of the plan," said Chang.

"This is better," said Larsen, studying the vague outline of the aircraft.

The murky green aircraft grew smaller as it climbed, eventually disappearing into the dark green sky. Four dark objects took its place a few moments later.

"I have four parachutes," said Larsen. "Do you know how they jump out of a Bronco?"

"Through a door?" said Chang. "Like every other aircraft?"

"Not exactly. The Bronco has a small cargo area, with a rear-facing hatch, which can accommodate five paratroopers. Jumpers sit nut to butt in the cargo hold and basically slide out of the aircraft when it climbs. Gravity does all of the work."

"Nut to butt?" said Chang.

"Just like it sounds," said Larsen. "Snuggled tightly. Nut to butt."

"I see," said Chang. "Where are they now?"

"Headed right toward us," said Larsen, backing up quickly. "Let's give them some room."

They retreated to the doors in front of the two-story glass lobby, Larsen watching the amorphous dark shapes morph into square parachutes supporting heavily laden parachutists. The parachutists executed a lazy circle over the drop zone, settling in for an easterly approach, directly into the prevailing wind. The four heavily laden operators released their combat equipment loads when they crossed into the open area, the bundles pulling taut under them—seconds before they landed. The team hit the drop zone a few seconds apart, none of them straying more than twenty feet from the ad hoc beacon. As their parachutes deflated, Larsen put a hand on Chang's shoulder.

"Stay here. If anything happens, run inside and head to the security hub."

"Nothing is going to happen," said Chang.

"I hope not," said Larsen, stepping out of the shadows.

The first parachutist to slip out of his rig immediately headed in his direction, sliding a compact rifle out of a rigged thigh bag and pointing it in Larsen's direction.

"Where's Chang?" she said.

She. There was no doubt about her voice.

"Chang's close by," said Larsen, extending a hand. "Welcome to the hot zone."

The operative ignored the gesture, glancing past him. "He's over here!"

Larsen lowered his hand and stepped toward her, gripping his rifle tightly, but keeping it pointed toward the ground. She didn't react. Instead, she glanced over her shoulder at the rest of her team, which was already on the move. When they reached her, she stepped to the side.

"Larsen?" said the lead operative, offering his hand. "Richard. Or just Rich."

"She didn't seem too keen on shaking hands," said Larsen, keeping both of his hands on his rifle.

"She's not very friendly," said the man.

"Neither am I," said Larsen.

"Then it's probably a good thing we won't be hanging out for long."

"Nice entry, by the way," said Larsen. "Haven't seen an OV-10 in a long time."

"The pilot wasn't very happy with the final details, but

he made a lot of money for a two-hour flight," said Rich. "Assuming he doesn't land in federal custody. No pun intended."

"We need to get moving," said one of Rich's men.

Larsen appreciated the sense of urgency. Given the sudden loss of city power, they really needed to get to Chang's aircraft sooner rather than later.

"I'll take you to the security hub for a quick mission briefing; then we'll get the hell out of here," said Larsen. "City power just went out. Not sure if you guys caught that."

Rich shook his head. "We've been screaming along fifty feet above the trees for the past thirty minutes, facing backward. How long has the power been out?"

"Five minutes," said Larsen. "Still. It's going to complicate things out there."

"Can we skip the briefing?" said Rich. "Things will get worse with the dark."

"We need a few minutes to get everyone on the same page," said Larsen. "We're moving with a mixed bag of people."

"All right," he said before glancing past Larsen. "Dr. Chang?"

"Yes?" said the scientist, still lurking in the shadows.

"Dr. Greenberg sends his regards. He's an amazing man," said Rich. "We're lucky to have him."

"Can you really get us out of here?" said Chang.

"That's our only mission," he said. "To keep you safe."

Larsen didn't like the sound of that, given their previous conversation with this guy's boss, not that there was anything he could do to stop them if they tried to take Chang. He could tell this was a serious group. The kind of operatives you didn't cross unless you had a death wish.

"Follow me," said Larsen, hoping this wasn't a colossal mistake.

Chapter Forty-Three

David didn't like what he saw when he entered the security hub. The four operatives sent to retrieve Chang's data and help them to the aircraft looked like bad news, casting furtive looks around the room and whispering among each other right in front of everyone. They wore the kind of hardened façades he'd only seen on career criminals. Types that would sell their own mothers to human traffickers if it got them ahead in the world. This crew would steal Chang at the first opportunity. He was convinced of it.

"That's everyone," said Larsen. "This is David. He's a local police officer—"

The female operative sneered and whispered something to the even scarier looking guy next to her.

"Problem?" said Larsen.

She shook her head, remaining expressionless. Who the hell were these people?

"David is also a former Marine and has been instrumental in getting Chang and the rest of us here alive. He'll take point, followed by—"

"I'm Rich. One of my people will take point," he said. "We're responsible for getting Chang to his aircraft safely."

"David knows what he's—" started Larsen.

"I'm fine with it," said David. "Believe me. More than fine with it." He didn't intend to stray more than a few feet from his son out there.

"All right. One of your people takes point," said Larsen. "We'll be moving along the eastern fence, so we'll only have to cover one hundred and eight degrees."

"Negative," said Rich. "We need to breach the fence at the closest point of approach to the aircraft. From what I understand, you can't win a running gun battle against the infected. Not in the numbers present in the city. We need to minimize our time on the outside."

David tried not to react visibly. *Minimize our time on the outside?* How did that make any sense? They planned to walk out of here with Chang's data after getting him to the aircraft. Or maybe they had different plans.

"No way," said Hoenig. "Nobody is breaching anything. I have close to two hundred people here counting on that fence."

"I didn't mean blow a hole in your fence," said Rich. "There has to be some kind of access gate. Something closer than the gate you're proposing."

"There isn't," said Hoenig. "Due to the close proximity to the interstate, we get no pedestrian traffic from that direction, hence no need for a gate of any kind. Deliveries and executive vehicles enter through gates on the western side of the campus."

"All we need is a few fucking ladders tall enough to reach the top of the fence," said one of the operatives. "Seriously. This isn't rocket science. We're on a one-way trip. Right?"

"He has a point," said Larsen.

"Are you sure you can climb a ladder?" said the female operator.

The man standing next to her gently nudged her with his elbow, giving her an oddly warm look under the circumstances.

"I'm fine," said Larsen. "Not the first time I got a boo-boo. Can we find some ladders?"

He kept watching the two of them, noticing that they stood awfully close to each other for mercenary commandos. If he had to guess, he'd say they were a couple. A close couple.

"Hold on," said Hoenig, adjusting his microphone. "Fitz, you guys find the breakers yet?"

"Negative," said Fitzgerald, his voice amplified in the room. "We're still stumbling around the maintenance building. It's a big facility."

"Have you seen any ladders?" said Hoenig.

"Ladders?"

"Yes. Metal. Wood. Any kind of ladders," said Hoenig.

"Yeah. We just passed through the landscaping garage. All kinds of ladders in there."

"How tall are the fences?" said Hoenig.

"Ten feet?" said Fitzgerald.

"That's about right," said Larsen.

"Fitz, I need you guys to grab the sturdiest-looking ladders in the garage. Anything that will reach more than fifteen feet. We're putting Larsen and his crew over the fence. Use your best judgment."

"Easy enough," said Fitzgerald. "Where do you want them?"

"Southeast corner of campus," said Hoenig. "We're putting them over as close as possible to their aircraft."

"Give us about twenty to thirty minutes," said Fitzgerald.

"Thirty minutes," said Rich. "Nothing takes twenty minutes."

"They're hauling ladders three-quarters of the way across campus," said Hoenig. "It'll take you ten minutes to even find the maintenance building. This is a big place."

While the newly arrived commandos grumbled, David decided to clear the air—or muddy the waters. It all depended on your perspective.

"Before we step off, I want to make something clear to the four of you," said David.

"Okay," said Rich, with a smug look.

"I don't know what your game is," said David. "But if you try to keep us off the aircraft, or snag Chang before we get to the aircraft, I will kill at least one of you. That might be all my meager police officer abilities allow me to accomplish, but I guarantee I'll take one of you with me."

"Jesus," said Rich. "You need to fucking chill out. Seriously. That's not what this is about."

"Really?" said David.

"Really," said Rich, actually looking sympathetic for a change. "I'd love for Dr. Chang to accept our invitation to slip out of the city without risking his life in the skies above, but he's made it clear that he's going to fly you, your son and the other couple to safety. I've accepted that. My boss has accepted that. That's the plan. No tricks. No bullshit."

David searched their faces, seeing nothing hostile. Most of them wore neutral masks, probably the result of doing this kind of work for years. Their leader looked genuine, though he quickly defaulted to his own version of a dispassionate expression.

"Chang?" said David. "What do you think?"

The scientist rubbed his face before taking a few steps toward the middle of the room.

"Greenberg trusts them," said Chang. "If Greenberg trusts them, so do I. And if the rumors are true, some of them have seen this before. Firsthand."

"Seen what?" said David.

"Whatever is going on in this city," said Chang. "A small unsanctioned group of American operatives are responsible for bringing this virus to Greenberg's attention. I believe a few of them are standing in this room."

The operative named Rich and the man standing next to the woman nodded at the same time.

"The mission was sanctioned by the U.S. government," said Rich. "Pretty far off the books, but sanctioned nonetheless."

"You've seen this before?" said Larsen.

"In Russia, but not on this scale," said the leader. "We entered a city of less than one hundred thousand mostly infected people. The Russians crushed that city. They basically executed an entire city, infected and uninfected alike."

"I never heard of any of this," said Jack Harper, who stood next to David's son.

"Nobody has," said Rich. "The U.S. government. The E.U., Russia. They kept this really quiet, for obvious reasons."

"We're wasting time," said the man standing close to the female operative.

"Then let's get moving," said Larsen.

David interjected. "We won't need a point man, or woman, if we're taking the closest point of approach. Is it fair to assume that your team is extremely proficient with their rifles?"

"Five in five times three stationary," said Rich. "Times two moving."

"Say what?" said David.

"Five headshots in five seconds against stationary targets. Three times in a row before a miss," said Rich. "Two times in a row against moving targets."

"That's pretty fucking good," said Larsen.

"Pretty fucking good?" said the female operator.

"Exceptional," said Larsen, looking at David. "Where were you going with your comment?"

"These four will defend the primary threat axis, shifting and reacting proactively," said David. "The rest of us will handle the easy shit."

"Sounds like a plan," said Rich. "Are we done here?"

"Almost," said Hoenig. "Overwatch reports helicopters inbound."

"Fuck," said Larsen.

"What's wrong?" said Rich.

"This can't be a coincidence," said Larsen, glancing at his watch. "This isn't the first flight of helicopters to spend some time in the area. They're probably responding to the OV-10 flyover."

"Then we wait for them to leave," said Rich.

"What if they don't?" said Emma Harper.

"Then we take them out," said the man still standing near the female operative.

"Three helicopters armed with miniguns?" said Larsen.

"Let's hope it doesn't come to that," said Rich. "My colleagues get a little excited when it comes to helicopters."

"We'll wait them out," said David. "One hundred rounds per second kind of intimidates me."

Everyone briefly laughed, finally cutting the tension in the room.

Chapter Forty-Four

Scaling the fence turned out to be far easier than Larsen expected. They placed two expandable, reinforced aluminum ladders side by side against the fence, and Rich's team was up and over within ten seconds. They fanned out, forming a tight screen around the landing point, and scanned for targets. To help those in the group who were not equipped with night-vision gear, Fitzgerald shined a flashlight fitted with a red lens at the ground on the other side. David and his son were next, dropping to the grass on the other side and rolling to absorb the impact of the ten-foot fall. Larsen cringed when they hit the ground. No amount of rolling was going to help his leg.

"Good knowing you, man," said Fitzgerald, holding a hand out for him.

He shook the security officer's hand, patting him on the shoulder.

"If the fence is breached," said Larsen. "Make sure Gary collapses everything on the main auditorium and seals that section. The cafeteria is open to the outside windows."

"I've talked to him about that," said Fitzgerald. "Good luck."

"You too," said Larsen, turning to the Harpers. "Up and over."

He followed closely behind the couple, making sure they didn't get caught up on the decorative spikes at the top of the fence.

"One at a time," he said. "Emma, you first."

Jack gripped her arm, steadying her as she placed her feet on the top rail of the fence, between the spikes. David stood below, coaxing her into jumping. A few moments later, Emma dropped on top of David, the two of them tumbling onto the concrete sidewalk in a tangled mess. Jack flung himself over in pursuit, landing in a deep crouch that must have pulverized half of the cartilage in his knees. The three of them were on their feet a few seconds later.

Chang was next, nimbly rolling to his right and taking a position next to one of the new operatives. Damn. That was too smooth. David glanced up and nodded, moving toward the fence to help him. Timing David's arrival, Larsen stepped between the spikes and launched himself forward, dropping like a rock onto the hard ground, his legs buckling to the point of near failure. He rose slowly and unsurely on his injured limb, shifting his rifle into position.

"Let's go," he said.

"You handled that landing like a pro," said Rich.

"Not my first rodeo," said Larsen.

"SEAL?"

"That obvious?"

"I was briefed," said Rich. "The guy on point was a SEAL."

"What about the rest of you?" said Larsen.

"It's a little more complicated than that."

"Sounds like the kind of story you tell with a few drinks."

Rich chuckled. "More like a few bottles."

A suppressed gunshot cut their conversation short.

"That's our cue," said Rich.

Two more snaps cut through the night.

"Twenty plus tangos approaching from the north," said the female operative. "Fucking helicopters started a party."

"I don't think they're headed in our direction," said Larsen.

The mass of people lingered in the street, stopping at the fence. A few decorative lampposts still shined deeper inside NevoTech's campus. The sooner Hoenig figured out the lighting situation, the better. A sharp metal-against-metal screech pierced Larsen's ears; one of the ladders scraped against the inside of the fence and slammed into the ground. One of the security guards must have knocked it over.

"They're headed in our direction now," she said.

Rich's team moved without any further coordination, creating a human shield facing north along East Street. They fired methodically and rapidly, their suppressors quieter than anything Larsen knew existed. Within ten seconds, the mass of approaching crazies had been stopped dead in their tracks. Literally. Several infected citizens poured onto the street, reacting to the cries of the fallen, and were dispatched just as quickly. The efficiency of their gunfire was unparalleled. The street quieted, remaining still—until more people appeared in the distance, followed by more gunshots and screaming.

"I suggest we get out of here," said Rich.

"David, it's you, me and Josh screening the front," said Larsen. "Rich's people will cover the city threat."

"Moving out," said David before starting across East Street.

David took them through the small park they had used to hide after leaving Chang's aircraft. The body of the man Larsen had shot between the eyes this morning lay undisturbed at the opposite end of the grassy flat, his feet still in the bushes where he'd suddenly emerged.

Larsen glanced around, making sure the park was empty. He paused long enough to guide Jack and Emma Harper toward David and Joshua.

"Can you guys see at all?" said Larsen.

"Barely," said Jack. "But enough to follow."

"Stay as close as you can to David," said Larsen. "I'll be right behind you. Chang?"

"Right here," said Chang, appearing to his left.

"Get in front of me," said Larsen, grabbing Chang's vest and tugging him forward. "Follow the Harpers."

"I can't see a thing," said Chang.

"You'll be fine. Once we get out of this little park, we'll head down the embankment to your airplane. Do not approach the plane until we clear the area around it," said Larsen before whispering forcefully over his shoulder, "How are we doing back there?"

Two operatives pushed through the bushes into the park, one of them splitting off to the right, where the dead body lay, the other heading in his direction.

"So far so good," said Rich. "We're mopping up stragglers as they appear, but I think we made a relatively clean break. They seem more focused on the fence."

"It's those damn lights on campus," said Larsen.

"Not our problem," said Rich. "I'm going to leave my team in the park for now. They can cover the city approaches. We just have to worry about the interstate. Let's go."

They broke through the bushes, heading down the grassy embankment toward the rest of the group. David and Joshua had already reached the airplane, spreading out to clear the exterior. Chang waited with the Harpers on the embankment.

"He really landed a fucking plane on the interstate?" said Rich.

"Yeah," said Larsen. "It was either that or face off against an Apache helicopter. I figured we were dead either way."

"You probably should be," said Rich. "How is he going to take off without lights?"

"The aircraft should have taxi lights," said Larsen.

"I meant runway lights," said Rich. "At a hundred and fifty miles per hour, I don't think taxi lights are going to be much use."

They reached Chang and the Harpers a few seconds later.

"You have headlights, right?" said Larsen.

"Taxi and landing lights," said Chang.

"Is that enough to take off?" said Larsen.

"It's a straight length of interstate," said Chang. "As long as it's still clear, I just need to see the lines right in front of me."

"Fuck," muttered Rich.

"I have to admit, this sounded better in theory than in reality," said Larsen.

"I'm just throwing this out there. So don't read anything into it," said Rich. "We can get all of you out of here on foot. It'll take a good twenty-four to forty-eight hours to do it right, but—I don't think I'd want to take my chances flying out."

A quick whistle drew his attention to the airplane. David stood in front of the propeller, giving him a thumbs-up.

"Chang?" said Larsen. "It's up to you. I'm good with either option."

"It's not just up to me," said Chang. "Everyone gets a say. Jack? Emma?"

Jack shrugged his shoulders. "Can you do it without lights?"

"As long as the highway is clear."

Larsen peered west down Interstate 70. "There's a car in the breakdown lane about four hundred yards from this overpass."

"I can hug the left until we get past it," said Chang. "Throttle up after that. We'll have plenty of highway left for the takeoff."

"I'd rather get the hell out of here," said Emma.

"That settles it for me," said Jack.

"David was pretty clear about his feelings," said Larsen. "He wanted to fly out."

"Then that's it. Get everyone loaded up and get out of here," said Rich. "Dr. Chang, get in touch with Greenberg when you land. They'll work out a way to get you to safety."

"Got it," said Chang. "Good luck out there. Stay safe."

"Will do," said Rich. "Larsen, what's your plan after this?"

"As long as Chang is in good hands, I'm headed west to meet up with my family," said Larsen.

"They're safe from this?"

"From the virus. Yes. From whoever is behind all of this? I don't know," said Larsen. "That's why I need to get to them as quickly as possible."

"I'll fly you to Colorado," said Chang. "I owe you that much."

"One step at a time," said Larsen. "We can hash this out later, once we've safely landed outside the quarantine zone."

Muted snaps cut through the night, turning all of their heads toward the park above them.

"Get out of here. Now," said Rich.

Larsen guided Chang down the rest of the embankment toward the plane, where David and Joshua waited. He looked back when they reached the highway shoulder, seeing that Rich had already retreated to the thick bushes framing the interstate side of the park, presumably watching over them from the high ground.

"How's it look?" said Chang, stepping onto the highway.

"The exterior looks fine," said David. "The cabin is clear. You want us in the same places?"

"That seemed to work out well last time," said Chang.

"Worked out well for everyone with seats," said David, patting Chang on the shoulder. "Just kidding. We're fine in back."

Larsen's attention drifted to the park above them. The rate of gunfire had increased, contrary to what he'd expected.

"We need to get out of here right now."

Chapter Forty-Five

Chang nudged the throttle forward, coaxing the aircraft forward along the highway. The moment he was clear of the overpass, he lightly tapped the right wheel brake, turning him toward the center of the highway. When the aircraft responded, he let off the brake and steered with the rudder pedal. Within seconds, he was pointed west, down their makeshift runway.

"Ready?" said Chang.

"Not really," said David, from the back of the cargo compartment. "Just kidding. Please get us out of here, Dr. Chang."

He flipped the switches for the taxi and landing lights, illuminating the highway and the concrete structure framing the overpass. Chang centered the plane between the guardrail on the right and concrete supports suspending East Street above the interstate—and throttled forward. The aircraft rapidly picked up speed, hurtling down the pavement, into the inky dark abyss ahead.

Chang eased the Cessna left, using the dashed lane markers to center the fuselage between the left two lanes of the four-lane highway, where they would avoid the vehicle stopped on the shoulder. The aircraft gained more speed, swiftly outpacing the illumination cast by the taxi lights on the road ahead of them.

"Let me know when we're past the stranded car!" said Chang.

He intended to go full throttle at that point, getting them airborne as quickly as possible. Larsen leaned toward the center of the cockpit, trying to get a clear view of the road ahead through his night-vision goggles.

"Coming up fast," said Larsen. "Three. Two. One. That's it! All clear."

Chang eased them into the center of the highway and pushed the throttle forward.

"Hang on, everyone! Here we go!"

The plane lurched forward, its dependable three-hundred-horsepower engine buzzing steadily. Everything felt and sounded right. He just needed the airspeed at this point. Maybe five more seconds. Once they were a few hundred feet in the air, he'd ease them into a steady leftward ascent, leveling off at five hundred feet. He'd stay at that altitude until they passed over Interstate 465, the inner quarantine boundary, where he'd drop to two hundred feet and change course to throw off any ground patrols that spotted them. Then they were home free!

"Turn left!" screamed Larsen. "Turn left!"

He fought every instinct to react, knowing that any sudden pedal or brake maneuver at this speed would be disastrous. They'd careen into the concrete center median or spin into the guardrail on to the right almost instantaneously, crippling the aircraft and likely killing all of them. Instead, he throttled back, hoping that the plane would slow down quickly enough for him to use the pedals to steer. His hope was short-lived.

A figure appeared briefly in the aircraft's lights, zooming past Larsen's window and striking the right wing with a heavy thud. Everyone screamed, and for a few seconds, Chang thought they might be okay. He even started to throttle back up for takeoff—before a metallic, crunching sound from the right side of the aircraft changed his mind. He brought the aircraft to a stop and hopped out the door without saying a word.

Chang gave the spinning propeller a wide berth as he jogged to the other side of the aircraft to examine the scantly illuminated wing. They were screwed. The wing strut was bent inward and splattered with blood, the strut completely disconnected from the fuselage. To make matters worse, the wing dipped noticeably downward. When he'd landed the plane this morning, he'd been worried about a nearly imperceptible half-degree dip. Now it was at least ten degrees lower than its normal position—parallel to the ground. There was no doubt that the wing was structurally damaged. The aircraft was grounded.

"What's wrong?" said Larsen, leaning his head out the passenger window.

Chang yelled over the propeller noise, "The wing is screwed!"

Larsen spilled out the passenger door, and for a brief moment, Chang thought the former SEAL was going to punch him for getting them into this mess. Instead, Larsen brushed past Chang and fired three quick shots at an unseen enemy.

"Get us back to the overpass!" said Larsen, firing three more shots into the dark. "Right now!"

Chang was back in the pilot's seat within seconds, throttling forward so he could turn the aircraft around.

"What happened?" yelled David, leaning between the Harpers in the row of seats right behind Chang.

"We hit one of the infected," said Chang. "Damaged

the wing. There's no way we can take off. I'm taking us back to the overpass."

"Jesus. This can't be happening," said Emma.

Larsen jumped into his seat a moment later, yanking his door shut.

"Step on it," said Larsen. "We have company."

"I'm doing what I can!" said Chang, tapping the brake hard enough to force a tight, right-hand turn.

"Threat axis?" said David.

"From the north," said Larsen. "Port side when we straighten out."

As the aircraft swung around, David hit one of the windows on the left side of the fuselage with the butt of his rifle, shattering it in place. Another hit knocked the glass free.

"What are you doing?" said Chang, looking over his seat.

"Keeping us alive," said David before firing through the window.

Larsen pushed his way between the front seats, taking a position between Jack and Emma in the second row.

"Get up!" he yelled at Jack. "Take my seat."

The second Jack had cleared the seat, Larsen started firing. Chang couldn't see what they were shooting at, but he got the distinct impression they had plenty of targets to choose from. Neither of them stopped shooting until he'd throttled up to forty knots, a little more than forty-five miles per hour.

"We're clear!" said David.

Chang eased off the throttle, bringing the aircraft's speed low enough to avoid stressing the wing any further.

"Now what?" said Chang.

"Back to square fucking one," said Larsen, pounding

the seat with his fist.

"What does that mean?" said Chang.

"Back to NevoTech. I highly doubt your friends stuck around," said Larsen. "I guarantee this thing drew a shit ton of attention, and it's going to attract even more when we return."

"I'll contact Gary," said David. "Maybe they can throw some of those ladders over for us."

"Or we can stop this thing on the other side of campus, where they have some closer gates," said Larsen. "Is that possible?"

"I can take us just past the Madison Avenue underpass, if I can find it," said Chang. "South Delaware street runs north-south along the western campus boundary. That's where all of the vehicle gates are located."

"Let Gary know where to expect us," said Larsen.

They taxied for a few more seconds while David tried frantically to reach Hoenig.

"Guys, I think I passed Madison Avenue already," said Chang, peering through the window next to him. "Or maybe we never got that far on takeoff."

"Are you serious?" said Larsen.

"I can't tell in the dark!" said Chang. "Sorry! It's an underpass. We might have gone right over it."

"Dammit. Then take us back to the East Street overpass," said Larsen. "They probably still have the ladders over there. It's our best bet. We might even be able to make it to the first gate. The one we used when we first arrived. David, please tell me you got Hoenig on the radio."

"I got him," said David. "But he said the streets are crazy around campus. He thinks we might be better off ditching the plane and heading south from the highway. Try to link up with Rich's team."

Chang couldn't see how that would improve their situation. The area south of the interstate was packed with apartment buildings and homes. They'd face the same problem, with no hope of finding refuge.

"We don't have a choice. We have to try to get back into NevoTech," said Chang.

Chapter Forty-Six

David pushed his earpiece into place. "Gary, this is David."

"Got you," said Hoenig.

Thank God he'd kept the earpiece and the radio. He'd almost left it in the security hub, but Hoenig insisted he keep it—just in case. Their current situation more than qualified as a "just in case."

"We're almost back to the overpass," said David.

"Fitzgerald and Mitch hear you approaching," said Hoenig. "Along with the rest of the city."

"How bad is it on East Street?"

"No worse than before," said Hoenig. "Chang's friends did a number on the first few waves of crazies."

"They aren't still there by any chance?" said David.

"The crazies? They're all over the place," said Hoenig.

"No. Chang's friends."

"Negative. They took off as soon as you did," said Hoenig.

"Except we never took off," said David.

David didn't hear Hoenig's reply. Larsen got up from his seat and kneeled next to the cargo compartment door, barking out orders.

"As soon as we stop, everyone gets out. Go around the back of the plane. The back!" he said, hitting the back of the front passenger seat. "That includes you, Jack! Around the back."

"I get it!" said Jack, annoyed. "Around the back!"

"We run like hell for NevoTech after that," said Larsen. "David, Josh and I will clear the way. Stick together, no matter what!"

The aircraft started to slow. "Coming up on the overpass," yelled Chang.

"Gary, we're seconds from stopping," said David. "Keep the information flowing."

"I'm focused on the eastern-facing cameras," said Hoenig. "I'll send Fitzgerald and Mitch back to the point where you jumped the fence. They can follow you down the sidewalk, from the other side of the fence, and add to your firepower if things start to spin out of control."

"Can you send more of the security team?" said David. "I'm thinking we might need everybody."

"I can do that, but Fitzgerald and Mitch are the only two officers on the ground with suppressed rifles," said Hoenig.

"I don't think it's going to matter," said David.

"Consider it done," said Hoenig. "I'll have some of them grab the ladders on the way over. It looks clear near that corner."

"It won't be that way for long," said David.

"Probably not," said Hoenig. "Good luck."

David didn't respond. The plane jolted to a stop, and Larsen sprang through the clamshell doors, reaching back inside to help Emma out. When she hesitated, David pushed her into Larsen's arms and turned to make sure Josh followed him out.

"Ready for this?" said David.

"I think so," said his son.

"Stay between Larsen and me," said David. "Do not shoot unless it's absolutely critical. Your rifle will draw too much attention."

He hit the pavement with his son, and they both ran for the back of the plane. David was worried about Josh more than anything else right now, but he couldn't show it. His son's best chance of survival lay in the group's cohesive, "fast-as-shit" passage from the airplane to NevoTech. If it didn't work out, at least they'd die together. Not a cheery thought on any level, but it was all he had right now. The Cessna's engine sputtered a few times, going completely silent.

Larsen grabbed him as they ran past the plane's tail. "What's going on with Hoenig?"

"We meet up with Fitzgerald and Mitch where we left them," said David. "If possible, they'll push the ladders over and cover us while we climb back over. He's sending the rest of the security force over."

"Let's go," said Larsen before moving toward the guardrail at a slow jog.

"Stay tight," said David, looking over his shoulder—and catching movement behind the group. "Contact. Rear. Everyone down!"

Larsen spun in place, aiming over the group, and David shifted to the left, each of them triggering their rifle-mounted infrared targeting beams at the same time. Green lines connected the rifles to the closest darkened shapes, but neither David nor Larsen fired. Call it gut instinct. Whatever it was undoubtedly saved their lives. Four beams immediately reached out from the figures, two reaching each of them.

"Jesus, you guys are jumpy," hissed a familiar voice. "Stand down."

"Rich?" said Larsen. "I can't believe you're still here."

"We were on our way out—"

"Save it for later," said David. "We need to get moving."

"Lead the way," said Rich.

David took off for the edge of the highway, but didn't get more than a few feet before Emma screamed. He started to turn, but a strong hand stopped him.

"Don't. We've been played," said Larsen, a green dot illuminating his face.

"We're taking Chang," said Rich, over the scientist's muffled protests. "No time to argue."

He turned his head far enough to see one of the operatives struggling to hold Chang in place, the crook of his elbow pressed over the scientist's mouth. David tensed, infuriated to see Chang held against his will. After everything they'd been through, it had come down to this. A kidnapping! Larsen must have sensed what was coming.

"Whatever you're thinking," whispered Larsen. "Forget it. Chang is lost. We need to focus on ourselves right now."

"Bunch of backstabbers," hissed David.

"Hey, we held up our end of the bargain," said Rich. "You had your chance. You don't get another."

The sound of a mob drew David's attention away from Chang. A sizable group approached from the direction of NevoTech. That was all he could ascertain standing exposed on the highway. They didn't have time for this. His son didn't have time for this.

"Are we free to go?" said David. "Things are about to unravel here."

"As long you understand Chang is coming with us," said Rich.

"I didn't think that was up for debate," said David. "Considering I have a gun pointed at my head."

"It isn't," said Rich. "And you have two guns pointed at your head."

"Then that's that," said David. "Dr. Chang, good luck to you. I'd like to say more, but—"

A gunshot echoed across the highway, followed by yelling in the distance.

"There's that," said David. "And the arm clamped over your mouth."

Rich muttered something, and the operative lowered the arm, still keeping Chang restrained.

"Thank you," said Chang. "All of you. I hope our paths cross again, under better circumstances."

"Keep us in mind when you win the Nobel Prize for Medicine," said Larsen. "I expect an invitation."

"We're counting on you to make the people responsible for all of this to pay," said David before nodding at Rich. "I suppose that applies to you, too."

"We're all on the same team," said Rich. "Even though it may not feel like it right now."

The operative standing next to Rich stepped forward. "I'll stay. Get them back onto the campus safely. Why not? We might need someone on the inside at NevoTech if there's a link to this mess."

"We don't want him," said David.

"Yes, we do," said Larsen. "We can use the help."

"He's yours," said Rich. "Keep them out of trouble, Scott."

"I'll try," said the operative. "Let's go."

What the hell just happened here? He glanced between

Rich and Scott, shaking his head.

"Don't look so confused. I told you we're on the same team," said Rich, motioning to the remaining two operatives, who started in the opposite direction with Chang. "Stay safe."

"You too," mumbled David before triggering his radio. "Gary? What are we looking at?"

"Pretty busy on East Street," said Hoenig.

"What are you seeing to the southwest?" said David.

"Hold on," said Hoenig.

"What are we doing?" said Larsen.

"East Street is busy," said David. "Checking for an alternate route."

His earpiece crackled. "Not looking good. You've attracted a serious following from the other side of the campus."

"Then we're slugging it out on East Street," said David. "Have your crew follow us along the fence with the ladders. We'll look for a break in the action to climb over."

"Sending all available shooters to the southeast corner of the campus," said Hoenig. "And I'm switching everyone over to this channel, with instructions to follow your orders."

"We're on our way," said David, patting Larsen on the shoulder. "Same place we came over."

"This should be fun," said Larsen. "Scott and I will take the lead. You coordinate with Hoenig and watch the flanks."

David grabbed his son. "I want you behind Jack and Emma, guarding the rear. If you see something on one of the flanks, call it out. If I don't respond, shoot it."

"Understood," said his son, nodding emphatically.

He leaned closer and whispered so the Harpers couldn't hear, "If things go completely to shit, you get right by my side," said David, hugging his son with one arm. He could feel Joshua's slim body shaking under his embrace.

As they started up the embankment, several figures broke out of the bushes to their right, running toward the airplane. Another group appeared about a hundred feet to their left, with the same apparent goal. Even in the complete darkness, the shiny white aircraft sat transposed against the dark highway, drawing them in like a beacon, while David's group moved undetected up the short rise.

When they reached the top, a small group of crazies piled through the scrub less than twenty feet from David's right. Three bright green beams reached out and connected with the closest targets, waiting to see if they continued down the embankment. All but one kept going; a man dressed in boxer shorts and a dark stained polo shirt cocked his head in their direction.

Scott's rifle clicked once, the man dropping in a heap where he stood. The operative's rifle was ridiculously quiet, the wet crack of the bullet snapping through the crazy's skull almost sounded louder than the gunshot. David immediately backtracked and checked on the infected that had piled through. The gunshot had gone unnoticed. Four figures scurried down the embankment toward the plane, joining another dozen or so that had just arrived from the overpass area. Across the interstate, David caught a glimpse of the team escorting Dr. Chang to safety. Despite the anger still fresh in his mind, he wished them well. Maybe Chang was better off in their hands.

He nodded at Larsen, and the group started toward

the NevoTech campus, their trip immediately halted by a short burst of gunfire nearby. The gunfire didn't sound random. Larsen and Scott edged forward in the bushes, the Harpers staying in place with Joshua. David listened to the bushes intently for any sign of immediate trouble. Sensing none, he contacted Hoenig.

"Gary, we just heard automatic gunfire. Sounded like it came from where we're headed."

"One of the security guards got spooked when a crazy hit the fence," said Hoenig. "You better hurry up. The streets are getting very busy. Wait any longer and they will be impassible."

Another staccato burst of gunfire shattered the night.

"Dammit, Gary," whispered David. "They need to get that shit under control."

"David, this is Fitz. Things are heating up at the fence. If you get here now, I can blast a path for you to the closest gate."

David really didn't like the sound of that. A dozen rifles blazing indiscriminately would draw every crazy in a one-mile radius to NevoTech. If they didn't get to the gate quickly, no amount of firepower would be enough.

"Dad," whispered his son.

"What?" he said, slightly annoyed by the interruption.

"We have a problem," said Joshua, his rifle aimed back toward the top of the embankment.

Larsen reacted immediately, sprinting in the direction Joshua's rifle was pointed. Holy shit. The gunfire had drawn them all back up the embankment! A head appeared over the top of the rise, instantly snapping backward from a bullet fired by Larsen. The ex-SEAL fired two more times before nearly screaming at David.

"Get in line with me!" he yelled. "Scott, you hold the

other side. Joshua, protect the Harpers."

David rushed into a position several feet to Larsen's left, at the edge of the embankment, pausing for a moment at the sheer insanity of what they faced. At least two dozen figures pressed up the rise, some fewer than twenty feet away. Only half were currently headed on a collision course with David's group, but that was about to change. They had no choice but to start clearing the hill. He triggered his rifle's green targeting beam and started firing.

Shifting their beams from target to target, they took down the closest threats, giving themselves some breathing room from the inevitable rush. The suppressed gunfire had drawn the rest in their direction.

"I got the left side!" yelled David, changing rifle magazines.

"Hurry up," said Larsen, already firing.

David knocked the crazies down in short order, none of them coming within twenty feet of their position. One bullet center mass. Move to the next target if they fell. This wasn't about killing them. It was all about stopping them. Buying time. A few still writhed in pain on the hill, bleeding out on the grass, but he didn't bother with a second shot. They were out of the equation for now. He couldn't believe he was thinking like this. Like the whole thing was a calculation. Was that how Larsen did it? How he seemed so disconnected from the killing?

"Let's go," said Larsen, tapping his shoulder. "Nice shooting."

Nice shooting. That was something you said about a tight center-of-paper target pattern at the range. He couldn't wait to get out of this hell. More importantly, to get Joshua out before the madness and fear consumed them both. Unfortunately, something told him they had a lot more humanity to burn through before either of them could escape.

Chapter Forty-Seven

Ragan walked cautiously through the silent apartment, noting the dead CHASE team member heaped on the floor in front of a bullet-stitched glass slider. The monochromatic green image presented by her night-vision goggles made it difficult to assess exactly what had happened inside the room. All she knew for sure at this point was that someone had really wanted to get inside Chang's apartment. The door had been breached with explosives. Not exactly a subtle job either. The charge had blasted half of the door away.

She approached the body, finally making sense of the blood-spray pattern. He'd been shot from outside the apartment. The contents of his skull had been blasted deeper into the space.

"Gunfire came from the inside," said McDermott.

"Blood pattern says the opposite," said Ragan.

"There should be bullet holes in the walls behind us. I think the shell casings in the hallway were from bullets fired into the apartment," said McDermott.

"That doesn't make any sense," said Ragan, puzzling over the two sets of contradictory data.

McDermott settled in next to her. "Damn. That's Stansfield. You're right. He was hit through the balcony slider."

"Single shot through the left temple," she said. "He was on Ochoa's team."

"Where's the rest of them?" said McDermott.

"That's the question, isn't it?" said Ragan before breaking off into the hallway next to the living area.

She passed an empty bathroom and a sparsely furnished office before reaching the master bedroom, where more of the story unfolded. The left half of the wide balcony slider had been shattered; large chunks of glass littered the hardwood floor and cement balcony beneath its frame. Dozens of shell casings lay scattered on the floor between the inner bedroom wall and the king-size bed. Someone had fired at least a full magazine through the slider. Possibly more. She didn't see any obvious holes in the wall where the bullets had been fired. Panic fire? She activated her radio.

"I think they had a sniper out there," said Ragan, quickly moving back into the hallway.

"Might still be around," said McDermott.

None of this added up. Larsen's team goes MIA. Now she finds a member of Ochoa's team killed by a sniper bullet?

"I'm starting not to care," said Ragan.

"Rags," said Cordova through her headset. "I hear that plane again. It's close. Getting louder."

"Are you sure it's a plane?"

Cordova was hidden in the lobby, three floors below, making sure no unwanted visitors showed up.

"I grew up next to a two-hangar airfield," said Cordova. "I know an airplane when I hear one. Sounded like it was trying to take off. Now it's taxiing. Cessna, if I had to guess. Single propeller."

She could hear the buzzing, but it didn't register as

anything but ambient noise to her.

"Can you tell what direction?" said Ragan. "How far?"

"Less than a mile," said Cordova. "I can't tell you what direction. The sound is bouncing off the buildings."

"I don't remember an airfield on the map," said Ragan.

"You thinking about hitching a ride?"

"More like hijacking," said McDermott over the net.

"I wouldn't turn down a ride if one was available," said Ragan. "Whatever happened here is finished. Chang is long gone, if he ever showed up in the first place. Control had to know this. At the very least, they knew something went down here—and they let us walk right into it. No warning. No nothing."

"When's the last time they asked for an update?" said McDermott.

"They haven't asked since we hid in the ambulance," said Ragan.

"And they know exactly where we are right now," said McDermott.

"Yep," she said, walking into the room with McDermott. "Still not a peep."

"I think they're done with us," said McDermott.

"The feeling is mutual," said Ragan, removing the CTAB and placing it on the kitchen table. "Cordova, do you think they could have landed the plane on one of the highways?"

"They'd need a long stretch of flat, straight interstate."

Ragan activated the map feature on the CTAB and zoomed in on their position. McDermott moved to the door to watch over the apartment. She quickly found two possibilities. Both nearby. Using a feature built into the map, she measured the two stretches of road.

"I assume a mile is long enough?" said Ragan.

"More than enough," said Cordova. "Easy takeoff. Even easier landing."

"One of the choices is the same north-south stretch of Interstate 65 that we just walked," said Ragan. "Part of it was clear before we hit the traffic jam."

"Not enough to take off. Maybe to land," said Cordova. "Maybe."

"The other is an east-west stretch of Interstate 75, about three-quarters of a mile southwest of here," said Ragan.

"My money is on that one," said McDermott. "The traffic jam we hit was caused by a pileup well before the 65-75 interchange. It's possible that the east-west highway is clear like the rest of the highway system."

"Let's find that airplane," said Ragan.

"We might have a problem with that," said Cordova.

"What? Is it gone?" said Ragan. "I don't hear it anymore."

"I think they shut down the motor."

"I'm sure we can convince them to restart it," she said.

"I don't know. I think they shut it down because we're not the only ones trying to find it," said Cordova. "The streets are coming alive."

"We'll be right down," she said, grabbing the CTAB.

McDermott put a hand over the device, keeping her from lifting it off the table.

"I think you should leave that here," he said. "Control might take a sudden interest in us if we go off-script."

She nodded, letting go of the CTAB. "You're right. I just hope you looked at the map longer than I did."

"We head west until we hit East Street," said McDermott. "Then straight south until we hit the interstate. Easy enough. If the plane doesn't pan out, we just hike back to 65 and follow it south until we hit a quarantine line. Talk our way through. It'll suck, but everything will get sorted."

"Control really wanted us to avoid the quarantine line getting in here," said Ragan.

"Because they knew the military would have stopped us," said McDermott. "And for good reason. This place is dead."

"Let's go," she said before heading for the door.

A short burst of automatic gunfire cut through the night. Military? She hoped so. Riding out of here in an armored HUMVEE beat flying out in a beat-up Cessna. Either way, they needed to get moving immediately. They'd caught a break when the power grid failed. Leveraging their latest generation night-vision gear, they were able to move through the scattered pockets of people undetected.

Gunfire was sure to draw more people onto the streets, and the last thing she wanted was to get caught up in a mob of crazies—in the dark. Night vision had its limitations, and so did her team, especially with their ammunition supply running low.

Chapter Forty-Eight

Larsen's injured leg throbbed as they ran for the fence. He suspected that some of the stitches had popped when they jumped down from the ladder. It had bothered him on the way to Chang's airplane, but he'd pushed it out of his mind, knowing he was minutes away from either escaping the quarantine zone or blowing up over an Indiana cornfield. Both with the same result. He wouldn't have to worry about his leg. Now that he was back in the thick of this nightmare—he was about ten steps away from hobbling.

He scanned the street running along NevoTech's back fence, finding it empty in both directions. They had emerged on the road about thirty feet from the southeast corner, where they had originally climbed over. All of the noise and commotion seemed focused in that direction.

"I don't see why they don't throw the ladders over right here!" said Larsen. "East Street sounds a little busy."

A hand gripped his shoulder and turned him around to face the long stretch of empty street he had just checked. Dark figures scrambled out of the bushes along the road, stretching all the way to the western side of the NevoTech campus.

"This keeps getting better," said Larsen, returning his focus to East Street.

"Just wait," said David before speaking quietly into his headset.

A long volley of semiautomatic fire shattered the night, causing Larsen to crouch.

"Let's go!" said David. "They're clearing a path."

Scott reached the corner fence support and peeked around the other side, up East Street.

"It's clear!" yelled the operative before disappearing around the brick column.

Larsen followed close behind, finding the street littered with bodies. To his left, on the other side of the fence, members of the NevoTech security team moved back and forth, reforming their firing line. A quick glance over his shoulder confirmed that the Harpers followed a few steps behind him. He moved to the right side of the sidewalk and made room for them.

"Get in closer," he said, and the Harpers filled the gap next to him.

Gunfire erupted from the fence line twenty feet in front of them, lasting far longer than necessary to stop a group of three crazies that had appeared between two of the houses on the opposite side of East Street. Scott could have taken them down with three quiet shots.

"David," he said, turning his head slightly, "we can handle small groups. They're—"

Suppressed gunshots cut him off, followed by David's voice. "Need some help here!"

Larsen wheeled left and started firing at a mob-sized group that had just emptied onto East Street from the direction of the park near the overpass. He snapped off two shots into the crowd before Hoenig's security force unleashed a torrent of gunfire that toppled the leading edge of the horde. They kept firing, some on full automatic, but the crowd kept coming. David and Joshua seemed lost in the frenzy, firing repeatedly at the surge of crazies pouring onto the street.

"We need to keep moving!" yelled Larsen, getting their attention.

David and Joshua stopped firing and let the security officers handle the mob. They still had at least a hundred yards to go to reach the first gate. It wasn't far, but they couldn't afford to stop or slow down. The blackout had pulled people out of their homes. The airplane noise drew them to the area. The gunfire would focus their attention right here, like a dinner bell, until they got through that gate.

Larsen jogged down the sidewalk next to the Harpers, who hadn't said a word since they got off the airplane. They were either in shock, scared out of their minds or playing it really cool. Whatever the case, he didn't care right now. They were responding quickly to directions, which was all that mattered.

"We need to pick up the pace!" said David, snapping off a shot. "The rear flank is about to collapse."

He turned and assessed the situation, shaking his head. The security team was panic firing at this point—most of them spraying automatic fire or bursts into the mob.

"Start running!" said Larsen. "We have a clear path to the gate."

A figure appeared on the other side of the fence next to Larsen, followed by a blur of heavily armed security officers running in the direction of the rear team.

"I'm shifting half of my people to the back!" said Fitzgerald.

The sharp crackle of rifles to the front caught them both off guard, each of them flinching. The rifle fire continued at a rapid, staccato pace.

"Shit," said Fitzgerald before speaking rapidly into his headset. "Thirty or more spilling off McCarty Street."

"We can handle that," said Larsen. "Just make sure the rear flank holds."

"I'm on it!" said Fitzgerald before taking off.

"David, Josh," said Larsen, "I need you up here. Fitz has our back."

"Are you sure about that?" said David.

"For now," said Larsen before moving on line with Scott.

The small mob ahead of them broke apart quickly, the combined guns from NevoTech security and Larsen's crew dropping most of the infected fifty yards out. Several crazies ran headlong through the barrage, barreling down East Street and passing the entrance gate. Larsen and Scott picked their targets on the move, knocking them down one by one until the street was clear again. They were almost there!

Movement in in his peripheral vision instinctively drew his rifle to the right, the green targeting beam intersecting a man running at them with a fireplace poker. A second crazy was right behind him. Both fell to the sidewalk across the street without anyone in Larsen's group firing a shot, a green beam slicing through the air where the two had just stood.

His first thought was to empty his rifle magazine into the tight space between the two houses, but he fought that instinct. If the shooter wanted him dead, he'd be dead. This was something else.

"Larsen?"

He recognized the female voice immediately. Ragan.

David stopped next to him. "You sure they're not

going to kill us?"

"They have to stand in line," said Larsen, nodding at the growing mob near the corner of the street.

"Good point," said David before taking off.

"You here to play nice?" said Larsen.

The green laser vanished, and Ragan appeared from the shadows.

"We just want to get out of here. All of this is beyond screwed," said Ragan. "I'm coming out with McDermott and Cordova."

"Hurry the fuck up, then!" said Larsen. "You picked a bad time to make friends."

As Ragan and her team crossed the street, the gunfire intensified to the south because Fitzgerald's shooters over-responded to a small group that managed to break through their shield of bullets. The momentary distraction, drawing most of their fire away from the main mob—essentially collapsed the rear flank. Larsen took off in the opposite direction, catching up with the rest of the group as they ran for the closest gate.

"Where are you going?" yelled Ragan.

"Back inside this fence!" he said. "It's the only place that's safe."

"What?" she said. "Why is the military here?"

"What military?" he said.

"The military inside the fence?"

"That's private security for NevoTech!" he said, looking over his shoulder.

At least twenty infected had broken through Fitzgerald's gauntlet.

"What the fuck is going on, Larsen?"

"I'll explain once we get inside!" said Larsen. "Until then—run and shoot."

They ran for a few seconds before a new volley of gunfire erupted in front of them.

"This isn't going to work," yelled David, who had stopped in his tracks.

A tidal wave of people rushed onto the road north of them, from McCarty Street, which was only twenty yards beyond the gate. Larsen's group was slightly closer to the turnstile entrance, but they'd never reach it in time to get more than one person through before they were overrun. They had to make a stand here and use the ladders—something they probably should have done in the first place. The grim realization that not all of them would make it over hit him like a hammer.

"David, tell Fitzgerald to collapse all of his security guards right here and get those ladders over!"

"I don't think—"

"Just do it!" said Larsen before grabbing Ragan and pointing back the way they came. "Form a tight line facing that way. That's your field of fire."

Ragan instantly assessed the situation unfolding on both ends of the street, a look of resignation settling over her face. She nodded and started organizing her team.

David yelled over the gunfire, "Dammit, Larsen! We don't have the firepower for this."

"We don't have a choice," said Larsen. "I got the north, with the rest. You reinforce whichever side needs the help, and keep coordinating."

David stared at him for a moment, like he'd spoken another language.

"We're all going to die out here," said David.

"Not all of us," said Larsen. "Get Fitzgerald's people moving. I want them right here, along the fence, putting out a steel wall. And we need those ladders."

David began coordinating with Fitzgerald while the lines formed up and started firing. The effect was immediate, but insufficient. Even with the NevoTech security team in place, Larsen couldn't imagine it being enough. It all came down to numbers. The number of critical hits per bullets fired balanced against the volume of targets. They simply didn't have enough skilled shooters to keep the crazies at bay long enough to get everyone over the fence—or anyone, if the ladders didn't show up very soon.

Chapter Forty-Nine

Major Smith's HUMVEE rolled to a heavy stop in front of the address Dr. Owens had given him. By the look of the place, he wasn't optimistic about finding Dr. Hale. The lobby entrance windows had been shattered, jagged chunks of glass lying on the sidewalk or on top of the steel frames. Similar to the windows, the glass door had been smashed, but the mess had been dragged inside. Almost like someone had jumped through it. He couldn't tell from here, but two bullet holes appeared in the upper right corner of the door frame.

"Third floor. Apartment three-ten. In and out in thirty seconds," said Smith over the squad tactical net. "Kick the door in if she doesn't answer."

"On our way," said Staff Sergeant Vaughn.

Four soldiers disembarked the HUMVEE behind Smith's and quickly moved into the building, spreading out inside the lobby. He tapped his fingers on the bullet-resistant window, willing Vaughn to move faster, though he knew she was balancing speed with caution. Stopping in the middle of the street made him nervous. They'd encountered dozens of infected on the way down here, aggressively maneuvering around each group and strictly avoiding the use of their mounted weapons.

In fact, he'd purposefully kept his gunners out of the

turrets. Gunfire attracted attention, and out here, the key to survival was not attracting attention. Hard to do when you were stopped in the middle of the street, in a rumbling, overpowered diesel vehicle. A lone figure holding a knife ran through the intersection ahead of them, paying no attention to the three armored vehicles. Pure luck.

"Kill the engine," said Smith, repeating the order over the net to the other drivers.

"You want me up on the two-forty, sir?" said Private First Class Roth from the rear driver's seat.

"Not yet," said Smith.

The HUMVEE cabin went still, the four of them waiting silently for news from Staff Sergeant Vaughn. A loosely spaced group of six figures dashed into the intersection, headed in the same direction as the first. One of them looked at the HUMVEEs as he ran by, slowing his pace. Smith held still, watching the man closely. His facial expressions were mostly washed out by the night vision, so he paid attention to the man's body language. The guy wanted to check out the vehicles. Shit. He just stopped.

"Sir?" insisted Roth.

"I got this," said Smith, grabbing the door handle.

A single pistol shot to the head would draw considerably less attention than a burst of 7.62mm gunfire from the turret-mounted two-forty. He started to pull on the door handle, when the distinctive crackle of automatic gunfire jolted the infected man's attention— and he vanished behind the corner of the apartment building.

"Vaughn, sitrep," said Smith.

"Just reached the third floor," said Vaughn. "Moving

toward—shit. The door is blasted in. Serious explosive breach."

More gunfire echoed between the buildings.

"Quick sweep and get out," said Smith. "I'm hearing sustained gunfire on the streets. It's going to get busy out here, really fast."

"I hear it. Webb and I are moving into the apartment," said Vaughn, pausing for a few seconds. "I have a body on the floor in the living room. Looks like a military contractor. Civilian clothes. Body armor. Suppressed rifle. Bullet holes in the glass slider facing the street."

"Get out of there," said Smith. "She's long gone."

"Copy that," said Vaughn. "Moving back to the vehicles."

Another long surge of gunfire cut through the night, but unlike the previous bursts, this one didn't stop. Instead, the shooting intensified, reaching the kind of ferocious pace he recognized all too well. A few blocks from here, a rifle squad was fighting for its life. He pressed the radio transmit button on his vest.

"All vehicles, get ready to roll. Gunners up in the turrets," said Smith. "Convoy will take a hard right at the first intersection. All vehicles stay on me and stay tight. We're looking for the source of that gunfire."

"Sounds like a final protective fire," said Sergeant Breene, starting the HUMVEE.

Most of the gunfire stopped for a few seconds. He could still hear some kind of shooting, but it was a lot quieter.

"Maybe it's over," said Corporal Mayer, in the seat behind Smith.

Before Smith could respond, the shooting started again, sounding more desperate than before. He glanced impatiently at the apartment building. Four soldiers appeared at the rear of the lobby, running toward the front door.

"Contact. Intersection," said Roth. "Request permission to fire, sir!"

Smith's eyes darted to the intersection. Four infected scrambled in their direction, armed with a variety of makeshift weapons. Harmless against the HUMVEEs, but he still had four soldiers in the open.

"Fire," said Smith.

The M-240 roared twice, its 7.62mm shell casings clattering against the metal roof. The people running toward the HUMVEE tumbled to the street like they had been switched off remotely. He triggered his radio again.

"Hunter convoy is cleared to engage hostile targets. I say again. Hunter convoy is cleared to engage hostile targets."

Roth yelled down from the protective turret, "You need to define 'hostile target,' sir."

She was right. Smith spotted a dozen or more infected beyond the intersection, all headed in their direction.

"Contacts approaching from our six o'clock," reported Specialist DeLeon, the rear vehicle gunner.

He couldn't put this off any longer. He'd wanted to shield them from shooting civilians, but they no longer had a choice.

"Hunter convoy, this is Hunter actual. You are clear to engage anyone on the streets," said Smith, wondering what he had just done.

Chapter Fifty

David jumped as high as he could and grabbed the bottom rung of the aluminum ladder with both hands, pulling it downward when he dropped back to the ground. The ladder flipped over the top of the fence from the sudden, violent momentum, crashing to the sidewalk between the two lines of shooters and skidding partway into the street. He yanked his son out of the firing line and took his place between Scott and Larsen.

"Get that ladder up and get over!" said David. "Take Jack and Emma with you!"

Jack heard what he said, and emptied the last few bullets from his revolver into the nearest crazy—less than ten feet away—before stepping out of the line to help Joshua with the ladder. David dropped the empty magazine from his rifle and removed another from his vest without taking his eyes off the approaching horde, noticing that most of his ammunition pouches were empty.

He slapped the magazine into his rifle and released the slide before connecting the green targeting beam with a man several feet away and pressing the trigger. David didn't wait to see the result. He shifted the laser to the next target and repeated the process. Scott and Larsen did the same thing, only much faster. None of them were using the optical sights attached to their rifles anymore.

The green beams, only visible to those wearing night-vision devices, moved back and forth across the crowd, pausing long enough on each target to guide a bullet.

A head slammed down on the sidewalk a few feet in front of him, the first crazy to get that close since they had reformed the group. Along the fence ahead of David, muzzle blasts from the NevoTech rifles flashed like a paparazzi camera frenzy, pounding the mob in a lethal crossfire. A man broke out of the pack, running toward David with a broken glass bottle. Two beams connected with him at the same time, Scott's rifle firing first. The crazy tumbled to the ground, the bottle skidding along the sidewalk between them. They were moments from being overrun.

David glanced over his shoulder. The long ladder sat against the fence at a forty-five-degree angle, extending several feet past the sharp spikes that curved outward to prevent someone from scaling the fence from the street. Two of the spikes protruded through the ladder rungs, still presenting an obstacle, but nothing that couldn't be avoided. Emma was already halfway up the ladder, while Jack stood on the bottom rung so it wouldn't tip when she got to the top. Much to David's dismay, Joshua stood under the ladder, firing at the rapidly approaching mob just beyond the other team.

He turned his attention back to the crazies directly in front of him, with one thought in mind. *Hold the line until my son gets over the fence.* Based on what he'd seen when he turned his head, he wasn't sure that was a realistic thought. The mob had completely broken through the NevoTech gauntlet.

A woman barreled into Scott, but he held firm, shoving her backward into the crazy behind her. David shot them both and barely got his rifle around in time to shoot a man point blank in the neck. The crazy's limp body knocked his rifle sideways, away from a tangle-haired woman coming at him with a kitchen knife. He stepped into the attack, deflecting the knife with his left arm while pulling his pistol from the holster on his right thigh and sticking it under her chin.

David was already searching for the next threat when he pulled the trigger, immediately turning the blood-slicked pistol toward a man swinging an aluminum baseball bat. He got off a single shot before the bat connected with his right forearm, knocking the pistol out of his grip and sending a shockwave of pain up his arm and down his hand. The man dropped from a gunshot blast to the forehead, replaced by another crazy—an endless tide. His only mission now was to buy a few more seconds for his son.

Unable to use his right hand, he gripped his rifle with his left and jammed the magazine against the crook of his right elbow, stabilizing the weapon. He managed to fire twice before he was knocked to the ground by a throng of infected. On his back, he saw Larsen still upright, firing his pistol point blank into several onrushing crazies. Scott grunted on the other side of him, driven to his knees by two men, one who was trying to push a switchblade into his gut.

David tilted his head up and caught a brief image of his son at the top of the fence, aiming the scoped M1 A1 rifle down at the mob piling onto him.

"Get out of here!" yelled David.

A thick, warm spray covered the left side of David's face, followed moments later by what felt like a bucket of hot worms spilling over his neck. The sound of rapid machine gun fire hit him before he could react, along with a steady flow of body parts. The crazies above him collapsed in a shower of gore, pinning him to the sidewalk and knocking his night-vision goggles out of place. He recognized the machine guns by their fast rate of fire. M240s.

"Stay down!" he yelled, his voice unable to compete with the repeated bursts of gunfire.

He strained his head sideways under the weight to find his son. In the dark, he could tell the ladder was bent, probably punctured in several places by bullets. He couldn't see anything beyond that. The bursts of machine-gun fire grew closer until tires screeched and the heavy engines surrounded him.

"Careful!" yelled an authoritative female voice. "We might have survivors. Start pulling them off."

"I got one over here!" yelled another serious voice. "At least two."

David desperately wanted to see his son, to know that he'd jumped over the fence in time, but he didn't want to move. The thought of making it this far and getting shot by a jumpy soldier kept him perfectly still. The weight pressing down on him lifted slowly, then was gone. He opened his eyes and smiled at the body-armor-clad soldier pointing a rifle in his face.

"David Olson, Westfield Police Department," said David. "There should be two more. One on each side of me."

Two pairs of hands lifted him to his feet. One of the soldiers kept him steady while the rest went to work sifting through the carnage. He lowered his night-vision goggles and looked around. Larsen stood on one leg, his arm draped around one of the soldiers. The team leader on the other side of the ladder was up, helping the soldiers pull dead crazies off her teammates. She gripped an outstretched hand and pulled one of her people clear of the mess.

"Medic!" yelled a soldier next to him.

Scott lay on his side, blood spilling out of his mouth. He grimaced in pain, roaring as one of the soldiers flipped him onto his back and started to unsnap his gear. David saw the problem before the medic. The switchblade was buried deep in his right side, and they'd just rolled him over it.

"Doc, he has a knife in his right side," said David.

"Shit," said the soldier, leaning back on his knees and unzipping the "unit one pack" next to him. "Major Smith!"

A soldier rushed past him, kneeling next to Scott and the medic. While the two argued over what to do with the critically injured operative, David searched the faces on the other side of the fence for Joshua. He didn't have to look for long.

"Dad! I'm here," yelled his son, waving frantically behind the fence with Jack and Emma Harper.

David raised his hand and gave them a thumbs-up, unable to form the words to express his joy. He just nodded and started to tear up, momentarily oblivious to the machine-gun fire and chaos around him. The moment was short lived.

"Breakthrough!" yelled one of the soldiers.

He knew what that meant and whirled to check his surroundings. A woman holding a golf club over her head bounced between the hood and back of two tightly parked HUMVEEs, lurching at David. He grabbed his rifle with one hand and fired twice from the hip, spinning her around. The soldier kneeling next to the medic jumped to his feet and dropped her to the street with two center mass shots. Still reeling from the surreal experience, David extended a hand, unsure what else to do.

"Thank you. You saved our lives."

"Major Nick Smith. 2nd Battalion, 151st Infantry Regiment. Indiana National Guard," said the soldier. "But don't thank me yet. One of your guys needs immediate emergency medical care. Like a hospital. Corporal Pillow is a good medic, but—"

The medic interrupted them. "This guy has serious internal bleeding. He needs a trauma doctor."

Smith cursed. "Believe it or not, I have one. I have a whole emergency room staff, but they're at least thirty minutes away—and they have limited medical supplies."

"Did you just come from a hospital?" said David, his mind instantly clearing.

"Methodist Hospital. We just evacuated all remaining staff," said Smith.

"We have Dr. Hale from Methodist. She's an ER doctor," said David.

"Holy shit," said Smith. "She's the only reason we're here. One of the doctors sent us to—"

"Dr. Chang's apartment. We've been there. Dead guy inside," interrupted David.

"Right," said Smith.

"She can help this guy. We also have plenty of medical supplies. Trauma-level stuff. Surgery kits. We just need to get him inside."

"We'll get you all inside," said Smith. "Is there a vehicle gate?"

David activated his radio. "Gary, get ready to open

one of the vehicle gates. Preferably close to the cafeteria. Get Dr. Hale prepped for an inbound stab wound. Heavy internal bleeding. The cavalry is here."

"I'm on it," said Hoenig. "See you inside."

"They have vehicle entrances on the west side of the campus," said David. "The other side."

"I'll make it happen," said Smith before taking a step away and issuing a series of orders to his soldiers.

A strong hand slapped his shoulder. He glanced over the gloved hand at Larsen, who grinned at him like a devil through a thick sheen of blood.

"Welcome back from the dead," said Larsen.

David shook his head. "Back again—somehow."

Chapter Fifty-One

Major Smith followed two of the men his team just rescued from a horde of crazies. David, a local police officer, and Larsen, some kind of Department of Homeland Security agent. They wound through the expansive NevoTech complex, trailed by Smith's medic and one of NevoTech's security officers, who carried the critically wounded man named Scott on a collapsible stretcher. The other Homeland agents trailed all of them at a distance. Two of them. Ragan and McDermott according to their ID cards. The third agent didn't survive the attack. He still had no idea how all of these people were connected, but it was obvious they had been through a lot together.

They took a quick detour around the cafeteria to avoid panicking the two hundred and thirty-eight civilians that had sought refuge on the company's campus. David must have mentioned the exact number several times while they wound through the hallways.

The "detour" brought them past a section of floor-to-ceiling glass, where Smith caught a long glimpse of the refugees packed around tables and sleeping on the floor. A very long glimpse. The only way he could have spent more time looking at them was if he walked directly through the cafeteria. David Olson, Westfield police officer, knew exactly what he was doing when he picked that route. He wanted Smith to see them, without drawing too much attention.

The infirmary was a few doors down, where Dr. Hale stood ready for her patient in a blue plastic surgical gown. A man and a woman dressed in spotless hospital-grade scrubs stood next to her. A full array of stainless steel surgical instruments sat on a similarly shiny tray next to every type of gauze, compress and bandage a field trauma surgeon could need. An IV stand with a plasma bag stood behind the table. It wasn't a high-tech emergency room setting, but it was the best scenario they could find within life-saving distance.

Hale's eyes followed David and Larsen as they entered the infirmary, remaining fixed as the rest of the group entered the room. He understood why. The two of them were soaked from helmet to boot in blood, their faces still bright red from the gore that had been blasted onto them from the HUMVEEs machine guns.

"What the hell happened?" she said.

"Bloodbath," said Larsen. "Literally."

The stretcher-bearers walked through the door, stopping next to Smith.

"Set him down here," said Hale, motioning to an examination table that had been covered with bright white sheets.

The two nurses helped transfer the critically wounded operator to the table, and everyone stepped back. Dr. Hale moved in, kneeling to get a closer look at the stab wound. The two Homeland agents entered the room, drawing her attention.

"Who are they?" she said.

"Long story," said Larsen.

Hale examined the hole in her patient's side. "How far in was the knife?"

David produced the knife. "At least an inch past the hilt."

"Fuck," muttered Hale. "I'm going to have to open him up."

"We'll get out of your way," said Smith, lingering for a few seconds. "Dr. Owens sent us to Chang's apartment. He insisted we get you out of here."

Dr. Hale nodded, fighting back tears. "I assume he's safe?"

"Safe as the rest of us," said Smith. "You'll see him soon."

"You're bringing him here?" said Hale. "That's not a good idea."

"No. I'm taking *you* to him," said Smith.

Hale shook her head. "I'm staying here. These people need me."

"No. You don't understand," said Smith. "Everybody is leaving."

"What?" said Larsen, cocking his head in what could be perceived as a threatening manner.

"We're not going to one of your quarantine prisons, Major," said David.

"I'm not going anywhere, so take this outside. I need to get to work here," said Hale, turning to her nurses. "Let's get the IV going. Remove his vest and cut away his shirt. Scrub him down."

"Hold on. I got ahead of myself," said Smith.

"I really can't hold on right now," said Hale. "This man is dying."

"I'm not taking any of you to a quarantine camp. I'm getting you to safety," said Smith. "At midnight—

tonight—the inner quarantine zone becomes a kill box."

"Jesus," said Larsen.

"What does that mean?" said Hale.

"It's a free-fire zone. No rules of engagement restrictions and no coordination required to fire on a target," said Smith. "No friendly ground forces will enter the kill box."

"In English, please," said Hale.

"Based on what I've seen out there," said Smith, "my guess is they're about to turn Indianapolis into an air force shooting gallery. I don't see any other way for the government to contain this."

Hale snapped on a pair of gloves and selected a scalpel.

"What's the evacuation timeline?" said Hale.

"I have to rendezvous with the rest of my convoy and get them through both quarantine lines. Owens and about a hundred members of the hospital staff," said Smith. "We've picked an out-of-the-way spot to drop them off, where they should be safe. My guess is I'll be back in two hours."

"It's already 9:30," said David, checking his watch. "That's cutting it close."

"They won't light up a military convoy," said Smith.

"Let's hope not," said Larsen.

"All right. I have to get moving," said Smith.

"We'll all get out of your way," said David. "Unless you need help holding him down."

"I'm going to hit him with a powerful local anesthetic. His team really came through with these kits," she said, nodding at her patient. "Did the rest of them get out okay?"

"What team?" said Smith.

"We'll catch everyone up later," said Larsen, trying to usher them out.

Something was off. He could tell by Hale's reaction to Larsen's answer.

"Is Chang okay?" she said, looking toward David and Larsen.

Why would she be asking them about Chang? Owens said Chang was out of town and had let her borrow the apartment between shifts. David hesitated to answer, looking pained to come up with a response.

"Chang is dead," said Larsen. "A crazy ran down the middle of the interstate while he was picking up speed for takeoff. Damaged the wing. He taxied us back to the overpass and we all got out to make our way back. A group hit us as soon as we got out of the plane. He died on the way back."

She turned to David, who took a moment to respond. "There was nothing we could do for him out there."

"Chang was here?" said Smith.

"Owens couldn't have known," said Larsen. "I can explain outside. It's kind of a long story."

"I'd really like to hear that story," said the female Homeland agent.

"Me too," said the other agent.

"I don't have the time," said Smith. "And it really doesn't matter. I'm sorry he's gone."

"I'll have Mitch take you back to your vehicles," said Larsen before turning to the two Homeland agents. "We can compare notes after that."

Smith sensed a rift between Larsen and the two, but he didn't have time to think about it, let alone worry about—not if he was going to get all of these people out of the kill box before midnight.

"I need to speak with your security chief for a moment before I leave," said Smith. "If I'm going to take all of you out of here, I need everyone in that cafeteria to follow a few basic ground rules. They probably won't like it, but everyone's lives will depend on it."

"What kind of ground rules?" said Larsen.

Smith didn't know how to say this any other way. "Strict communications restrictions. No cell phones. A slow trickle of pickups wherever I leave all of you. A hundred cars converging in the middle of nowhere will attract attention. A barely used cell tower suddenly maxing out? You get the picture."

"Why would they care?" said David.

"My orders were to leave the remaining hospital staff behind. One hundred and eighteen of them. I obviously didn't obey that order. The government doesn't care if any of you get out of here. In fact, I think they'd prefer you perished in the kill box. We need to be cautious."

"I hope Chang—" started David. "I hope Chang's research burns the people responsible for this to the ground."

Smith started to grin, but kept a straight face. Chang didn't die out on the highway. He had no idea what was going on here, but hoped that David was right. That this Dr. Chang was the key to bringing these people down.

Chapter Fifty-Two

Hale barely watched them leave. She needed to focus on her patient, whom she strongly suspected wasn't as critically wounded as they had all reported. His vitals were steady, and the bleeding from his mouth looked superficial. Blood loss from his wound was sustained, but not alarming. She'd still have to do some cutting to assess the damage, but overall he looked like a case that could be stabilized for a long trip to a hospital.

"Dr. Hale?"

She glanced at the door, finding David. He looked nervously at her two nurses.

"Chang's fine, isn't he? Larsen has the worst poker face," said Hale, waiting a few seconds for him to respond. "You can trust them."

"We did collide with one of the infected on takeoff," said David. "Crippled the plane. The other team took him south. This guy, Scott, volunteered to help the rest of us get back. Take care of him."

"We will," said Hale. "Do you trust this Army guy?"

"Indiana National Guard," said David. "Local guy. I trust him. Your friend Owens trusted him."

"I guess that's good enough," said Hale.

"Sounds like we don't have a choice," said David. "See you wherever Smith takes us."

"You're leaving?"

"I'm getting Joshua out of here," said David. "I can't count the number of times I've almost lost him over the past twenty-four hours. I need to focus on my son from this point onward. I'm all he has—and he's all I have."

"He's lucky to have you," said Hale. "I don't know if this means a lot coming from a nonparent, but I think you're an amazing dad. My guess is that he feels the same. Good luck, David. If I don't see you later."

"I'm sure we'll see each other," said David, starting to leave.

"David!" she said, rushing over to the counter on the other side of the room.

He stepped back inside. "Yeah?"

She grabbed the Ziploc bag with Chang's experiment vaccine. After distributing pills to everyone on campus, she still had a few dozen yellow pills left.

"Give these to any of the soldiers that were handling you, and to your two new friends. I don't think the virus is contagious in the usual sense of a flu virus, but you guys are covered in infected blood. One should be enough for anyone that got a dose earlier today. Two for everyone else."

Her own fever had dropped since taking the pills earlier in the day, a positive sign that Chang's vaccine might also be effective as a post-symptomatic treatment and not merely a vaccine. Might. Only time would tell, and it appeared that Chang's treatment had, at the very least, bought her more time.

As soon as David departed, Hale turned to the two nurses she'd handpicked from a dozen medical professionals among NevoTech's refugee population. Jen worked as a perioperative nurse in the birthing center at St. Vincent Women's Hospital. She undoubtedly knew her way around the abdomen far better than Hale. Doug was a registered nurse that worked in a Medicaid clinic on the fringes of east Indianapolis. Together, Hale figured they could handle just about anything that came through that door. Just about anything.

Chapter Fifty-Three

David rested against a thick maple tree, his son sleeping in his arms. He wasn't letting go of this kid for any reason. He meant what he'd said to Dr. Hale. Joshua was his only mission now. As soon as he got his turn to make a cell phone call, he'd get in touch with his dad in Evansville. He wanted to take his son as far from all of this madness as possible. The southwestern tip of Indiana should be far enough away, especially given what he'd seen on the ride out of Indianapolis.

Once Major Smith's HUMVEEs broke out of the area immediately surrounding NevoTech and reached the interstate, the trip had been mostly uneventful. Heading south on Interstate 65, they'd sailed through the National Guard inner quarantine zone barricade. Soldiers at the fortified checkpoint had waved the vehicles through without stopping them.

They'd joined the bulk of Smith's convoy several miles past the checkpoint, and proceeded together to the outer quarantine boundary, where soldiers from the 10th Mountain Division conducted a short, cursory check of the vehicles—while David and his son hid in the back of Smith's HUMVEE. After they cleared the final quarantine line, everything appeared normal on the roads. David quit paying attention after that, drifting asleep amidst the gear and ammunition packed into the vehicle.

When he woke, the convoy had stopped on a road that looked like it could have been anywhere in Indiana. Cornfield on one side. Trees on the other. David took a quick look at one of Major Smith's maps while the soldiers offloaded the hospital staff and got them settled in the woods. It looked like they were somewhere outside Rushville, Indiana, fifteen miles beyond the outer quarantine boundary. It would take his dad four or five hours to get here, though he didn't intend to ask him to drive through the night. It was already one in the morning, and the back roads he'd have to take to steer clear of the quarantine line would take him through Hoosier National Forest and the hills of Brown County.

Jack and Emma Harper took a seat against the tree facing them, exhaling deeply as they settled onto the forest floor. He couldn't see their faces, but he could sense that they were beat. He had to hand it to them. For two "yuppie" millennial types, they had held up pretty damn well. He'd never forget the image of Jack standing on line with three seasoned shooters, firing and reloading that revolver like a boss.

"Did you guys make your call yet?" said Emma.

"Not yet," said David. "They have some kind of system. Trying to stagger arrivals. What about you? Are Ma and Pa Harper on the way?"

"I was told to have them leave in two hours. They have a six-hour or so drive around Indianapolis. Since they have to cut between Indy and Fort Wayne, Smith's soldiers came up with a lot of back roads. I guess there's a lot of military activity between the two cities. Fort Wayne was hit with the virus, too."

"They're coming from northwest Indiana, right?" said David.

"Munster. Right on the Illinois border. Just under Hammond," said Jack.

"And things are under control up there?" said David.

"Supposedly. She said things have been pretty quiet up there. Most of the trouble has been in the south side of the city. They've quarantined specific areas, but not all of Chicago."

"You, Emma and your parents are more than welcome to follow us to Evansville," said David. "The closest infected city is Louisville, and that's at least eighty miles away. You could all wait it out for a little while. Make sure the situation in Chicago doesn't spread."

"I'm not tied to your parents' house," said Emma. "In fact—I like the idea of moving away from any of this craziness better than getting closer to it.

"I agree with you," said Jack. "But it's really up to them."

"No, it's not," said Emma. "We're going with David. Your parents have always been talking about taking a trip to southern Indiana. This is the perfect opportunity."

"They're going to kill me," said Jack.

"Blame it on me," said Emma.

"Don't worry," said Jack playfully. "I will."

"David Olson?" said a voice from the edge of the forest. "David Olson?"

"Must be our turn," said David, easing his sleeping son out of his arms and leaning him gently against the tree. "He's completely out."

"Go ahead. We'll watch him," said Emma.

"I feel like the two of you should be his godparents," said David.

"That would be an honor," said Jack. "Even if we're only like ten years older."

David stood up, his knees audibly crackling. He felt like he'd been thrown out of a fast-moving train. This had to be what it felt like. At least he wasn't wearing that vest and helmet anymore. He didn't think he could stand up on his own at this point under the weight of anything other than the fresh clothes that had been generously donated to him by one of the families at NevoTech.

"You gonna make it?" said Jack.

He laughed. "Barely. But I'll manage."

"David Olson?"

"Over here!" he yelled.

"Major Smith asked me to grab you for a minute," said the soldier, walking into the forest.

"Be right over!"

He snagged the rifle leaning against the tree next to Joshua and offered it to Emma, along with two spare magazines from his pockets.

"Hold on to these until I get back," said David.

Emma took the rifle and cradled it in her arm, tucking the magazines into her waist. David hesitated, not wanting to leave Joshua.

"We got him," said Jack, getting up and standing over David's sleeping son. "Nothing will come between him and the two of us."

"Thank you," said David. "Be back in a few minutes."

David followed the soldier out of the forest, where a long, mixed convoy of HUMVEEs, canvas-covered trucks and armored transport trucks sat parked in the grass, at the edge of a cornfield, on the other side of the two-lane road. Two vehicles down, a group of soldiers had set up a makeshift table, where they were processing the phone calls placed to families around the state. They turned in the other direction and walked along the road until they reached Smith's vehicle at the head of the convoy.

Major Smith stood with two other soldiers around the front of the HUMVEE, examining a map spread out on the hood with red-colored flashlights.

"Major, Corporal Webb, I have David Olson."

One of the flashlights pointed in David's face for a few seconds.

"I almost didn't recognize you," said Major Smith. "You look like you're headed to the golf course."

The soldiers laughed, and so did David after a few seconds.

"Glad to find you in a good mood," said David. "I assume this is about the thing we discussed?"

"It is," said Smith.

"You want us to take a walk, sir?" said one of the soldiers.

"No. I think this is good news," said Smith.

David's mind was too exhausted to interpret Smith's statement. At this point, the only good news he could imagine was that his ex-wife had been officially declared dead. He didn't want her to be dead, but given what he'd seen on the streets, dead was better than strapped to a bed like one of the infected. He wasn't sure how he would break this to Joshua, though he was pretty sure his son strongly suspected the truth.

"I ran your ex-wife's name, date of birth and social security number through IDN, narrowed by incident zone. No Meghan Olson tagged to incident zone one-four. That's the Indianapolis zone. We ran her maiden name, Meghan Harris, through zone one-four and still came up empty, so we widened the search. We found her tagged to zone one-five. Fort Wayne."

"Fort Wayne? How the hell did she end up there?" said David. "I guess it doesn't matter. What do they do with them?"

"What do you mean?" said Smith.

"With the infected?" said David. "She almost killed her boyfriend."

"David, your wife isn't tagged as infected. She's in a class Charlie quarantine camp at Grissom Air Joint Air Reserve base," said Smith.

"Class Charlie?" said David. "Grissom Air Base?"

"I probably shouldn't tell you this," said Smith.

"I think we're well past keeping secrets at this point," said David.

"Quarantine camps are broken into four classifications. Alpha. Bravo. Charlie and Delta. Delta camps are for noninfected, nonsymptomatic people originating outside the primary quarantine boundary, but inside the secondary line. In this case, anyone outside Interstate 465, but inside whatever arbitrary outer boundary they've set.

"Charlie is for noninfected who are confirmed to have been in direct contact with someone infected, or are strongly suspected of having been in contact. Additionally, anyone originating inside the first quarantine boundary line, Interstate 465, will automatically be placed in a class Charlie quarantine camp—unless they're symptomatic.

"Anyone showing symptoms like fever, aches or neurological glitches is placed in a Bravo-level camp. These are more like detention centers. We delivered most of the hospital patients to a class Bravo camp just outside Greenfield. It was pretty grim."

"I can guess what Alpha is for," said David.

"Full-spectrum infected. That's what they call what we saw on the streets," said Smith. "I don't know what goes on at those camps, and I don't want to know."

"So she's probably fine," muttered David.

"I couldn't say for sure," said Smith. "But it looks promising."

David could barely believe what he was hearing. Joshua's mother was alive and well, sitting in a quarantine camp a few hours north. This changed everything.

"How do I get her out of there?" said David.

Smith took a moment to answer. "I have no idea. This is all brand new to me."

"Do you think we could drive up there and turn ourselves in? Say we heard there was a big quarantine camp and drove up here from Carmel to see if we could find her. They'd put us together, right?"

Smith's silence was the answer.

"Who am I kidding," said David. "Right?"

"Grissom is home to all four classes of quarantine camps," said Smith. "It's a massive facility, according to IDN."

"IDN?"

"Integrated Data Network," said Smith. "I pull all of my mission information from the network. It's how they're managing to coordinate the response of dozens of government agencies and military units."

"Sounds like Big Brother," said David.

"It's not too far off," said Smith. "I have no idea how I'm going to explain the time I've spent away. There are only so many flat tires and reroutes I can justify."

"Can't they see where you've been?"

"Not yet," said Smith. "We're not transmitting any data. Receive-only mode. Almost everything we need is cached, anyway. I'll have some tap dancing to do tomorrow."

"Speaking of tap dancing. What would you do in my shoes?" said David.

"I don't think it's a good idea to show up at Grissom," said Smith. "The chances of ending up somewhere other than with your ex-wife are pretty high. Most of these facilities are barely functioning, slapped together in a few hours with little supervision or instruction. Pure chaos. I haven't witnessed a lot of independent thinking over the past twenty-four hours. You stand in the wrong line and get the wrong medic asking questions, and who knows."

One of the other soldiers spoke up. "Sir, I doubt the camps are co-ed. That's something else to consider."

"Shit," said David.

"I didn't think of that," said Smith. "You might be better off waiting this out. You know where she's located. Let things simmer down and take a trip up there. You go now, anything could happen."

David agreed, but he wasn't sure he could convince his son. Then again, he could keep this information a secret—until it was safe to try to get her released.

"Thank you, Major," said David, offering his hand.

"Nick," he said, shaking his hand. "Good luck getting her back. For your son's sake."

"Right," said David.

For my son's sake.

Chapter Fifty-Four

Larsen thanked Captain Gresham and hopped out of the backseat of the HUMVEE, shaking his head at Ragan and McDermott, who sat next to each other on the ground, their backs against the rear tire. He helped them up and muttered a curse.

"We don't exist. There's nothing mentioned on any network bulletin that remotely resembles our activity or mission."

"It is a top-secret program," said McDermott.

"The kill box order listed every unit—military, government or law enforcement—that had been ordered to enter the city. If our job was so critical to national security and the crisis at hand, like we've always been told, they would have added our call signs and updated our locations. It's not like they didn't know most of our locations at all times."

"That's why Control didn't want us making any kind of contact with the military or law enforcement," said Ragan. "We're bullshit. Some kind of top-secret, illegal mercenary army put together by the same fucking nut jobs that caused the mess out there. Everything compartmentalized. Everything a secret. Nothing legitimate. Think about how many supposed VIPs were murdered or imprisoned over the past twenty-four hours. Hundreds. All probably just like Chang. People that could unravel or explain exactly what happened to our country."

"The ID badges didn't turn up anything?" said McDermott.

"Smith's unit has a universal card reader. Part of the IDN system," said Larsen. "I swiped the card and scanned the bar code. Nothing. If we'd approached a quarantine checkpoint, they would have arrested us, stripped away our gear and thrown us in a quarantine camp. Treated us like some kind of crazy militia types."

"Disposable and deniable," said Ragan. "I'm going to kill that Cooper fuck back at Grissom. He had to know about this."

"Nobody's going back to Grissom," said Larsen. "It's one of the biggest quarantine detention centers in the Midwest—and I'm sure the 'colonel,' whoever he really is, was long gone by the time we parachuted. My guess is the entire CHASE facility is empty, like it never existed."

"Did someone say they were headed back to Grissom?" said a familiar voice.

A dark, nonmilitary-looking shape stood several feet away in the dark. Larsen lowered his night-vision goggles for a moment, taking in the new and improved David Olson.

"Did I miss the showers? And the Gap Outlet," said Larsen. "I'd hug you, but I'm still covered in blood and intestines."

"I'll pass," said David. "What did you say about the Grissom Joint Air Reserve Base?"

"That's where our unit is based," said Larsen. "Though it appears that we never really existed, in the traditional sense of legitimate government units. I think we were created specifically for this bioweapons attack.

To remove people like Chang from circulation. That was his theory."

"Whose?" said David.

"Chang's," said Larsen. "Why the interest in Grissom?"

"My wife's in one of the quarantine camps there," said David. "Class Charlie camp, which is supposedly a good thing. Noninfected. Sounded like your colleague was considering a road trip to visit an old friend at Grissom."

"Something like that," she said.

"You don't want to go up there," said Larsen. "Not right now at least. Nothing good will come of it."

"That's what everyone keeps telling me," said David.

"You need to take your son somewhere safe," said Larsen. "And just be with him. You go up there—you might never see him again."

David wiped his face, finding the voice to respond. "You're right," he finally said. "What about you? How are you getting to Colorado?"

"I don't know," said Larsen. "I haven't gotten that far in the planning process yet. I was kind of hoping the code on my Homeland ID badge would trigger some kind of all-mighty power of appropriation to take one of these HUMVEEs. Apparently, I'd have a better chance of talking them out of a HUMVEE by flashing a plastic badge from Party City. At least the system didn't order them to arrest me. That's something, right?"

"I'm taking Joshua south to my father's place about five hours from here," said David. "You're welcome to come with me. All of you. I mean that."

"I couldn't—"

"It's southwest of here. Toward Colorado," said David. "You can take some time to figure out what you're going to do from there. If the whole country doesn't implode, I might even consider driving your ass out there myself. I haven't been to Colorado in years."

"It's the best time of year to visit," said Larsen.

"I don't doubt it," said David before pointing toward the trees on the other side of the road. "I'm right over there. Waiting for my turn to call. There's a creek about a quarter mile into the woods. Not saying my dad will care one way or the other if you stink like road kill—but you really do stink like road kill."

"Thanks, David," said Larsen.

"Just thinking about camp hygiene."

"No," said Larsen. "For the offer. I'll take you up on it."

"I didn't realize I had given you a choice, Eric."

Larsen laughed. "We made one hell of a team."

"We did," said David. "These two kind of came in at the end and took a lot of the credit—"

"Right. If we hadn't shown up—"

"We'd all be dead," said David. "I expect both of you to take me up on my offer, too. Unless you have family nearby."

"I'm from Sacramento," said Ragan.

"Vermont," replied the other.

"Yeah. You're coming with us," said David. "We'll figure out how to get you home."

Larsen watched David head back into the forest, noting where he came to a stop. That was where he was headed after he washed the day away in that creek. A long nap under a tree, and a fresh start in the morning. He could barely wait.

Chapter Fifty-Five

Dr. Hale shuffled down the road in the clogs she'd been wearing for four days straight. Great shoes for standing all day in the ER, but in the forest or on uneven pavement—she couldn't wait to get rid of them. Hale peered into the shadowy woods, looking for David Olson or Eric Larsen. The tops of the trees glowed golden orange, but the trunks near the forest floor blurred together in the murky, predawn darkness. The sun was still hidden behind the vast cornfield lining the other side of the road.

The road felt lonely without the National Guard convoy. Major Smith and his soldiers had stayed long enough to implement the evacuation plan, but his unit was already long overdue when they'd left a few hours ago, after the first wave of families and friends arrived to pick up their survivors. Looking over the list that Smith had left behind with Gary Hoenig, it appeared that everyone hiding in the forest had somewhere to go.

"Dr. Hale?" said a voice, followed by movement in the trees ahead of her.

Eric Larsen emerged from the forest. He was still dressed in tactical gear and carrying a rifle, but he'd obviously made an effort to clean off the blood and gore that had covered him last night.

"Expecting me?" she said.

"No. Everyone's up," said Larsen. "We're hiking out of here in a few minutes. Don't worry, we were going to swing by to say goodbye."

"Yeah. Sure," she said, smiling. "Hiking? I thought all of you had a ride out of here with David's father?"

"We do. His dad is caravanning up with a few neighbors. They'll be here in about two hours," said Larsen, checking his watch.

"So why hike anywhere?"

"Call me paranoid, but I don't want to be here that long," said Larsen. "If they tracked Smith's convoy—who knows."

"He disabled all of that," said Hale.

"I'm still taking a little walk this morning," said Larsen. "Put some distance between me and this place. What brings you out our way?"

"We have some unexpected guests arriving at any minute," said Hale.

"Spoken by anyone else under these circumstances—those words would terrify me," said Larsen. "I'm surprised they got out that fast."

"Me too," said Hale, looking over his shoulder. "I think that might be them."

Larsen turned to face two rapidly approaching vehicles.

"You guys having a party without me?" said David, appearing among the trees next to her.

"Sort of," said Larsen, nodding at the vehicles. "We're waiting for some guests to arrive."

"How's your son doing?" said Hale.

"He's still sleeping," said David. "This is a kid that can sleep until noon after doing nothing all day. After yesterday, I don't expect him to open his eyes until about nine tonight."

"Wave some pizza under his nose," said Hale. "I bet that'll do the trick."

"I'd kill for some pizza right now," said Larsen.

A silver Suburban and a well-worn, soft-top Jeep Wrangler rapidly approached from the south.

"Let me guess," said David. "Chang and his new friends."

Hale cocked her head. "Nice guess. How?"

"Just a feeling."

They stepped out of the road as the vehicles arrived and came to a sudden stop next to them. Chang smiled at her through the Suburban's rear passenger window, but didn't open his door. She recognized the Suburban's driver as one of the operatives that had carried medical supplies into the infirmary, but she couldn't identify the others through the tinted glass.

Two men armed with submachine guns got out of the Jeep and took up a position facing the way they had come. Chang opened his door and stepped onto the road, followed closely by the driver. She caught a glimpse of the operative in the backseat next to Chang, recognizing her as the other operative she'd seen in the infirmary. She looked just as serious with her helmet off. The group's leader was already out of the front seat, crossing in front of the Suburban.

"We need to make this fast," he said. "Dr. Hale. Rich. It's a pleasure meeting you."

"Likewise," said Hale, turning to Chang. "This is like a small miracle."

"More like a big miracle," said Larsen.

"We had a little outside help," said Rich, glancing toward the two men watching the road. "Where's Scott?"

"About fifty yards down the road," said Hale. "Same distance into the forest. I have some people waiting for you. You need to get him to a hospital. I got the bleeding under control, but I don't know what else is wrong. It's a deep stab wound."

"He's still in good hands," said Rich. "Thank you for taking care of him, given the circumstances."

She shrugged her shoulders. "This is what I do. Doesn't matter who he is or how he got here."

Rich glanced furtively at Larsen, who stood next to her.

"What?" said Hale.

"They didn't tell you," said Rich.

"Tell me what?" she insisted.

"You did the right thing," said Larsen. "Even David would agree."

"Barely," said David. "But, yes."

"What are you talking about?" said Hale.

"I took Chang—"

"Kidnapped," said David.

"Rescued," said the driver, staring them down.

"Whatever," said Rich. "When they taxied back with a busted plane, I grabbed Chang and took off. I honestly didn't think any of you would make it back to NevoTech alive—even with Scott's help. In my mind, he signed up for a suicide mission."

"But you let him go anyway," said Larsen.

"I wouldn't have let him go if I thought it would jeopardize our chances of getting out with Chang," said Rich. "It was his choice."

"I would have treated him the same, regardless of the *circumstances,*" said Hale. "That's what I do. Part of the oath I took as a doctor."

"Which is why I thanked you," said Rich. "Don't ever stray from that path. It leads to dark places."

"Very dark," said Rich's driver. "We need to load up our guy and get out of here before that darkness catches up with us."

Who the hell were these people? The driver got back in the Suburban and drove down the road slowly, stopping when her two nurses stepped out of the forest and waved him down.

"Joshua is okay?" said Chang.

"One hundred percent—asleep," said David.

Chang nodded, his eyes tearing up. "I can't describe how helpless I felt when they dragged me off. I knew it was the right decision, but I felt like I had killed all of you."

"What?" said David. "No. That's not how any of us felt. It was a heated moment, but bringing you back to NevoTech would have been the wrong decision. Rich saw it clearly. I get the feeling he's made a lot of similar calls in his career. We survived out of sheer, unforeseen luck. Seriously. Rich made the right call."

"And it all worked out," said Larsen. "Not sure how, but here we are."

"And here we go," said Rich, glancing at the stretcher being loaded into the back of the Suburban.

"I thought we'd have more time," said Hale. "I need to tell you something. I think it could be important to your research."

"My research is pretty much dead," said Chang.

"Maybe not," said Hale. "The vaccine you developed may have post-symptomatic efficacy."

"I doubt it. Even the high-dose, intravenous administration of potent antiviral drugs barely makes a difference in the mortality rate once a patient shows the symptoms of herpes simplex encephalitis. And that's when doctors catch the symptoms extremely early."

"But you haven't conducted clinical trials for post-symptomatic efficacy," she said. "Right?"

"No. That's not the market NevoTech wanted to pursue," said Chang. "Wait. Have you seen someone's symptoms regress? I thought everyone inside NevoTech was asymptomatic. Checked every four hours."

She nodded. "Someone slipped through the cracks."

"Who?" said Chang.

"Me."

"You're infected?" said Larsen.

"I started running a fever late in the morning," said Hale. "It reached one hundred and two at one point, and I started to have headaches. I was going to report myself, but within a few hours of taking two of Dr. Chang's pills, I felt considerably better. I'm not running a fever now."

Chang stared at her, slowly shaking his head. "That's—that's incredible. The implications…"

"Are huge," said Rich.

"Game changing," said Chang. "I mean, this could be used to save lives right now. They could treat mild to moderately impaired patients before the virus consumed them. It would definitely save lives in the future."

"Can they make enough of it that quickly?" said David.

"NevoTech can't," said Chang. "But I know someone who can. Greenberg."

"Greenberg?" said Rich.

"He said they had massive production facilities just waiting to produce any kind of biological warfare vaccines the government could license from private industry."

"Who's they?" said Hale.

"The military," said Chang. "Greenberg works for the Department of Defense. Bioweapons Defense Division."

"Worked," said Rich.

"It doesn't matter anyway," said Chang. "Not until we can prove that the vaccine can do what Dr. Hale suggests."

"Then use me to test the theory," said Hale. "Can't you run some kind of lab tests on me?"

"Yes. Would you be willing to come with us? Is that okay?" he said, looking at Rich.

"As long as she's not contagious, and she volunteers," said Rich. "I'm done kidnapping—for today."

"I volunteer," said Hale. "Dr. Owens and a few other hospital staff have things under control."

"Don't you have someone coming to pick you up?" said David.

"No, actually, I don't. I hadn't made any arrangements. My parents are on vacation in Costa Rica," said Hale.

"You're kidding," said David.

"Not kidding," said Hale. "Good timing, too. They live in St. Louis."

Chang didn't look overly excited by that statement, and she knew why. If they hadn't left at least a week ago, it was possible they could be infected.

"They've been gone for three weeks. Thirtieth-anniversary trip," she said.

"That's really good timing," said Chang.

"Then that's it," said Rich. "You're coming with us. The rest of you are good?"

"Are you offering a ride?" said David.

"How many do you have?"

349

"Seven. We were just about to hike out of here," said David. "My dad's a few hours out."

"How far were you planning on walking?" said Rich.

"A few miles," said David. "We just wanted to—you know."

"Put some distance between yourself and this very tempting government target?" said Rich.

"Something like that."

"I can take two in the Jeep and two more inside the Suburban," said Rich. "The rest will have to split up between the two vehicles and stand on the running boards. I'll take you down to Rushville. It's about three miles south. We came through there on the way out. Pretty quiet. I'm headed east after that."

"As long as you're headed away from Indianapolis," said David. "Count us in."

"I need to say goodbye to Dr. Owens and a few others," said Hale. "I hate to leave them here like this."

"Half of the people are gone already. The rest will be gone by noon," said Larsen. "You're not cutting out that early. They'll survive without you."

Larsen was right. Everything was on autopilot at this point. Scott was their most critical patient, and he was coming with them. Barring any driving delays, everyone hiding in the forest would be on the road by lunch. Her work was done here. She had a different mission now. Not really new. Just bigger. Instead of saving one life at a time, she had a chance to save thousands. She took a step toward the Suburban in the distance, stumbling on her clogs.

"First stop is a new pair of shoes," she said over her shoulder, laughing with the rest of them.

Chapter Fifty-Six

Karyn Archer sat in front of a curved flat-screen monitor, sifting through the last of her prioritized electronic reports. Incident Zone One-Four had gone quiet from her perspective. KILL BOX protocols had cleared all of her intelligence sources from the city. All she saw now was unimportant clutter tagged by overeager military and law enforcement commanders at the quarantine boundaries. Reports that barely met the relevancy parameters set by program analysts. The CHASE agents assigned to her incident zone were either dead or vanished. Based on what they'd found over the past twenty-four hours at three of the four target locations, she was pretty sure they were all dead. There was no way to know for certain—but she'd taken steps to feel good about the assumption.

At 2:05 a.m., she requested two precision-guided, one-thousand-pound bombs. The "colonel" offered, so she took him up on it. Ragan's CTAB hadn't moved from Chang's apartment for close to six hours at that point. Archer guessed they had decided to stay put for the night. Routine aerial reconnaissance taken at 3:11 a.m. indicated that Chang's apartment building was a pile of smoldering rubble. Hopefully, Ragan's team was at the bottom of it.

The only outlier was Eric Larsen. Three members of his team had been found dead at Chang's house, inside a reinforced "safe room." Their deaths could *only* be described as utterly bizarre. Forensically, the three appear to have shot each other. Circumstantially, it looked like Larsen had shot them and deserted. She'd liked that version better and forwarded it to her superiors. If Larsen ever showed up, she'd have carte blanche to bring him in—or drop a one-thousand-pound bomb from a circling stealth bomber on his head. She'd be happy either way.

Then there was Chang. Somehow he'd managed to run the gauntlet and disappear. That was the truly bad news. Chang was the real mission. Cleaning up the CHASE mess was just a side job. Archer was stuck here until Chang was confirmed dead or captured. And if he showed up on the evening news, she could expect a few one-thousand-pound bombs to drop on her own head.

She was about to get up to find a cup of coffee, when a red-flagged report hit her message box. What the fuck? Archer reread the contents of the message. The report was over five hours old! She picked up her phone and dialed a prefix that rang in the adjacent hangar.

"I thought we were done," said Ecker, sounding half asleep.

"All teams out the door in three minutes," said Archer.

"Three minutes? What the hell is going on?"

"Larsen's still out there."

If you enjoyed reading KILL BOX, grab a copy of
FIRE STORM
Book 3 of this conspiracy action-thriller series

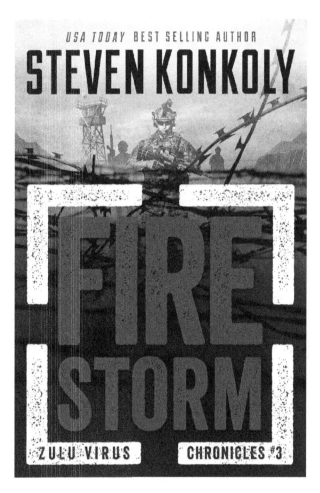

Available at Amazon Books
and other leading book vendors

Please consider leaving a review for KILL BOX. Even a short, one-line review can make all of the difference.

Thank you!

For VIP access to exclusive sneak peeks at my upcoming work, new release updates and deeply discounted books, join my newsletter here:

eepurl.com/dFebyD

Visit Steven's blog to learn more about current and future projects:

StevenKonkoly.com

About the Author

Steven graduated from the United States Naval Academy in 1993, receiving a bachelor of science in English literature. He served the next eight years on active duty, traveling the world as a naval officer assigned to various Navy and Marine Corps units. His extensive journey spanned the globe, including a two-year tour of duty in Japan and travel to more than twenty countries throughout Asia and the Middle East.

From enforcing United Nations sanctions against Iraq as a maritime boarding officer in the Arabian Gulf, to directing aircraft bombing runs and naval gunfire strikes as a Forward Air Controller (FAC) assigned to a specialized Marine Corps unit, Steven's "in-house" experience with a wide range of regular and elite military units brings a unique authenticity to his thrillers.

He lives with his family in central Indiana, where he still wakes up at "zero dark thirty" to write for most of the day. When "off duty," he spends as much time as possible outdoors or travelling with his family—and dog.

Steven is the bestselling author of nearly twenty novels. His canon of work includes the popular Black Flagged Series, a gritty, no-holds barred covert operations and espionage saga; The Alex Fletcher Books, an action-adventure thriller epic chronicling the events surrounding an inconceivable attack on the United States; The Fractured State series, a near future, dystopian thriller trilogy set in the drought ravaged southwest; and THE RESCUE, a heart-pumping thriller of betrayal, revenge, and conspiracy.

He is an active member of the International Thriller Writers (ITW) and Science Fiction and Fantasy Writers of America (SFWA) organizations.

You can contact Steven directly by email
(stevekonkoly@striblingmedia.com)

or through his blog:
StevenKonkoly.com.

Made in the USA
Las Vegas, NV
16 July 2022

51700082R00215